Frank let himself into his house with a very strange feeling inside – it was almost as if he didn't belong there any more. When he picked up on the awesome silence with no sound of the radio, TV or stereo and worse still, no sound of Anna or his twins, James and Oliver, tears came into his eyes. Drawing a deep breath, he told himself to get a grip before strolling along the passage and into the kitchen. His intention had been to come in and collect the rest of his clothes and let Anna work it out for herself that he was leaving her. But now, he was having second thoughts. He was in a bit of turmoil. He felt as if he was going from a dream into a nightmare. The dream was of he and Bridget living in their fantasy world, and the nightmare was Anna letting him go without so much as a goodbye. Never mind that she was already out there with George Blake . . .

Sally Worboyes was born and grew up in Stepney with four brothers and a sister. She now lives in Norfolk with her husband and three children. The author of sixteen previous novels, she has also written plays for TV and radio, and adapted her own play and novel, *Wild Hops*, as a musical, *The Hop Pickers*.

By Sally Worboyes

NOVELS

Wild Hops
Docker's Daughter
The Dinner Lady
Red Sequins
Keep on Dancing
Down Stepney Way
Over Bethnal Green
Whitechapel Mary
At the Mile End Gate
Banished from Bow
Girl from Brick Lane
Down by Tobacco Dock
Where Sparrows Nest
Time Will Tell
Jamaica Street
Room for a Lodger

MEMOIR

East End Girl

Lipstick & Powder

Sally Worboyes

An Orion paperback

First published in Great Britain in 2007
by Orion
This paperback edition published in 2008
by Orion Books Ltd,
Orion House, 5 Upper Saint Martin's Lane
London, WC2H 9EA

An Hachette Livre UK company

A CIP catalogue record for this book is available
from the British Library.

Typeset by Deltatype Ltd, Birkenhead, Merseyside

Printed and bound in Great Britain by Clays Ltd, St Ives plc

The Orion Publishing Group's policy is to use papers that
are natural, renewable and recyclable products and made
from wood grown in sustainable forests. The logging and
manufacturing processes are expected to conform to the
environmental regulations of the country of origin.

www.orionbooks.co.uk

*This book is dedicated to my lovely niece, Sarah Brody,
and my youngest nephew, Billy Lipka.*

My thanks to the team at Orion
for the lovely welcome into the group
that I received, especially from Kate
Mills and Jon Wood.

Chapter One

After what had been a run-of-the-mill June day, Anna Watson, who was approaching her twenty-sixth birthday, yawned and stretched as she got up from her comfortable dark red and gold sofa – the sofa that her once caring husband, Frank, had bought her at an antique shop in Portobello Road when she was pregnant with their twins. This chaise-longue type of a couch was something that he knew she had always hankered after because, for one thing, it reminded her of her late gran's little two-up-two-down, a few turnings away from where she was now living.

Anna had spent a lot of time with her maternal grandmother as a child, when the quietly spoken woman had looked after her before she was old enough to go to school. And this evening, for no reason in particular, she had been thinking of those early days when her own mother, Ivy, worked full time at the local umbrella factory in Cambridge Heath Road. This work, which had afforded her a decent take-home pay at the time, had been Ivy's saving grace, because not only had she worked every God-given day but she had also to take care of her family of three daughters.

Apart from this, the woman had also to endure the stigma of her husband having left her for another. But all this of course was now considered part of a former life, the ghost buried, and Anna, just like her two elder sisters, was looking out for their mother without too much fuss being shown. Back in the early days Ivy had been fiercely independent but now, in the comfort years of retirement, she was content to let her adult offspring feather her nest as and when they felt like it. She had her memories of good times as well as bad. Over Bank Holidays she had taken her daughters to Margate by train to picnic on the beach, enjoy a little nap in a deckchair, and traipse back home again in the late afternoon. Those had been lovely days out for Anna and her sisters.

In her sitting room, her little comfort zone, Anna had been looking through an Avon catalogue in between thinking about her life and her marriage, and all to the low sound of *Coronation Street* in the background. This evening had been quite relaxed because her six-month-old twins had been – and still were – happy to lie in their playpen enjoying each other's company as well as their attached colourful mobile toy. Their tall and handsome dad, Frank, would be working late as usual, and no doubt coming home after midnight with the smell of drink on his breath and perfume on his shirt.

Glancing at herself in her old wax-polished pine mirror above the Victorian fireplace, Anna ruffled her shoulder-length dark blonde hair and then twisted it into a pleat at the back, wondering if it was time for a new cut and style and maybe a colour tint. 'I suppose you could try being a redhead for a change ...' she quietly told herself. 'That should go all right with those green eyes of yours.' Then, her smile fading, her confidence on the wane, her shoulders slumped and she sighed loudly as she stared at her reflection and let her hair tumble down. She wondered if it might be time to take her sisters' advice and get out of the house now and then to meet up with old friends. Most of her mates, like herself, were married now, but from the few telephone calls that she had had before they gave up on her it had been clear that, even though they were no longer single, they were keeping in touch with each other. One or two had joined a fitness club and another, who had attended pottery classes one evening a week, was now selling handmade and hand-painted pots from a stall in Hackney market. One of her very best friends during her schooldays had broken a barrier and was working as a part-time driving instructor and was one of the first women to do so.

She glanced across to the small bureau in the corner of the room on which stood a lovely framed photograph of her and Frank on their wedding day, when they had been deeply in love and gloriously happy. Shaking off the memory of that day, she contemplated the idea of fetching her address book out of the dark and phoning some friends to see what kind of a response she might get after her long spell of silence. It was nobody's fault but her own that the phone had stopped ringing, because she had all but cut her mates dead. When she and Frank were first married Anna had drawn a circle around what had been her wonderful little oasis and, not too long after this, there had been the exciting house-hunting episode which had taken up most of her spare time. Then came her all-consuming desire to have babies – which hadn't been as easy as she thought it would be.

Taking the bull by the horns she collected her address book and a biro and went into the passage to sit on the padded stall next to the little shelf on which the black telephone perched. Flicking through the pages, she couldn't decide who to call first so started at the beginning. Beryl Andrews was the first name and this brought a smile to her face. Amongst other girls, she and Beryl had each at one time been captain of the netball team at both the junior and senior school and, since Beryl had been a bit of a daredevil flirt, it had come as no surprise that she was the first to marry at the age of seventeen having got herself pregnant by a favourite boyfriend.

A touch eager now, Anna dialled her old chum's number and felt a rush of euphoria as she waited for her to pick up the phone. But it wasn't Beryl who answered. It was an older voice. Momentarily silenced, Anna quickly collected herself and said, 'I'm sorry to have troubled you but I think I might have dialled the wrong number. I was hoping to reach an old friend of mine called Beryl.'

'Well, the only way you can do that sweetheart is to go to your local church. My Beryl died from breast cancer three months ago,' said the voice on the end of the line.

Stunned by this news all Anna managed to say was, 'I'm so sorry … I didn't know she had cancer.'

'Well, that's probably because people won't mention the word, will they? Anyone would think it was some kind of punishment from God for being a devil

4

worshipper. You'd be surprised just how rampant cancer is, and still it's hushed up. I've moved in to look after her little family though, so the kids will be fine.'

Shocked by this news Anna could hardly speak. When she finally found her voice all she could say was, 'I'm really sorry.'

'You and me both, darling. The good Lord is looking after her now. Take care sweetheart.' And that was it. Anna heard a click and then the dialling tone. She had only just recognised the woman's voice from the few times she had been in her house as a schoolgirl, spending time in her friend's bedroom listening to her records and talking about boys and sex. Pushing this horrible news from her mind, she collected herself and turned the pages to call another of her old school friends but there was no answer. She tried another but all she heard was the unobtainable tone. Deflated by her failures she drifted back into the sitting room, sat down on the sofa and shed a few tears. She had never felt as alone as she did right then.

Anna had had a lot of fun with her friend Beryl in particular because in the old days they had been like two peas in a pod. She smiled sadly as she remembered how, when just thirteen, they had wished for each other's eyes and joked about exchanging them via surgery. Beryl's eyes had been big and round and a lovely warm tone of brown but she had longed for them to be like Anna's, wide and sloping and a soft shade of green.

She snapped herself out of this worsening dark mood that seemed to have been dragged into the house, possibly because of the old romance that she had been watching on TV that afternoon while feeding one twin after the other. The film apart, though, worries over her failing marriage had clouded her mind as she remembered a time when her and Frank's world was filled with laughter and socialising, parties and music. A time when she always wore lipstick and powder whether she was going out or not. Slowly shaking her head, she spoke softly to herself. 'You've got to get out more, Anna. You're behaving like your own jailer – shutting yourself away. Life is too short and the proof of that is Beryl. She shouldn't have suffered and she shouldn't have died so young. She was full of life.'

The gentle sound of her babies gurgling in their playpen brought a faint smile to her lips. She looked around the room and brought to mind the time when she and Frank had first purchased this house. They had been so in love, content to spend hours together talking about the way they might decorate their nest. They had agonised over things that now seemed trivial, such as choosing between the Heal's modern Seventies look or keeping the mid-Victorian feel with appropriate replica wallpaper which they had seen when browsing in the Sanderson's gallery off Oxford Street.

Anna had no idea why something so frivolous, compared to what she had just heard about an old friend, should have floated to the surface other than the fact that she didn't want to think about the tragedy. In the early days, furnishing their home had been the most important thing in her and Frank's life and the centre of their little love world. They had enjoyed every minute of window-shopping and delivery once this house, which they had renovated together, was ready. They had stripped dark varnish away from the solid pine floorboards before giving it a coat of wax polish and a good buff so as to match the carved pine fire surround. They had decorated the ceiling and walls a brilliant white and thrown down red and black Afghan rugs, bought cheaply at a warehouse in Aldgate East.

The jewel in the crown for Anna was the brass Georgian companion set and matching fender that contrasted beautifully with the colourful patterned Victorian fireplace tiles. The fender, purchased from a second-hand stall in Whitechapel market, had been black with age before Anna cleaned and polished it until it shone like gold. All of this had, of course, taken place earlier on in their marriage when the inseparable couple loved to curl up by the small coal fire and watch the reflection of the flames on the small burnished copper scuttle while listening to love songs playing on the stereo. One of the best things to have come out of the so-called Swinging Sixties, as far as Anna was concerned, was the trend of mixing new styles with old and, especially, stripped pine furniture.

Wrapping her arms around herself, she looked about the room where she had always felt comfortable and snug and wished that she wasn't spending so much time in it by herself. Pulling herself out of this low mood she turned her attention to the outside world and a heartening smile spread across her face as she glanced through the glass panes of the door that led onto her walled garden. She could just see the head and shoulders of Rachel, her old Jewish neighbour next door, tending to her plants in the soft glow of the light shining out from the woman's back door, and recalled how neighbourly she had been on the day she and Frank moved into the turning. She smiled again as she remembered Rachel saying, 'These houses might be old fashioned but they are a lot safer than what they build nowadays. Look at what happened to Ronan Point. What a disaster.' The woman had been referring to a brand new high-rise block of flats that had partly collapsed while people were living inside. And during other little chats over the garden fence with her neighbour, Rachel had criticised the government for dismantling London Bridge for dispatch to a tourist park in Arizona and praised Bernadette Devlin who, at the age of twenty-two and the youngest MP, had demonstrated against government trying to remodel union law. Anna was always amazed at how the old woman kept up with everything that was going on in the world.

When Frank and Anna had purchased this late Victorian two-up-two-down terraced house from a private landlord some three years ago, being a local girl meant that Anna's family was not far away. Her grandparents had lived close by to this quiet and scantily tree-lined back street before they passed away and this in itself had been a reason why she wanted to be in this little corner of East London. She felt so much at home here. There had always been a relaxed neighbourly atmosphere, another reason why she and Frank felt that they could not have wished for a better place to bring up children. And as for Rachel . . . she was like an old-fashioned adopted grandmother who upheld an old-fashioned wartime spirit of *one for all and all for one.*

Soon after they were married Anna had wanted to start a family and had often sat huddled up with Frank on the sofa, talking about their future and what it would be like to be parents. As it turned out, she hadn't found it quite so easy to conceive as she first thought and after trying for two years and failing she had been advised by a gynaecologist to take a fertility drug. This had proved successful for hundreds of women with problems similar to her own and eventually resulted in Anna getting pregnant with not one baby but two. Twin boys. Oliver and James.

Frank had been over the moon at the news of her pregnancy and, protective where his wife and their unborn were concerned, put caution before passion when in bed for fear of anything going wrong. So, for most of the nine months while she was carrying, Anna did little more in the bedroom than kiss and hug her young husband and satisfy his desires in her own sweet way. She had hardly been able to believe it when, towards the end of her term, every now and then she thought that she could smell a hint of someone else's perfume on Frank's shirts when she was putting them into the washing machine. Why all of this was filling her mind now was no mystery. She knew why she had been thinking about better times and doing her best to force away the dark stomach-churning worries inside. Little cameos of better and worse times had been floating in and out of her mind all afternoon, even though she had tried to lose herself in her favourite serial, *Crossroads*.

And now, in the silence broken only by the chimes

of the distant clock tower striking seven, she instinctively glanced at her wristwatch to confirm that it was time for her babies to be fed. She drew the curtains and then smiled down at the twins as they vied for attention, gurgling and kicking their legs excitedly. At least they were happy and content in their unhurried safe little world. Looking from one to the other she felt as though her heart was melting.

'I'll never be able to thank the Lord Jesus enough for you two, will I?' she murmured as she wiped her eyes with the back of her hand. Then, lifting her face, she closed her eyes and whispered, 'Please, God, if I am left to look after the twins by myself, help me to be strong.'

As much as Anna loved her twins there were times when she felt as if she could scream with frustration. Times when one or the other or both would cry non-stop even though they had been fed, changed and cuddled. But at least they were there, and one-sided conversations were better than having nobody to talk to. Much better. And now it was time for her to feed and get them ready to go down for the night. She needed a little break from them so that she could think seriously about what she could do to improve her lonely world. She had her future to think about as well as theirs. A future which was looking a touch bleak and one that she didn't think anyone else knew about. She was going through a private hell and had been for quite a while. But it helped to know that there were others in the same boat, others who were possibly listening to or watching the same programmes and who would understand what it was like to move around in silence or have only the radio and television for company.

Earlier that afternoon she had read an article in a magazine about unmarried mothers and how they not only had to cope alone but also live with the stigma of not having a husband.

Anna had been caring for her twins almost single-handed but at least she was married. She had been keeping up the appearance of everything being all right while she went about doing the housework and taking care of the laundry. She glanced across to the Moses basket next to the garden doors and felt anxiety sweep through her for not having done the task she liked least – the ironing. The basket was full to almost overflowing with the white shirts that Frank wore to work, as well as other dry laundry that was ready for a steam press.

Shrugging off her sense of guilt at having watched television for most of the afternoon, she decided to leave the ironing until the next day. In any case she could see that the twins were brewing up for a crying session to let her know they were hungry. Her saving grace this evening was that her neighbours' seventeen-year-old daughter, the lovely Jackie, had promised to call in with her Summer Avon products catalogue and this she was looking forward to. Jackie had said that she would spend time with Anna, enjoying a glass of wine while she chose and placed an order for scented products in pretty pots and jars. Such little interludes as this were important contacts with the outside world because, while Anna had her catalogue, she felt that she was one of a club of hundreds of other housewives who were turning and admiring the same pages and choosing the same products.

Asking herself if perhaps the time had come for her

to enjoy more than just motherhood and wondering if she should reinvent herself by going on a little shopping therapy trip, she went into the kitchen to warm the twins' bottles which had been made up earlier and kept in the fridge. She thought about Jackie, the young redhead who was so full of aspirations and dreams as well as a determination to work every hour that God sent so as to save enough money to travel on economy through Europe. Jackie's dream was to go from one country to the other working in bars, restaurants, or on the land picking fruit crops for a living. This wasn't so out of the ordinary because some young folk had, since the late Fifties, been catching the ferry to France then traipsing around the Continent. It had all been part of a new and growing fad. This ambition of Jackie's was something that had brought her and Anna a little closer than they might have been if all they had in common was the Avon products. Anna had toyed with the idea of travelling herself at the age of sixteen once she had left school but, as with most girls, hadn't done anything about it. The only difference that she could see between the pair of them apart from their age was that, whereas her husband Frank had been her first love, Jackie was enjoying more than one relationship and had said that she had no intention of tying the knot until she was thirty.

In her late teens and already independent the girl didn't seem to give a toss if she was labelled 'spinster' and the irony of this made Anna smile. The word 'spinster' was such an old-fashioned expression for a Seventies girl to use. The differences between Anna and Jackie was that Anna had always been a home-girl, with the maternal instinct from as far back as the days when she played with her dolls. But during the Sixties, once she had started to earn a living, she had saved a little each week so as to be able to enjoy one or two annual cheap package holidays on the Costa Brava. This had been more than enough to satisfy any lust for travel. The dream of working during long summers picking grapes in Spain or grafting as a chambermaid in hotels had not been on her agenda. She had loved London all through the Sixties when she was working as a telephonist for an insurance company in Covent Garden. That was when she had really got into fashion and the general swing of all that was going on around her, right through to when Biba in High Street, Kensington in the late 1960s copied the fashion of the Twenties and the Thirties when girls had worn floppy hats and flowers in their hair.

With memories of these times floating through her mind, Anna bottle-fed one baby after the other, enjoying the recall of her teens when she had been as free as a bird to do as she pleased. And now, on the surface, she had little to complain about because she had her adorable babies and her standard of living was all right. She and Frank enjoyed a good income from Prima Pasta, the restaurant that they had started up four years earlier, and she didn't have to worry about money. Her own mother, Ivy, one of the closest people to her, had not been able to enjoy the small luxuries earlier in her life that Anna and her sisters were now almost taking for granted.

In this somewhat prosperous time though, her mother was enjoying a bit of the affluence that seemed buoyant in comparison with the way it was before, during and after the Second World War. Ivy was more than happy with this bubbling new era – and happier still with a little of her other two daughters' ill-gotten gains coming her way every now and then. Hazel and Linda, Anna's sisters, enjoyed a vibrant lifestyle while running their exclusive brothel in old Bethnal Green.

After the twins had been fed, bathed and were sleepy, Anna thought that she would have little trouble in settling them down for the night but she was wrong. Once in their matching cots in their small shared bedroom, decorated in pale blue and primrose, Oliver, the less contented of the two, began to grizzle, which in turn started James off. Leaving the room, Anna slowly pulled the door shut behind her and went downstairs, intending to pour herself a glass of red wine to take into the sitting room, but one of her babies was not letting her off that easily. Oliver, who was a little more prone to stress than James, was now crying loudly. Doing her best to sit it out and not fall into the trap of spoiling either of them, she pulled her favourite LP from the rack on a shelf and placed it on the turntable.

She wanted to listen to the Beatles and her favourite song from the early Sixties, 'Please Please Me'. This reminded her of the time when she had seen the group at a concert in North London before she had met Frank. A time when she and a friend had tried to pose as staff so as to slip in through the back door and up to their dressing rooms. Of course they were thrown out along with other fans that had had the same idea.

With this and other past events floating in and out of her mind, and with the setting sun casting a warm glow into the sitting room, Anna did her best to try and block out the sound of her babies crying above. Cursing under her breath for having to look after them all by herself all of the time, she made herself busy by folding their playpen and carrying it into the front of the house to the dining room, which hardly got used now. 'You're a selfish man, Frank,' she murmured. 'You should be here with me taking care of your sons.' She only just stopped herself from throwing the playpen across the room. 'They're your babies as well as mine! You should be here with me!' Drawing a long and trembling breath she then shook her head, saying, 'I'm not going to do this. I'm not going to let you push me to the edge. I *can* take care of the twins. We don't need *you*.' She then slowly dropped to her knees and cried into her hands in the room with the delicate black and white William Morris patterned wallpaper and the red fitted carpet that she and Frank had chosen together. The room where they had once enjoyed so many dinner parties with their friends. She could almost hear the laughter in the now silent unlived-in room.

Their friends who had once been an important part of their lives had gradually fallen away because of Frank having been too busy at work during the week and too tired to entertain or socialise at weekends. And as so often was the case, this evening the house seemed too quiet and empty, her only company her babies howling above.

Tired though she was, she went back upstairs, supporting herself on the old polished pine handrail as she went. Once in the twins' bedroom she picked up Oliver, who really seemed unusually distressed as tears

15

trickled down his face and into the collar of his pale blue Babygro. Pacing the floor with him and patting his back, she smiled down at James who had quietened since she had come into the room. Patting one and soothing the other with a gentle voice she gradually quietened the pair of them and before too long Oliver was asleep, his head resting on her shoulder. To the sound of an occasional sob she gently lowered him back into his cot, which was a touch premature because he woke up straightaway and began crying again. She tucked him in and gently patted his back in case he had trapped wind and this seemed to do the trick. She sat on the chair next to the cots and quietly sang the same lullaby that she could remember her mum singing to her many years ago. Eventually both babies drifted into a contented sleep until she was left sitting there wondering why she felt so empty when she had them to love.

Glancing from one baby to the other she realised that James was awake again and, in his own sweet way, about to make it clear that it was now his turn. Leaning over his cot, a dull ache now in her back, she turned him onto his side, tucked him in and gently shushed him back to sleep. This done, she crept out of the room and went downstairs only to hear one of them start up again. She told herself to be strong and not go back upstairs and so left him to it, and this as it turned out was the right thing to do. After a few minutes there was silence.

She poured herself a small glass of sherry and went back into the sitting room to put her feet up and relax properly now that she felt sure that they were settled for the night. With the sound turned down low she switched on her old record player – her first record player – one that she had been given as a present when she was fourteen and which she had refused to get rid of. Her taste in music had changed along the way but she loved to listen to her old favourites.

When Frank had brought home his much treasured and brand new Bang & Olufsen a few weeks before, he had wanted Anna to pack hers away but she had resisted. Frank's music centre was his prized possession and lately, when he *was* at home, he was often stretched out on the sofa, his head sunk into a big feather cushion, his personal bulky black earphones on. In one hand would be a glass of malt whisky and in the other a small cigar. Here he would listen to favourite tracks from his favourite LPs. He had wanted to shut out all other noises and sounds but Anna felt that his earphones were also a way of excluding her from his private little world of love songs.

Settled in an armchair by the fireplace where no fire burned tonight, she tried to think of where she had gone wrong: why it was that Frank didn't seem to love her any more and how she might win back his affections. She thought about a new wardrobe and whether this would be the answer. Perhaps some new and sexy underwear? A different hairstyle or a new shade of lipstick? Too upset by the cause of having to think like a single person again she glanced at her wristwatch and saw that it was almost eight o'clock. She could hardly believe how quickly the time had passed and presumed that Jackie had changed her mind about calling in. But then, just as she was resigned to another evening alone, she heard the lovely welcoming chime of her doorbell.

For no particular reason she glanced at herself in the mirror over the Victorian mantelshelf and pushed her dark blonde hair into place as she checked that without make-up she didn't look too washed out. All that was called for was a visit to the hairdresser for that new cut and style which she had been wondering about. The soft chimes of her doorbell went again and she went to let in Jackie, anticipating her smart blue and black Avon case filled with samples. She smiled inwardly as she left the room because this visit was not only going to mean a bit of company for her but a chance to choose whatever she wanted from the new catalogue.

When she opened the front door though, there was no Jackie, but a familiar red Jaguar sports car parked outside, and on her doorstep were Hazel and Linda, her beautiful classy sisters, who shared their stylish converted house in old Bethnal Green from which they ran their upmarket team of attractive and fun-loving prostitutes. When she could, Anna enjoyed herself at their home, sipping champagne with the girls in the gaudy gilt-furnished plush sitting room, listening to their illicit talk about the fun side of the business and the clients.

This evening, looking as stunning as ever in their up-to-the-minute designer clothes, the girls were armed with a Chinese takeaway and a bottle of best port, the favourite drink of all three of them. They breezed past Anna, smiling broadly as she gazed back at them, a touch bemused. They looked in the mood for a celebration and were intending to have one by the look of things because, apart from the bottle of port Hazel was carrying, there were two bottles of red wine in an off-licence carrier bag. Too taken aback to think of anything to say, Anna smiled when they joked about the shocked expression on her face. 'We'll 'ave to do this more often,' said Linda with the long wavy brown hair, who was just two years older than Anna.

'Or better still find a reliable babysitter so that we can drag Madam out and about town,' added Hazel, who was the eldest of the three girls at thirty, and had beautiful long black hair.

Following them through to the sitting room Anna wondered why they had come round to see her. She knew her sisters like the back of her hand and to her this buoyant mood was a veneer and they were covering the real reason for this visit. But after just a few minutes of asking no questions and from the expressions on their faces she decided that they were simply in high spirits and that was all. She assumed that this was because they had notched up another name to add to the client list of their small and lucrative business – the Call A Girl Company. The highly successful so-called dating agency situated on the border of old Bethnal Green and Shoreditch, in what had once been a small Victorian boot and shoe factory, was now a beautiful home from which business and pleasure were conducted.

'So ... what's brought about this little surprise visit then?' said Anna as she collected three wine glasses off the shelf of her pine Welsh dresser. 'Gonna name-drop, are you? Someone famous under your wing, is there? Who is it this time, a rock star or a notorious villain?'

'This is purely a social call, babe. A night in with good food and wine. We're here to sister-sit.' Hazel smiled. 'Nothing wrong with that is there? You spend too much time on your own, Anna. And besides, we want to see our godsons more often – it's our right. I'm going to go up and look at them in a minute. Might even cough a little so as to wake 'em up for a cuddle.'

'Oh really,' said Anna teasing her sister. 'Do I detect a hint of maternal longing, Hazel? Or have you already gone and got yourself pregnant by one of your millionaire clients?'

'Pregnant? Me? No chance, sweetheart. We leave that kind of domestic wonderland stuff for you to wallow in. Keep on churning them out, babe.'

'I don't think so.' Anna went quiet and then said, 'I'm happy with what I've got. I don't need any more.'

'Famous last words!' called Linda from the adjoining kitchen as she opened the cartons of takeaway Chinese. 'I'll put this little lot on the kitchen tray and we'll eat it while it's hot so we won't 'ave to warm the plates up!'

In the sitting room, Anna handed Hazel a corkscrew for the bottle of wine and looked directly into her sister's face. 'So what's this all about then? This impromptu visit with no phone call first to say you were coming?'

'God – you're a worrier,' said Hazel, shaking her head. 'We fancied having a girls' night in. That's all. Lighten up, babe.'

'Fair enough.' Anna smiled. 'I'm not complaining. I'm glad you're here. I was feeling a bit low as it happens . . .'

'Oh? And why's that?'

Regretting the little slip of the tongue, Anna covered her tracks and showed a smiling face. She didn't want anyone to know what she was going through. 'Time of the month probably,' she said, shrugging it off.

'Oh, right . . . but you weren't hoping to be pregnant again were you, sweetheart?' Hazel asked, with a touch of concern in her voice. 'Because that would be daft and far too soon after our twins.'

'No. No, I don't want any more babies, Hazel. One of you two can deliver Mum with granddaughters that she can hug. I'm more than satisfied with my boys. And let's face it – it wasn't easy for me to fall as it turned out, was it.'

'Will be now though,' said Linda coming back into the room. 'All you have to do is take the fertility drug again and Bob's your uncle. There shouldn't be any stopping you now. If you wanted a bigger family, that is. Or, more to the point if Frank wants another baby – a little girl perhaps?' For reasons of her own, Linda had deliberately brought Frank into the conversation. 'You know what men are like with daughters.'

'Never mind what Frank wants or doesn't want. I might try for a little girl in a few years' time. I'm hardly old and I might even be married to someone else later on. Someone who *wants* to spend time with his offspring.'

'Oh dear . . . Frank been neglecting you, 'as he?' said Linda, outwardly smiling but sick inside at the thought of her brother-in-law.

Anna lowered her eyes. 'I suppose he has been neglecting me a bit, yes. But I don't mind. I'm lucky to have my twins; they're as much as any mother could wish for.'

'They're our little miracle babies,' said Hazel, cutting in with a smile and a wink. 'And you deserve them. Let's hope they don't grow up too much like their daddy.'

Anna looked from one sister to the other and after a short pause, said, 'What's that supposed to mean?'

'Well, I s'pose he's no different from all men in that they can't keep their dick from rising when a tease comes along. And that waitress you both took on is a bit of a tease, babe.'

'Is she? I wouldn't know.' Anna wanted to change the subject. 'Anyway, who gives a toss? And getting back to my boys – you're right, they are our little miracle.' She smiled at Hazel as she recollected the many months when she had been disappointed at not having conceived. The day when she found out that she had still had a wonderful magical ring to it. This was when Anna had left the small room of her private gynaecologist in a cul-de-sac just off Harley Street, and had to do her best not to walk along grinning like a Cheshire cat. She had been going to the London Hospital as an outpatient for two years before her GP asked if she could afford to go private. Having said yes without hesitation, whether it meant she would have had to take out a loan or not, she was referred to a specialist, one of the top men in his field who was tall, slim and handsome and turned out to be Anna's knight in shining armour.

'I reckon you deserved a medal the way you just kept

on picking yourself up after every disappointment. You were a star then, babe, and you still are.'

'If you say so. I don't think I could go through all of that again though.' Anna slowly shook her head as she remembered the disappointments every month for over two years, before she fell pregnant with the twins. 'I was ecstatic when I got that positive result, wasn't I,' she said. 'I don't think I've experienced anything like that before or since. I walked away from Harley Street as if I was on some weird and wonderful planet and was happier than I ever imagined I could be.'

'We know that, babe. You came and told us that same evening, if you remember. You were miles of smiles that night.'

'I know. It was incredible,' she said, helping herself to a spring roll. 'You should have seen me when I came out of that little clinic. I had to stop myself from telling complete strangers about it. And before I knew what I was doing, I was pushing open one of the huge glass doors of John Lewis's and heading for the nearest counter. And when the girl offered me a free squirt of the perfume she was pitching that week, I was so stupidly bowled over that I said, "I didn't come in for perfume. I came in to tell you that I'm gonna have a baby."'

'As if she would 'ave been interested,' said Hazel, quietly laughing at her sister.

'I know, but ... well ... on that day I have no idea how many strangers I told.' She slowly shook her head as she remembered it all. Then, her smile dissolving, she murmured, 'I was *so* happy.' Shrugging, she let out a little sigh and looked from one sister to the other. 'I've

23

got something to tell the pair of you that you're not going to like.'

'Fire away,' said Hazel as she piled hot food onto her plate. 'It can't be the insurance man you're having a fling with because they don't come door to door to perk up bored housewives any more, do they?'

'No,' said Anna, 'they don't. If they did and a handsome salesman knocked on my door I might just drag him in for company though.'

Hazel leaned back in her chair and studied her sister's face, then said, 'That's not like you, Anna. We two old scrubbers might come out with something like that but not you. What's the matter, babe?'

'You're not scrubbers. Don't use that word.' Anna pushed a hand through her hair and drew a trembling breath. She didn't want to break down in tears but there was no denying that they were welling up behind her eyes. She smiled sadly at one sister and then the other. 'I love the twins more than I thought possible and I was fantastically happy when my gynaecologist broke the news to me that they were in there. The two women in John Lewis seemed really pleased for me when I told them.' Then snapping out of the past, she said, 'Frank wasn't as thrilled with the news as I thought he would be though.'

'He looked as proud as Punch to me,' said Hazel.

'I know. And I think he was once it really sank in. But I can't forget the response I got when I phoned him from a telephone kiosk in Oxford Street to give him the news. He was short and offhand and this, if I'm honest, knocked me sideways.' Her eyes glazed over a little and she went quiet again before saying, 'Do

24

you know what he said to me when I phoned him after I had got those results . . . when he was serving behind the bar in our restaurant?'

'No, but you're gonna tell us,' said Hazel.

'I whispered to him – because it felt like our private bit of news of the century – "I'm pregnant, Frank. I'm actually pregnant." And he said, "Great. Fantastic. I'll talk to you later. Gotta go darling. Busy." Then he hung up. He didn't even make the effort to come home from the restaurant earlier that night. One of his brothers would have stood in for him, he's given them a helping hand at Tower Hill enough times. Still does.'

'So Frank didn't come rushing home? No surprises there then.' Hazel drew breath and forced herself to stay on track. She had to get a message across to Anna who she still saw as her baby sister. 'What else did you expect, Anna? Frank lives for that place, for the work, the kudos, and the women he loves to flirt with. Flirting for the sake of the business is no bad thing, I suppose.'

'He doesn't flirt, Hazel. He keeps the customers happy and that's what brings them back. They're just as bad as he is and it's all a bit of fun. It's ginger-nut Bridget that's the problem. *She* flirts with *him* and in front of customers. Sometimes in front of me for that matter. She hangs over my husband like a dangling scarf. I wish her husband, Trevor, would make her pregnant and cart her back to the country village where she came from.'

Hazel glanced at Linda and gave her a sly knowing wink before topping up Anna's glass. They had got Anna talking much sooner than they had hoped. And getting her to open up about her marriage was the very

25

reason they had breezed in out of the blue. 'She's a good little worker though, babe, isn't she? And that's always good for business surely?'

'Yes, she is a good worker, Hazel, but I don't know about her being good for business. Other women who are in for a night out don't want a bloody flirt swanning around the place and teasing their men. It makes my stomach turn over every time I see her up to her tricks on the rare occasions that I do go in these days.'

'The trouble is – with girls like her – you have to watch they don't go too far,' said Linda. 'Before you know it that little tease might well start to lure Frank up into the flat above the restaurant for a cuddle. And men being men, who would blame him if he did follow that pert little wiggling arse of hers up the staircase to heaven.' Linda already knew that the waitress at Prima was familiar with the flat above the restaurant. She was simply drawing Anna in to see just how aware she was of what was going on. 'At least she keeps the punters happy . . . not to mention Frank.'

'Oh?' said Anna as she leaned back in her chair and stared into Linda's face. 'And you'd go along with that, would you? You'd make allowances if Frank was at it with her in what used to be our little flat when we were first married?'

'Men will be men, sweetheart. But then I doubt that she would do something like that while either of us two is in the restaurant. But there's no telling. I'm just letting you know what I think she's like, that's all. I wouldn't give Frank too much free rein if I were you – that's all I'm saying. Remind him that he's a family man now and then – while *she's* in earshot.'

'Or better still expand your family,' said Hazel. 'Try for a baby girl. You know what men are like with daughters.'

Uncomfortable at the way her sisters were throwing advice at her, which she hadn't asked for, Anna said, 'I'm quite content with my twins thanks. I don't need any more babies. You kick into action, Hazel, or persuade Linda to.'

'You and Frank were over the moon once you'd hit the target, you know that you were.' Linda poured more wine into the three glasses and said, 'Get that down you and don't look so serious.'

'I'm a responsible mother of twins don't forget,' said Anna, still wondering why they had made this impromptu visit. 'I have to take things seriously. It's all right for you two – footloose and fancy free. She sipped her drink and waited. She wasn't daft; there was something on both of their minds and by the look of it, something else was on the tip of Hazel's tongue.

'You know what?' said Hazel, as predictable as ever. 'I don't think I've ever seen a happier face than Frank's after you'd told him you had two babies growing and not one. He walked differently after that. Shoulders back, chest out, proud as punch. That soon wore off though, didn't it?' She looked from one sister to the other and sipped her drink.

A touch miffed by this reminder of how happy she and her Frank used to be, Anna felt herself go cold as her stomach churned. Even though she was angry with him she was just as much in love as she had ever been, but from the way her sisters were talking she could detect a tone of warning. She wondered if both girls knew more than she did. On the surface everything looked rose-tinted and reasonably good when it came to her marriage. She and Frank were seen as the young handsome couple who were able to live a comparatively comfortable lifestyle in the East End. They had their lovely refurbished terraced cottage in a corner of London where they had been born and bred, which was now being promoted as the next best link to the City in years to come. It was also being seen by medical students attached to the London Hospital as an interesting historic place to lodge and this, in turn, was bringing other students attached to various colleges to lodge in the surrounding area.

For others, with ready cash and an eye for a bargain, the area was now reputed to be the place for developers to snap up cheap run-down properties that would soar in price in years to come. With its wealth of history, museums, the Whitechapel art gallery and the vibrant markets, tourists from abroad were also coming into the area, if only to see where the likes of the Kray twins had lived. Similar in a way to 1888, when people from all walks of life poured in after Jack the Ripper hit the headlines.

The pubs down by the river in and around Wapping had long since been the haunt of the young middle- and upper-class students swigging beer and belting out naughty ballads. But the old East Enders were still thick on the ground and this was why Anna loved living so close to where she was born, in Stepney Green. But now, with this particular impromptu visit from her sisters, she felt that her little world was about to be blown apart.

Bringing herself back to the here and now she spoke quietly, saying, 'I have a feeling that we all know that Frank's not interested in us having any more children ... don't we?'

'You tell us,' said Hazel, giving nothing away as she topped us Anna's glass of wine.

'You do sound a bit heavy, sweetheart,' said Linda, knowing full well what was wrong. 'What's the matter, babe?'

Anna shrugged as she splayed both hands. 'I'm just being a misery. Take no notice, I won't slit my wrists.'

'Now stop that. That's not what I meant. We just don't think you're all that happy, that's all. And maybe it's time for you to start going out again? In the evenings? With us, or get in contact with some of your old friends.'

'No thanks. I'm all right as I am. Yes, I will admit that I do sometimes feel a bit low, but it's nothing to get depressed over. I've got my lovely neighbour next door to talk to whenever I want. Rachel's smiling lined face has brought me out of the gloom more than once. Then there's Jackie the Avon girl coming and going with her catalogue ...'

Her sisters hid their feelings well. Of course they were gutted by Anna's pathetic attempt to make light of what was clearly appearing to be a lonely world that she moved around in. Neither of the girls felt comfortable in the silence that now hung in the air after Anna's back-handed confession. Glancing at each other, they couldn't be sure what was coming next or whether or not Anna knew that her husband was having an affair with his assistant manager, Bridget, the girl with the soulless dark brown eyes who dressed to kill. Taking the bull by the horns, Hazel spoke in a quiet voice, saying, 'We weren't sure what to do about the way things were going, babe. Or whether we were reading things wrongly.'

'With Bridget and Frank, you mean?'

'Well, that's not what I was gonna say—'

'Yes you were. So something is going on then?'

'A bit more than flirting, that's all . . . but it might be the time to nip it in the bud. We don't think it's too serious, babe, and we don't think that it's anything for you to worry *too* much over.'

'It's all right, Hazel.' Anna offered a knowing smile. 'You needn't look so worried. Nor you, Linda. I've known for a while what that pair were up to. Well, not *known* exactly, just suspicious – which is worse in a way. But I didn't think that you'd cottoned on to anything going on between them. I would have thought that you would have swung her around by that long curly ginger hair of hers if you had spotted her brushing up close to Frank. Or are you gonna tell me that it's all my husband's doing and that Bridget's just a simple innocent creature that's been lured in by his come-and-get-me eyes?'

'Like hell we are,' said Linda, taking a cigarette from her slim gold case. 'She's lucky I've not scratched her face beyond recognition. And trust me I would have liked to have done. But that's not the way to go about things is it? We don't want her crying on Frank's shoulder, do we?'

Anna suddenly felt sick. This was all sounding too serious for words, as if a proper affair was going on and not just a bit of flirting. 'So what is it you're trying to tell me?'

Hazel looked from Anna to Linda with no words needed. They had come here tonight to warn their younger sister to watch her step where Bridget, the sometimes coy and sometimes brazen flirt, was concerned. 'We're not trying to tell you anything, Anna. We just wanted to make sure that you knew what she's like around men. And Frank in particular.'

'Well, now that you do know that I know, we can drink a toast to it, can't we. I'm glad that you know but at the end of the day it's my problem not yours.' Fighting to control the tears welling behind her eyes, she said, with forced gaiety, 'So ... let's keep the wine flowing and eat, shall we? And while we do, you can fill me in as to what you've picked up in Prima. Is it for instance a bit of flirting and no more than that? Do they have a secret kiss and hug now and then?'

Hazel reached across the table. She squeezed Anna's trembling hand and smiled weakly at her. 'There's nothing we can tell you that is *fact*, babe. But come on, you're obviously ill at ease with this conversation. It's us you're talking to. Your big sisters. You don't have to cover your feelings.'

'Fair enough. Well go on then. Lay it on the line. But don't tell me half of it because that would be worse than you not saying anything.'

Hazel drew breath and leaned back in her chair. She knew that there was no going back now and she hadn't thought for one minute that they would have got this far this quickly. It was actually going better than she had thought it would. So, with both girls' attention on

31

her she quietly laid the cards on the table. She admitted that she and Linda had seen what had gone on and was still going on between Frank and Bridget. She told of the private little innuendos between them and the knowing looks they gave each other which gave them away. They spoke of the little asides that they shared in between serving the customers and the irritating little-girl laughter from the silly cow when the pair of them were behind the bar enjoying a drink or two together. And before they had even got round to dropping the bombshell that they slipped upstairs to the flat now and then, Anna gestured to indicate that she had heard enough.

Unable to take any more, she pursed her lips and covered her face with her hands, still trying her best not to break into tears. Then, taking a deep breath, she managed to say, 'I think I realised, if I'm honest with myself, that by keeping his distance Frank's been hiding his guilt for a long time.' She looked from one sister to the other before breaking into a feeble smile as the tears escaped.

'Even though the bastard's got the looks of a handsome movie star,' she said, as she dabbed her face dry with a tissue, 'he can't act to save his life. Guilt's written all over him.'

'I don't know about a movie star, babe,' murmured Linda, gutted to see her sister this broken. 'But I agree with you about the guilt. He blushes deep red every now and then whenever me and Hazel and the boys are in the restaurant. Especially lately.'

'And what about Bridget? Does she blush or just flash her silk knickers?'

'She flashes those all of the time at all the men, sweetheart.' Linda smiled. 'It's that Trevor Plumb, her husband, that I feel sorry for. It's painful to watch sometimes. There he sits in a corner of the restaurant when he's come in to give her a lift home, trying his best not to let on that he sees what she's up to. She only flirts with the attractive customers and hardly gives the plain and ugly ones a glance. I can't imagine what must go through Trevor's mind at times. Poor sod.'

'I couldn't agree more,' said Hazel. 'He seems a really nice guy. And he's got an honest face. I've seen him in there quite a few times when he's turned up to give that cow a lift home in his second-hand Anglia. He's a tall and handsome feller but obviously can't satisfy her lust for excitement. I love that sandy hair and those freckles. He's better looking than your Frank – in a way.'

Anna didn't need them to tell her who Bridget was married to because she already knew. She also knew that Trevor was a lovely guy, a swimming instructor who taught children locally in and around the East End as well as the disabled in the Stratford East swimming baths. She had found this out during conversations with him when he had dropped into the restaurant when she had been there.

'We don't have much to say to Bridget when we're in Prima,' said Hazel, offhandedly. 'She's makes herself busy coming and going from the kitchen to the tables and the bar when we're in. She's good at what she does when she is in working mode – I'll give her that.'

'I agree,' said Linda. 'But then she would keep busy and out of the way just to keep up appearances. Prima is our sister's restaurant as well as Frank's let's not forget.'

'Exactly,' said Anna. 'She knows when to act as if butter wouldn't melt in her mouth. But all of this apart I'm still jealous of the way Frank pays her more attention than he does me. And I'm frightened that she's stealing him away.' Covering her face and trying not to break down she shook her head. 'I don't want to lose him. I've never loved anyone else. And I never in a million years thought that he would be taken from me by someone else. Especially not her.'

'Us neither,' said Hazel. 'You were the ideal couple. But don't give up on yourself, babe. After all, what's to say you wouldn't meet someone else and fall in love? You'd have to prise yourself out of this house though and start to socialise a bit. Have some fun perhaps? You never go out in the evenings and you're on duty with the twins practically twenty-four hours a day. Mum would baby-sit, you know she would. You're only twenty-six for Christ's sake.'

'It never occurs to me to go out. I'm a married woman with two babies. I didn't even consider it to be an option.'

'Well, maybe it's time you did start getting back to your old self. Once upon a time there was no keeping you down. Remember that cold day in February in Hyde Park three or so years ago when thousands of postal workers came out on strike in favour of a pay claim for telegraphists? There you were giving support even though you were a telephonist and not a telegraphist. Nothing or nobody could have stopped you from shouting the odds against unfairness once your back was up.'

'*Nearly* twenty-six,' said Anna.

'All right, nearly. And you being *nearly* twenty-six is why we're here. We want to arrange a night out doing a pub crawl or going up West to a nightclub. Us three and our wayward girls as Mum calls them, and your old friends. We want you to pick up the phone and ring round.'

Anna raised an eyebrow. 'Your wayward girls are prostitutes. What would any of my old friends make of that? In any case that's exactly what I did earlier on. I phoned Beryl. You remember her?'

'Of course we do. She was your best mate when you were at school, wasn't she?'

'Yes. And for a little while afterwards.'

'That's right. So what about her?'

'She's dead. Her mum answered the phone. She's there looking after the little ones.'

'Good God,' murmured Hazel. 'I can't believe that.'

'Me neither, babe,' said Linda. 'What happened? Was there an accident?'

'No. She had cancer.'

'Jesus wept.' Linda slowly shook her head. 'Cancer at her age?'

'Yep.'

'Phew ... that must 'ave knocked you for six, sweetheart, cos it's kicked me in the guts and she wasn't my best friend.'

'I know. Anyway ...' Anna shrugged and sighed. 'A night out would be great but I don't know about including my old mates.'

'Because of our girls?' said Hazel. 'You don't have to say what they do for a living, babe. And anyway, each and every one is an attractive up-market hostess who sometimes entertains their clients in the classy rooms at the top of our house. They're not common prostitutes. And you know they're a lot of fun to be with.'

'Give me time to think about it. My birthday's not for weeks. Anything could happen in the meantime. I might have kicked Frank out by then or sent Bridget packing so that me and my *husband* can pick up where we left off before *she* came along.'

'Fair enough,' said Linda. 'You've got three weeks to think about where you'd like to go on your birthday.'

'Never mind my birthday. I want my life back. And I want Bridget out of my marriage. I *am* jealous of her – I am. I'm jealous and I hate the feeling. It eats and eats away at you. It takes you over. Wakes you in the night and stops you from thinking about much else during the day.'

'But you've got nothing to be envious of, sweetheart,' murmured Hazel. She was upset to hear her baby sister talking like this. 'You're much better looking than she is. And no one's taken in by that phoney innocent expression of hers. She's a calculating little cow who's not only interested in getting your husband into bed but most likely had her sights set on owning your half share of the restaurant.'

'She's welcome to it.'

'No she's not. And don't you say that again or it might just happen. You fight for every single penny that's rightfully yours . . . if it should come to that. I've seen women who've been so fucked up by this kind of

36

thing that they've taken a packed suitcase to walk away and end up with nothing. Why do you think that some girls turn to prostitution? Because they decided when they were innocent little children that this is what they wanted to be when they grew up? A good majority of young women have been left high and dry by their husbands who've gone off with someone else.'

'Don't exaggerate,' said Anna.

'Exaggerate? No, sweetheart. It's real. Respect and faded love goes right down the drain when it's balanced against money. So don't even think of talking like that again or it just might end up happening to you as well. You've got our twins to think of if not yourself.'

Anna went quiet and leaned back in her chair, looking from one to the other of her sisters. When she eventually spoke it was in a more sensible and calm tone. 'All right. You've made your point and it's a good one. Enough said. I know what the pair of you are trying to do. And I *will* pick myself up. I *will* get the old Anna spirit back. And if necessary I'll fight for Frank with both fists and my feet because I want my husband back. I want us to be the way we were.'

Downing her wine in one, Anna reached for the bottle to top it up again. 'I suppose I've been partly to blame for the flirting that's been going on. Frank's been lying through his back teeth as to why he's late home every night and deep down I think I knew why but I didn't want to believe it, never mind face up to it. I was too scared to ask what was going on between him and her if you want the truth. Too scared to ask because I was dreading the answer. Because, after all, what could I have done if he openly admitted it? If he said that he wanted to be with her and not me? I can't nail 'is feet to the floor, can I?'

A silence filled the room until Hazel quietly said, 'I know what you mean, babe. This is more or less what we were worried about. We've seen the chemistry that's developed between the pair of them. And thinking about it, ginger-nut might well have *wanted* us to see it.'

'You could be right there, Hazel.' Linda leaned both elbows on the table and cupped her face as she looked into Anna's. 'She might well have been hoping for this. Hoping to push Frank into telling you. Which, after all's said and done, was not all that bright, was it? But never mind, at least we're ahead of the game now. All three of us. She won't have a leg to stand on if she carries on the way she's going. A broken knee cap can be very painful.'

'Oh stop it,' said Anna, 'stop talking like that. I don't like it. But I have taken on board all that you've said. Now I just need to sit and think about things quietly. I can look at it in a different light now that we've talked. I don't feel as if I'm on my own now. I'll do what I think is best for me and the twins.'

Hazel gave Linda a look to let her know that enough had been said and they had achieved what they had set out to do. She then helped herself to a prawn cracker and shrugged. 'It's the same old story every time. And who is it that gets the blame? The wives at home, getting on with all the drudgery and all the while they haven't got a clue what their old man's getting up to.'

'Tell me about it,' said Anna. 'Tell me about it.'

38

Chapter Two

Just before the girls left, Hazel suggested that Anna might want to pay a little visit to the restaurant the next day for a coffee while Ivy took care of the twins. But she needn't have worried because this was exactly what Anna intended to do in any case. The girls had made their parting brief, leaving their sister at the table with the half-empty containers of Chinese food and enough wine to send her off to sleep for the night. They wouldn't have been too surprised to learn that once she heard the street door close behind them, Anna wept. While her sisters were there, she had held on tightly to her emotions even when she had felt queasy deep down inside. But now that she knew for certain that Bridget hadn't managed to pull the wool over their eyes, relief balanced the suffering that she had been going through night after night after night.

Soon after midnight Anna, having patiently waited in the silence for Frank to come home so that they could have a little chat, had done her very best to give him the benefit of the doubt and had told herself over and over agan that this affair must be just a flash in the pan – that he had succumbed to a professional tease who could be sacked and sent packing. But she was so tired that she could hardly keep her eyes open and decided to go to bed; perhaps she could talk to him once he was home and in bed, but just before she switched off the lights she heard a black taxi pulling up and its engine running. Her heart felt as if it would leap out of her chest it was pounding so much and she had to ask herself why she was allowing herself to get into this state. Frank was back from Prima, that was all. And if he wasn't too drunk to have a sensible conversation then they would have one. It was that simple. So why then was her heart thumping?

The stumbling footsteps she heard in the passage told her she would get little out of him tonight. He came into the room and stood peering at her as he swayed on his feet and tried to say something, but his speech was so slurred that it was incomprehensible. Anna looked at her husband, wondering why she had not complained before when he had come home in this state. Or why she hadn't got angry over it. Bracing herself, she spoke quietly, saying, 'Why don't you come and sit down. I've opened a nice bottle of red wine.'

'Have you?' he said, still swaying. 'That's nice.'

'Do you want me to pour you a glass?'

'Why not? That would be lovely.'

'Are you hungry? Would you like a sandwich?'

'No. A glass of wine will be enough.' He slumped down onto the sofa and kicked off his shoes. 'Bloody busy at the restaurant, Anna. Fuck me, it was busy. Rushed off our feet. But never mind – it's putting money into our coffers, darling.'

'And that can't be a bad thing,' she said, as she went to the sideboard to pour his drink.

'No. That's not a bad thing. A little house in the countryside, Anna. That's what it's all about. We'll put all our money by and get us a second home. People with a bit of spare cash are doing that now you know. I hear things in that restaurant.'

Anna handed him his glass of wine and sat beside him on the sofa. 'Do you know what I think,' she said. 'I think it's time we had a family holiday. In the country perhaps. Devon or Cornwall for a week. The fresh air would do our babies the world of good.'

'I'm sure it would, darling, but I won't be able to take time off this year.' He put an arm around her shoulders and looked into her face but the smell of drink on his breath made her want to pull away. He had been drinking gin and tonics – probably large ones.

'But you could go away with our boys,' he said. 'You could go with your mum to Butlins for a fortnight. You'd like that wouldn't you?'

'No, not really.' She laughed quietly at him. 'I don't think you would suggest it if you were sober.'

'Wouldn't I?'

'No.'

'Oh. Sorry. Shall we have a cuddle on the sofa instead of talking about holidays then?'

'Like we used to you mean?'

'Yeah. Like we used to.' He slumped back, closed his eyes and quietly giggled. 'We were like fucking rabbits weren't we?'

'Not lately though, Frank. Not lately. Why do you reckon that is?'

'Tired ain't I. Exhausted from running that fucking restaurant. Anyway, it'll all work out. Always does.' He heaved himself up and stumbled out of the room saying, 'Going to bed.'

41

And that was it. That was all he had to offer her. She could hardly believe just how much he had changed over the past nine months or so. They had been the idyllic couple. Always laughing, always making love, always cracking jokes. Until Bridget came along. She found herself wondering if deep down Frank had always been selfish, always put what he wanted before anything else. She decided not to go there, to resist weighing up the pros and cons, the good and the bad points. The trouble was he hadn't lost his attractive looks, which made her want to be held close by the bastard. His dark blue eyes, tanned complexion and black hair still had her longing to fall into his arms, even though he had gone from a fun-loving guy to someone who seemed like a stranger. This was still what she wanted.

Tired though she was, Anna was not in the right mood to sleep and didn't feel in the least bit like lying next to Frank in bed as if everything was normal. And neither did she want to give vent to her feelings and tell him that the girls had been round and that they knew about Bridget. Her mind switched from one thing to another as she remembered little innuendos that she had heard from her regulars whenever she had been in Prima. She realised now that they had, in their own gentle way, been giving her subtle messages about the affair. So many other little incidents involving the sneaky pair were floating in and out of her mind now, almost as if they were re-runs of an old film. It was all so obvious: Frank and Bridget had been at it from as far back as when she had stopped working at Prima, when she was four months pregnant and Bridget had been promoted from head waitress to assistant manager.

For her own reasons, Anna decided not to let on to Frank that Hazel and Linda had been round that evening. Before he had staggered in she had made sure there were no traces left of their visit. She had dropped all of the takeaway containers and leftover food into a black bin bag and dumped the lot into their dustbin at the back of the garden, knowing that the bin men would be collecting the next day. She had then opened all of the downstairs windows and sprayed the entire ground floor of the house as well as the staircase with fresh air spray to get rid of the lingering smell of the Chinese food. She wanted to keep him totally in the dark as to what she knew for certain and what she wasn't quite sure about.

In her soft, pink and blue checked pyjamas and matching housecoat, as she sat in an armchair close to the fire where no fire burned, she tried to think of what to do for the best. She despised Frank for the damage he had done to their marriage, but at the same time she loved him for all of the good times they had shared together. She wanted to strangle him one minute and hold him close the next as all kinds of conflicting emotions swept through her. Frank had, as usual, made a display of being too exhausted to do much else other than utter those few words before he climbed the stairs to the bedroom with no thoughts of justifying another of his late nights. She knew that there would have been no point in her trying to have a proper conversation with him because he would have dismissed whatever she had to say as boring and gone to bed in any case.

43

She recalled his expression a week or so earlier when she asked why he was so tired all of the time. His only response was to wipe his forehead and look at her with an expression of apathy before strolling out of the room shaking his head. Tonight, though, she had managed to smile sweetly at him when she had said, 'I'm sure you must have had a hard time at the restaurant, Frank.' And then called him a two-timing bastard under her breath. By keeping her mouth shut and her temper in its place she had proved that she did have the strength of mind to know when to hold her tongue. The only thing that she wasn't comfortable about was that she was going to have to get into the bed next to him and carry on the charade of there being nothing wrong. She didn't want him in her space, never mind their bodies possibly touching when he turned over in the night because, since he hadn't taken a shower, she knew that the scent of Bridget would be on him.

Feeling that she should brave it out, she drew comfort from the fact that when she looked into his face he could have no idea that she knew what he had been getting up to. She realised that this feeble sense of triumph was a sad replacement for feeling loved, but at least it was better than nothing. Much better.

Topping up her glass of wine she quietly spoke to herself, saying, 'It's *her* fault that your heart feels as if it's being gripped and squeezed, but it's your own fault, Anna, for being a coward and not facing up to the truth that has been staring you right in the face.'

She sipped her drink and slowly shook her head. 'You knew all along what you were doing, Bridget. You even had me believe that you were my friend. *My* friend and not Frank's. Well ... I might be a little bit drunk now but I won't be tomorrow when I walk into Prima and sack you.' She smiled at the thought of it and then raised her glass, saying, 'Good riddance to bad rubbish. At least horrible suspicion's no longer eating away at me. Hazel and Linda are girls who tell it as it is without frills or exaggeration. So I have no reason to doubt what they told me about you. They're right as a rule about most things and their timing tonight was spot on. I should have known my sisters wouldn't allow someone to pull the wool over my eyes. I should have known they would have seen through all of your phoney sweetness and light.'

Too tired to think anymore, Anna let the tears come. 'You were the only one of my boyfriends that I loved, Frank, the only one I gave myself to – and you've let that cow ruin it all.'

Swallowing against the lump in her throat, Anna wiped away her tears with the back of her hand then gazed at her wedding ring. She felt completely alone in the house even though she was not the only one there. A touch giddy from all the wine, she again whispered to herself. 'This isn't you, Frank ... this isn't my Frank who was always so caring before she came along. You *did* love me – I know you did.' She dabbed her face with the hem of her soft blue dressing gown and told herself that she had to be strong, had to look forward and not backward.

Her head now gently throbbing from trying to work things out, she tried to imagine a gentle hand sweeping all of the questions and worry away and a soft voice telling her that it wasn't her fault. That she mustn't blame herself for having been snared in this battlefield of changing emotions. And that she wasn't the only injured party. Bridget's unassuming young husband, Trevor, was also in the ring and now Anna wondered if he knew what was going on. In fact, since it had been so blatantly obvious to others, she wondered how he could possibly have missed it. But none of this mattered in any case because the ball was now in her court and the match was only just beginning.

Ready for her pillow at last, she switched off the lamp and left the comfort of the snug for the bedroom. Once in bed though, with Frank sound asleep, she gazed at his handsome strong face and his broad, naked olive-skinned shoulders and felt her anger rise as vivid images of him in bed with Bridget filled her mind. As she turned over so as to have her back to him she caught a faint, now familiar, whiff of perfume – not one that she ever wore. Pulling herself up again she switched on the bedside lamp and tipped the shade so that the light would shine onto Frank's face. She stared at him as he lay on his side, and had to use every bit of will power to stop herself from grabbing and tugging at his thick dark hair or pressing her pillow over his face.

Moaning contentedly in his sleep Frank, however, was clearly on cloud nine within the dream where she imagined him to be playing the role of the handsome hero screwing the leading actress in a B movie. 'You rotten, stinking, lousy two-timing bastard,' she murmured. 'I hate your guts and I don't want to sleep in the same bed as you.'

Too drunk, and possibly too wrapped up in his own

little world of wet dreams for her animosity to have any chance of filtering through, Frank turned over onto his front without waking up. Now she had a full view of his beautiful strong back which had once been a major attraction. She still couldn't believe that he had changed from a great hunk of a guy to a sneak-around, mendacious bastard. He had had a lot to drink by the time he had arrived home, and had worked a long shift, so perhaps he could be forgiven for hardly having said a word, but he hadn't given their sleeping babies his usual fatherly stroke either.

Staring out at nothing and in no mood to read her book, Anna could hear the echoing sound of her neighbour Rachel bolting her back door. Her ageing friend, who always seemed to have long soft wisps of grey hair escaping from the French pleat at the back of her head, was in her eighties and going to bed later than Anna was. Rachel, whose lined face spoke volumes about her having had a hard life, was energetic enough to plant out her seedlings at night in her walled garden. At least this brought Anna a faint smile because the old girl had said more than once, 'The moon is just as important to bring on seedlings as it is to light the way in the dark when a man can't find his way home.' Anna wondered if she had been alluding to Frank's late-night homecomings. She also wondered what her neighbour, who was full of Jewish jokes and clever sayings, would think if she saw this little scene of a young handsome couple in bed. She glanced at her spouse again and felt nothing but contempt. Here she was, nearly twenty-six years old, and in bed with a book while her husband dreamed of his lover.

*

Rachel had lived by herself for quite a while in her old fashioned two-up-two-down rented house next door. She had been kind on the day that Anna and Frank got the keys to this house, and had remained kind ever since. She sometimes gave Anna homemade soup in a Tupperware container. And occasionally, when Anna had been reclining on her sun-bed in her small walled garden with a broken section between their houses, Rachel would give her a buttered bagel and a glass of orange juice. She was a shining example of an East Ender who had come through a lousy life of rotten fortune and broken dreams but still made the most of every God-given day.

Not only did Rachel have a canny outlook on the world and its people, but she could also cut through a quarrel between neighbours with a one-liner to stop them in their tracks, and have them laughing or ashamed of themselves. And even more poignant where Anna was concerned, the old girl was always there for her when she was feeling a touch on the lonely side and in need of a friend to talk to over freshly drawn tea in a china cup.

Living on a state pension, the woman was excellent at making a small amount of money go further than anyone because she only ever shopped in the local markets, and always minutes before the stallholders were packing up. So instead of living hand to mouth, as most old folks did, her larder was stocked up for little emergencies – a habit left over from wartime. Sometimes she would come home from one of her trips to the local markets with her large basket on wheels crammed with vegetables of one sort or another that she would sell for a small profit to the corner shop at the end of the turning.

A widow of five years, she told warm stories of the man she had married some fifty years ago, who had dropped down dead in his vegetable patch. She was also good at giving gentle advice and, occasionally, Anna had been tempted to open up to her, but as it turned out there was no need because she had already worked out for herself that Anna was lonely. She had sometimes asked why the twins' father spent so much time away from the home and this, Anna felt sure, was Rachel's way of leaving her back door open should she need a shoulder to cry on at any time of the day or night.

With so much going through her mind and her resentment towards Frank growing, she couldn't bear to lie next to someone who had become like a stranger and smelled of someone else's scent. Drawing back the covers, she slipped out of bed, out of the room, and crept down the stairs so as not to disturb her sleeping twins. Collecting the spare quilt from the linen cupboard on the way, she felt sure that Frank wouldn't notice or care that her side of the bed was empty and going cold. Animosity wasn't the only reason for her leaving the room – she wanted to be by herself so that she could plan how to go about things the next day; what she would say and what she might do to Bridget when she paid her a visit at the restaurant.

After collecting some herbal pills that Rachel had given to help her sleep just before the twins were due, Anna went into the sitting room and made herself comfortable on the sofa ... her makeshift bed. Once settled, she asked herself why she hadn't done this before: left Frank to dream and snore alone while she had the peace and quiet of the ground floor to herself. By the soft glow of her small table lamp, she curled up, pulling the padded quilt to her chin, and glanced at her Welsh dresser and the cut glass decanter half filled with sherry. She smiled wistfully to herself because the decanter had been a wedding gift from Ivy, her altruistic and doting mother who she would be leaving the twins with the next day.

Closing her eyes, she whispered, 'You'll make it all right, Mum, I know you will.' She then sank her head into her feather cushion and sensed a kind of intoxicating calm flowing gently through her as she closed her eyes and blocked out all thoughts of her long lonely evenings. Her sisters had told her that they had known for a while that she wasn't happy and that she spent most nights watching television by herself, because Anna's lovely old neighbour had taken them to one side and whispered it long before now.

So, as the quiet dark streets outside settled down for the night, Anna promised herself that she would get back to the person she once was – a light-hearted, fun-loving girl. She imagined herself going out to nice restaurants again, with her sisters, while Ivy looked after the twins. Earlier on, Linda had been firmer than Hazel, insisting that Anna put all that had happened between Bridget and Frank in the dustbin where it belonged and that it would be Bridget who would lose out in the end.

She had said the girl would not only lose her husband but get the push from Frank as well, once their little affair was out in the open and in the public domain. This was all pie in the sky as far as Anna was concerned, and by the time Linda had got round to telling her that she wasn't to torment herself over what Frank might be getting up to, she had already got to this point herself as if it had been written into her diary. She was ready for battle.

It infuriated her the way Frank walked around in a little world of his own, behaving as if she didn't exist and happier when getting ready for work in the mornings than when at home at the weekends when the restaurant was closed. Even when he *had* spent time with his family at weekends he was prone to singing along to a favourite LP, and often with those bulky black earphones of his on. With the herbal pills making her feel drowsy, Anna snuggled deeper into her bedding and told herself that she wasn't alone, that she had her beautiful twin babies, her family, and her lovely friend next door. Comfortable on the big squashy sofa that was her bed, she sank her head deeper into the silky feathered cushion and drifted off into sleep.

In his usual buoyant morning mood, Frank left the house at nine o'clock sharp to go to his brothers' restaurant at Tower Hill — as he did every Tuesday, their busiest day — not only to give them a hand but because he liked the change of environment. So, knowing that her husband would be working a full day in another area, it seemed a perfect time for Anna to pay her visit to Bridget. Frank had not asked her why she had slept on the sofa but, just in case he had bothered to ask, she had been ready with an answer, a deliberate cliché, that she had had a 'headache'. But he hadn't mentioned one word of it and she wondered if this was out of guilt. He didn't want to ask questions because he didn't want a confrontation. Anna couldn't quite work it out but neither did she want to.

She could no longer leave things be and wait to see how they panned out. Now she had to send the interloper packing. With all sorts of questions and worries flying through her mind, she went into the sitting room again and looked at the bedding. Since she was always the first one up so as to see to the twins, Frank could have been forgiven for not having realised that she had left their bed while he was still asleep, but there was no escaping the fact that the spare padded quilt was on the sofa.

'Forget it, Anna,' she told herself, as she went upstairs to gather a clean set of clothes for each of her babies from a large drawer in an old waxed pine chest. 'Don't waste your energy. If he wants to go then good riddance. If he wants to stay, then he has to come clean and make an apology. Enough is enough.'

Standing between their cots and looking from one to the other of her twin boys, she said, 'We'll be all right. We'll be fine. We've got your grandma and we've got your aunties who love you to bits.'

Smiling up at their young mother and gurgling, Oliver and James brought warmth back into Anna's heart as nothing else could. She leaned over to kiss one and then the other as she whispered, 'Your daddy's gone off the rails a bit that's all. It'll all come out in the wash.' She picked up Oliver first to dress him in his outdoor clothes and, as she held him in her arms, he looked at her amd smiled and she noticed that a first tooth was just beginning to show. This seemed like the best present she could have been given. A little pearly milestone.

An hour or so later, her mind flying from one thought to another once she had the twins dressed and ready and sleeping soundly in their twin pram, she relaxed in an armchair to enjoy a freshly percolated cup of coffee. Her view of her small walled garden lifted her spirits. There was a mass of beautiful forget-me-nots and some pansies opening up around the old gnarled apple tree. So, while the twins slept peacefully in the passage, Anna began to get herself ready in her own time, determined to look good. Once showered, she brushed her hair until it shone and spent more time than she had done in a while in front of the mirror putting on her eye makeup and, in particular, her favourite Corn Silk powder and lipstick chosen from her Avon catalogue. She wanted to feel and look her best when she faced Bridget.

In her pale tan leather boots with Cuban heels, flowing green and rust skirt with matching jacket set off by her black polo neck, and her chunky gold neck-chain, she felt as if she was almost back to her old self again. Checking her appearance in the full-length mirror on the passage wall, she realised that it had been a long time since she had been given a reason to get dressed up and memories of her days as a single girl came flooding back. A time when Frank hadn't been able to take his eyes off her when they were out and about, going to parties and nightclubs. A time when they were often on the dance floor until the band packed up and they then sat with the night owls drinking and chatting.

Since giving birth, she had simply pulled on a pair of corduroys or jeans and a sweater in the mornings before getting on with her role as mother, laundry maid and housekeeper without any thoughts of powdering her nose or swiping on some lipstick. Frank, on the other hand, had taken to primping himself and dressing as if he were a prince among men, wearing expensive aromatic aftershave to go to work and leaving the house as if it were a hotel and not a home.

Noticing the faint scent of his aftershave in the air, she put on her gold bangles and her rings, feeling how she imagined her sisters must do every day of the week. But Anna was happy enough if this one day of excitement was all she was going to get for a while, because she was about to shine a spotlight on the secret little love planet where Frank liked to escape. Ready to go on her mission, she eased the twins' navy and chrome pram out of the passage and into the tiny front garden with both her baby boys sleeping soundly. For a brief moment she thought about Frank as she looked from one little face to the other and it dawned on her that it was he who was the loser, not she. He was missing out on this very special time, especially today when that first pearly tooth showed itself.

'Your daddy's loss is not mine,' she said, and took a deep breath as she willed herself not to lose her confidence. This possible breakdown of her marriage wasn't what she wanted and was the last thing that she ever thought she would be doing. Going on a mission to sort out her husband's lover? No way. But if it was to turn out all right for her and the twins she had to try and keep her blood on the boil and be in the right mood when she walked into her and Frank's family restaurant to see off Bridget once and for all.

All she could hope for now was that some of her old regulars would be in today to silently will her on. Several of those who frequented Prima's had been there in the beginning when they first opened and knew Anna and Frank as the happy couple running their restaurant together and making a success of it. She couldn't imagine what they were making of Bridget who, from all that her sisters had told her, had kicked her shoes under the bed in the small flat above Prima that most knew Anna and Frank had onced shared. The bed in the little love nest that had been their first home after they were married – their cosy one-bedroom flat above their workplace, the restaurant which had previously been a truckers' café before they turned it into the successful friendly place it now was.

'Oh well ... look what the wind's blown in,' said Ivy, glancing from her daughter's face to the twins in the pram. She then turned her eyes to heaven before cautiously saying, 'I take it your sisters paid a visit last night or you wouldn't be here?' She knew they had but was trying to make light of it.

'Well, if it's a problem,' said Anna, going along with the little bit of play-acting, 'I'll take Oliver and James over to Frank's mum. You know how much she loves having them to herself for a while.'

'Suit yerself,' said Ivy, from the doorway of her masionette in Peabody Street as she glanced from left to right hoping to spot a neighbour so as to show off her grandsons. All she could see was an elderly Asian couple in traditional dress coming along. She knew them quite well; they had four daughters who, between them, seemed to be forever pregnant and proudly pushing a pram or two. 'There won't be any white faces around here soon,' murmured Ivy as she waved her daughter through the open doorway and into the wide passage where she could park the pram as usual.

Easing the front wheels up and over the doorstep, Anna drew breath. 'You'll get done for being racist if you keep on saying things like that, Mum.'

'That wouldn't bother me, I'll be among friends in Holloway Prison.' She laughed, then looked over her daughter's shoulder, nodding and smiling at the old couple.

'Did it go all right down at the housing office, sweetheart?' she said, her voice raised and all friendly.

'Much better than so far!' said the gentleman. 'It looks like they will give us one of those lovely flats in skyscrapers. We are over the moon!'

'That doesn't surprise me,' said Ivy, 'and I'll tell you why! That little terraced house you're renting will be sold off to private buyers just like all the others round this way. They'll get a fortune for your place once it's been renovated.'

Laughing, the neighbours from along the turning showed a hand. 'We don't care what they do with it, Ivy! We are going to get a brand new council flat! And soon!'

'Good luck to the pair of yer! Don't forget to give me the address before you go!'

'We won't! Don't worry!' said Mr Dayjoo as he placed a hand on his heart. 'You, my friend, will be the first guest that we invite in for a cup of your favourite British tea.'

'I'll hold you to that,' said Ivy, smiling as she closed the door.

Anna slowly shook her head. 'You're so two-faced at times, Mum. And the word's renovated, not renoviated.'

'I know that. And as for the pretending to be racist, I just like to keep both sides of my friends happy, that's all.' She smiled at Anna and could see that her lovely soft eyes looked greener than ever with the sun coming into the room and shining onto her daughter's face. Coming up to her fifty-sixth birthday, even though life had been a little hard on her, Ivy was still a handsome woman herself, medium height and with a soft curvy figure and no spare fat. If push were to come to shove, she would have to admit that she, just like Anna, believed that there was a Lord keeping watch over the lot of them even if at times the Lord was dozing.

She pushed her fingers through her short wavy fair hair and said, 'Gwen from next door will 'ave been at the curtains eavesdropping when you arrived so my racist comment, as you call it, was to keep her happy. I told her not to knock once you were here but I bet she will.'

'Oh, right. So you sowed a nice little seed of mystery then?'

Ivy ignored that comment and leaned over the pram, slowly shaking her head and smiling at her grandbabies. Then in a whisper she said, 'Angels, sleeping angels.'

Anna, warm and comfortable in her mum's company and ever amused by her went into the kitchen and filled the kettle. She hadn't bothered to phone and tell Ivy that she was on her way over, nor ask if she would baby-sit, because her sisters had told her the night before that they were popping in to see their mother on their way home. She guessed they would have filled her in on everything. Hearing a low sigh escape from her mum as she came into the room, Anna turned and held out her arms for a hug. Obliging, and a little too choked to speak, Ivy squeezed her tightly and then looked intently at her youngest daughter. 'It'll all come out in the wash, sweetheart, don't you worry.'

'I know it will, Mum. And *you* don't have to worry about *me*. Not now that you all know and I don't have to keep secrets as if *I've* done something wrong.'

'Fucking men,' said Ivy as she set two big china cups onto saucers. 'They use their dicks like torches to hone in on a bitch on heat in the dark. They're worse than stray dogs. But I never thought that Frank would turn out like this. I suppose he's just forgotten how to behave decently, that's all.'

'You haven't told Frank's mum have you? Only I did say to the girls to tell you not to. I gave them that message. Did they remember to tell you? I don't want to upset her just yet.'

'That's not what you mean, Anna. I'm not daft. You don't want her to fly off the handle – which she will do once she does know. You've been more like a daughter to that woman than you have to me.'

'Oh Mum, please! I'm not in the mood for your baiting and I'm not stopping long. And it's not entirely Frank's fault all of this – it's that girl we took on in good faith. Now then, I've made the bottles up and all you have to do—'

'Is to stand them in a pan of boiling water to warm up.' Ivy cut in. 'I've done it before, you know. What time is their next feed due?'

Anna glanced at her wristwatch. 'In about an hour.'

'And if they don't wake up for it?'

'Give them ten minutes over and then do what you usually do, Grandma.' Anna smiled warmly at Ivy. 'I don't know what I'd do without you.'

'Nor do I,' said Ivy, keeping her emotions in check. Once Anna had gone, then she would shed a tear, or swear angrily and mentally throttle Frank before mentally squeezing the life out of the waitress who had got her claws into her son-in-law. The girl who dressed to kill and who had been taken in by his handsome looks, Italian suit, gold cufflinks and soft black leather wallet.

'I'm not sure now, though . . .' Anna sighed. 'I'm having second thoughts as to whether it would be best if you did phone Frank's mum today and tell her. But can we trust her not to phone Frank to give him a mouthful?'

'What if she did? He fucking well deserves it.'

'I know he does. But I want a whole day with him having no idea that I know.' She leaned against the kitchen sink and looked Ivy in the face. 'I'm angry, but worse than that I'm really hurt by this, Mum. It's that lush Bridget that's pulled him in by crossing and uncrossing her legs and showing off her fancy knickers. But I want to do it *my* way. Catch the bitch off guard and give her a good right hander.'

Ivy drew breath and then pointed a finger at her daughter, saying, 'Don't you dare lay a finger on her, Anna. From what I've heard she's a canny little cow—'

'Whose mouth wouldn't melt butter. I think I've got the message. But I will try not to leave 'er with a broken jaw.'

'Don't be silly. And besides, your sisters could 'ave got it wrong. Whenever I've been in she's been as nice as pie. And I've not seen 'er flirt once with Frank.'

'Of course you wouldn't have done! She's too clever for that. You're his mother-in-law for Christ's sake! She's hardly gonna squeeze up close to him while you're around, is she?'

'That's true. But I still don't think you should move too quickly, that's all I'm saying. And apart from that what if Frank doesn't take your side which ... I very much doubt that he will if you show him up at the restaurant and in front of customers.'

'Frank's at his brother's place at Tower Hill today. I'm not daft – I wouldn't punch her on the nose if he was at Prima Pasta.'

'Well, if she is mostly to blame, you'll be playing right into her hands if you so much as touch her. She'll get Frank's sympathy whichever way it goes. This ain't the way to play it, sweetheart.'

'I'm not playing a game, Mum. And I know this must be painful after what you've been through. You still wish you hadn't broken Dad's tart's nose—'

'Too bloody well right I do. And you know why if you think back to all the rows. He wouldn't have left me for that ugly cow if I had played it differently, if I'd have acted the little girl hurt bit, shed a tear, said I could

60

forgive and forget. He would have stayed with us if I had made me an easier option than him going off to Wales with her.'

Still leaning against the surface, her arms now folded, Anna said, 'And that's what you would have wanted is it? That's what you could have lived with? Dad here now and harbouring the over-romanticised thoughts that he'd given up the love of his life for you because you'd been so good about it all?'

'Bollocks to that. You know I wouldn't put up with that. Fucking liberty taker is what your father was.'

'Well, then?'

'Oh, do what you think is best, Anna.' Ivy dropped down onto a kitchen chair and held a hand to her forehead. 'I don't know who makes me more sick – dopey men or husband thieves.' She raised her eyes to meet Anna's. 'How can they sleep at night? Women who go out of their way to take someone's husband? I can't believe that anyone would do something like this. You've got twin babies between you for Christ's sake. And she's married to a lovely feller. You and the girls must 'ave got it wrong, love. Surely this can't be right?'

'I've seen the way she looks at Frank when I pop into Prima.'

'But she's never given you any reason to pull her up?'

'Of course not. She's too clever for that. Types like Bridget don't give a toss about anyone but themselves. By the time she's finished she will have turned his family against me. She must have seen Frank as a target when she first walked into our restaurant for that interview. The handsome, successful restaurateur that only need open up for five days a week? She was straight in. As soon as I was gone in *she* went, flashing her legs, pouting her lips, and fluttering the eyelashes.

'The thought of Frank holding another woman close wasn't even a tiny question in the back of my mind at that time. You know what we were like. We shared the same sense of humour; the same likes and dislikes. We had the same dreams. And we really did love each other, it didn't even have to be voiced. We just knew it. And, all right, he might not have been as over the moon about my being pregnant with the twins as I thought he would be, but deep down he was as proud as Punch.'

'I know, I know,' said Ivy slowly, the disappointment showing in her face. 'But I've seen Bridget in the restaurant and she doesn't come across as a lousy husband stealer. She obviously spends a lot of time in front of the mirror and she is nice looking, but that's no reason to be jealous of her, is it? I mean, we don't know for sure that he's been sleeping with her ... Do we?'

'Of course he has. And I'm not jealous! I'm angry! I've been totally humiliated! From the moment I set eyes on her I saw what she was up to by the way she looked dispassionately at me but smiled sweetly at Frank. I should have *known* she would be a marriage breaker. When that type wants something they just zone in and go all out, regardless. She all but lays her body on the bar and has the gall to act like a little girl, all sweetness and light, while doing so. It's *sickening* to watch.'

'Well, maybe I'm the fool for missing it then?' said Ivy, thoughtfully.

'No. You just weren't looking because decent people

don't. We don't expect women to perform the way that tease behaves. Frank didn't stand a chance, trust me.'

'Oh, give me a break, love. Frank? He's no different to the rest of 'em. Men can smell a bitch on heat from a mile off and then forget that they're married with—'

'Mum! Stop talking about the twins' dad like that.' Anna, suddenly on the verge of tears, went on. 'Why didn't you say something when that woman gave Dad the eye in the pub? Would you 'ave taken any notice of your mother if she had told you that Dad was being lured in by a charlatan?'

'No I wouldn't. I would have gone *potty* if she had of accused your father of being taken in by a silly cow. But now I know different of course.'

'Well, there we are then. Enough said.'

'But on the other hand—' The sound of the ding-dong doorbell stopped her short. Slowly shaking her head she said, 'I bet you my bottom dollar that's Gwen come to have a look at my grandsons. She can't resist little babies.'

'Well, don't tell her about Frank and Bridget,' warned Anna.

'As if I would,' said Ivy as she went to open the door.

Anna knew very well that as soon as she was gone Ivy and Gwen would be debating as to what either of the two of them would do to Frank if they saw him out on a dark night. But really, this didn't bother her as much as she made out. Gwen from next door was Ivy's best friend and the doting mother of John, the thirty-two-year-old who had at last told her that he was gay.

It had taken John two years to pluck up the courage

to stop dropping hints ever since the November of 1970 when the Gay Liberation Front was formed. When he did finally tell Gwen that he wasn't the marrying type, and explained why, she had surprised him. Even though his mother was every bit the old-fashioned housewife, she had simply shrugged it off, saying, 'I knew you was too pretty to be a boxer from the moment you opened your eyes for your first drop of breast milk.' She hadn't treated him any differently since, and continued to welcome his friends into her humble home whenever they knocked on the door.

When Gwen had moved into the maisonette next door to Ivy soon after her husband had passed away, she had been a touch isolated because her son and only offspring was a sociable, popular guy, always out and about with his fashionable friends. But at least she had a claim to fame. Every now and then John could be seen on the telly – on *Top of the Pops* – mingling and dancing with other young people.

Coming into the room followed by Gwen, Ivy was telling her friend that she was going to baby-sit for Anna, who was going out on a little shopping trip for some new clothes. A little white lie to appease her daughter, which Gwen accepted without much thought even though the rapid excuse had been a dead giveaway.

'Don't you look lovely today, Anna. You look prettier than that Jean Shrimpton,' said the woman, pulling up a chair and smiling. 'Look at that slimline figure – and you having lugged them twins about inside you for nine months as well.' She sat down and leaned forward to peer into Anna's face. 'You get your lovely looks from your mum, and thank God for it. Although I must say I have noticed a certain lack of interest lately where your mother's concerned. A bit of lipstick and powder goes a long way and you're the living proof of that.

'I had my hair curled and shampooed yesterday by Harry, the Jew boy in Becky Zeid's little hairdresser's in the Old Jago. You can't beat a Jew when it comes to a good cut and style even if most of them are manic, always shouting at each other. But put a pair of scissors in that man's hand and he works miracles. I keep telling your mother to go and get hers permed there but I think by doing that I was more of a hindrance than a help.'

'I don't *want* old-fashioned chipolata curls thank you,' said Ivy. 'Short and wavy with a few dark grey hairs coming through suits me fine. And it's natural. The colour and the waves. So don't keep going on about that fucking hairdresser.'

'See what I mean, Anna?'

'Don't push your luck, Gwen,' Anna chuckled. 'And anyway don't mind me – all this talk of a hairdresser is reminding me that I'm due for a visit. I might go to Vidal Sassoon's for a new look altogether.'

'Money for old rope,' said Ivy. 'Them poncey blokes haven't got a clue – West End salons or not.' She looked from Anna to Gwen and slowly shook her head. 'You can sit there pulling faces for as long as you like, it won't bother me.'

'I'm not saying that your hair don't look nice, Ivy. It's too short, that's all.' She glanced slyly at her friend. 'You look like a man when you're wearing slacks and a shirt blouse. I wouldn't be able to sleep a wink if I'd 'ave gone out looking like that in the daylight.'

Ignoring the baiting banter from her neighbour, Ivy poured her a cup of tea. 'I did dye my hair dark auburn once, to look like a movie star, but no sooner had I gone through all of that rigmarole than the blonde roots came through. Waste of time. So what do you think of them twins in the pram then, Gwen?'

Gwen stretched her body and neck to glance at them. 'They're the same ones I saw last week and the weeks before that. Why do you ask?'

'Our Linda reckons that they're gettin' to look more like me than ever.'

'She always did 'ave a sense of humour. No, they're beautiful, them boys. It's a good job you never 'ad quins like that woman in south London, Anna. She took one of them fertility pills as well, according to the newspaper. You might well 'ave delivered one of them who did resemble your mother if you shoved five babies out. I mean to say, you never know what's gonna 'appen when you start taking them new drugs, do yer?'

'Right, ladies,' said Anna, not wishing to be drawn in. 'I'm gonna love and leave you. Don't wake the twins up with your gossiping.' She then opened her tanned leather shoulderbag and took out her lipstick to swipe a little more on.

'That's a lovely shade of pink, Anna,' said Gwen. 'You'll have all the young men following you for a kiss on them cupid lips of yours if you're not careful.'

'It's the latest shade, Gwen. Pale Apricot. And thanks for the compliment. They've been few and far between lately.' Anna dropped her much-treasured golden-cased lipstick into her bag, then kissed her mother lightly on the cheek before squeezing Gwen's bony shoulder. 'Don't leave it too long before you come round to my place for a cup of tea with Mum.'

'Oh I won't, don't you worry. It takes me right back to when I was little and visiting my old nan, your house does. All right, so you 'ave got a fitted washing machine, tumble dryer and a fridge in yer kitchen, but your sitting room reminds me of all the dust that used to show up in my gran's house when the sun shone. I can't fathom why the young these days want old-fashioned brass ornaments and Victorian knick-knacks. Bloody dust collectors. The kitchens might be small in our maisonettes but they're streamlined – and with enough cupboards above and below the working surfaces. Who needs them bloody big old-fashioned oak dressers that take up space and light, eh?'

'I know what you mean. We're living in the bloody past, us young people.' Anna winked at her mother's friend and then, to cover the sick feeling in her stomach, smiled as she took her leave. This visit she was about to make was not something that she had ever thought possible.

'Shopping?' said Gwen, once she heard the front door close behind Anna. 'Pull the other leg, it's got bells on. I think she might have been telling you pork pies, Ivy. She's going to meet a feller on the sly if you ask me. I've not seen her looking so pretty like that before. And she touched up her lipstick before she left when it wasn't necessary. It's a dead giveaway that is. Applying fresh lipstick and powder during the daytime every now and then. And I smelt that perfume . . . Well, good luck to 'er an' all. Good bloody luck.'

'My Anna's not like that. She's the rosy apple in the bowl that one. Her sisters are a different kettle of fish. And speaking of lipstick, you've not brought that Rose Red back that I let you try out last week.'

'Haven't I? Oh, I must have forgotten.'

'I'm sure,' said Ivy. 'It suits your face as much as it suits mine so you can borrow it whenever you want. But fetch it back!'

'Of course I will. Anyway, I still say that there was a certain look in Anna's eyes today that I've not seen in a long while. A kind of self-assertive smile, if you know what I mean. And if I didn't know better, I would say that she's got a bit of a grudge to bear. Not going to sort things out in the restaurant, is she? Cos no matter what's going on under the surface, she looked quite confident to me. As if she's gonna give the boot to that waitress you was telling me about.'

Gwen leaned back in the kitchen chair and undid a couple of big buttons on her thick apple-green cardigan. 'I'll be bloody glad when I stop having these hot flushes. I shall throw myself in the Thames if this goes on for much longer.'

Ivy quietly chuckled. 'You stopped having them years ago, Gwen. How old are you?'

'I'll be fifty-nine next birthday. I wonder if those foreigners work the same way as we do. I mean to say, you never see a West Indian woman breaking out in a sweat do yer? Lucky mares.'

'I expect they're exactly the same as us but they don't make a song and a dance and a show of it.' Ivy smiled.

'It's probably down to their black skin. I bet that's what it is. When they lived in the jungle in Africa their skin 'ad to adapt. That's what it'll be. Lucky bastards. *She* was a darkie – the woman my old man ran off wiv.'

Ignoring this because she had heard it all before, Ivy poured a little milk into each of their teacups while her friend fanned her flushed face with Ivy's rolled-up newspaper folded in her hand. 'We're all better off now even if there are more foreigners around. We've got central heating and takeaway Chinese shops. And look at the nice clean white baths we've got to sit in. Our maisonettes are lovely.' She glanced, with a touch of nonchalance, down at the kitchen floor.

'I'm not keen on these cheap tiles you've fitted mind you. I don't think you can go far wrong with lino on the kitchen floor, same as in the lav and bathroom.'

'Each to their own,' said Ivy. 'Each to their own.'

'I still use my old recipe for polishing the floors you know. You can't beat it. It gives a lovely shine and yet you don't slip arse over head.'

'I don't s'pose you miss having coal fires neither?'

'No, I bloody well don't. You can't beat an imitation electric flame. My chap's coming round later on to watch telly by the fire whether it's sunny or not. Ask him how our places compare to that grand old block of flats he lives in. All right, his is free and goes with his job as a porter, but I wouldn't want to live there.'

'Well, you've changed your tune,' said Ivy, topping up her cup with more tea. 'It wasn't so long ago when you was bragging about your new chap living in a grand block of flats up West that 'ad a posh reception, lift and porter.'

'Yeah, but at that time I never knew that he *was* the porter. Crafty fucker never told me that bit. The velvet lined curtains are dusty and faded and smell of stale pipe tobacco, and the glass shades everywhere are beautiful but thick with grime – and most of the bulbs are dead.'

'Just off of Tottenham Court Road by a tree-lined square is what I think you said . . .'

'I did, Ivy, but I don't think the rent is that much. Not by the type of people I seen coming and going. Shoddy old out-of-work actors is what they reminded me of.'

'So your chap's gonna move in with you one day is he? Into your little flat with a sparkling white bath to soak in?'

'No he fucking well ain't! I waited a long time to see the back of my old man and be a single person again. God rest 'is soul, the two-timing bastard. Couldn't keep 'is dick in his trousers for five minutes. The old tart he shacked up with was more than welcome to 'im. My new chap did once ask if he could stop overnight now and then and so I told him to sling 'is hook and not to come back any more if all he wanted me for was my body.'

'But he does 'ave your body, whether he stops over or not.'

'But I only do it to keep him happy and not give him grounds for complaint. He's got a mate you know,' said Gwen, sipping her tea. 'We could go out in a foursome. You look all right once you've put a bit of makeup on. His mate looks smart when he's wearing his suit and tie.'

'Oh yeah? And you've seen 'im have you? This mate of his?'

'Just the once or twice when I went on visits. He lives on the fifth floor, the top floor of the building. Horace. I think he comes from good stock.'

'Oh right. I've come across that type when I cleaned in a gentleman's club in Soho for a while. Black shoes polished so you could see your face in 'em but bloody great holes in the leather soles.'

Quietly chuckling, Gwen slowly shook her head. 'Who gives a fuck so long as they're good lovers? Mine is.'

'Is he now,' said Ivy, sensing a slight tingle inside which she hadn't felt for a long while. 'Well, you'd best ask your Wilfred if he's got a friend for me then, hadn't you? An ordinary good-looking bloke who's neither posh nor poor.'

'Posh or not Horace is a character, and just like you he can play a lovely tune on the piano.'

'Oh? Well that's different. I suppose I could go for a drink with him to see how we get on. How old is he?'

'Course you could. A nice little foursome. And I should fink he's about sixty-odd.'

'Suits me.'

'All right,' said Gwen, draining the tea from her cup. 'I'll broach my chap on the subject this evening before we make love. That kind of talk should turn him on. A lover for you and a lover for me and a foursome on the settee if he fancies it.'

'If your John could hear you now he'd blush redder than a rose. You're a filthy cow at times.'

'He can talk. Now, do you want me to feed one while you feed the other?'

'Could do,' said Ivy. 'Share and share everything alike, eh? Even our lipstick and powder – and you can't get more personal and friendly than that.'

Later on, around two-thirty in the afternoon, safe in the knowledge that her babies were in their grandmother's tender care, Anna made her way to Prima Pasta on a double-decker bus and was a touch angrier than she wanted to be for letting things go on as they had been for too long. As the bus approached Stratford East, she decided to get off one stop short of hers to give herself time to calm down a little and think things through logically as she walked through the back streets. So deep in her thoughts was she, that she hardly noticed the people around her or the traffic.

Her biggest regret was taking Bridget on as assistant manager. Other than a clairvoyant though, nobody could possibly have known that Bridget had been set from the very beginning on having her husband – with the restaurant thrown in as a bonus. But now that Anna did know what was going on, the anger in the pit of her stomach was actually helping her, as if it was a friend willing her on and there for the ride. She knew that what she was about to do could easily be a recipe for disaster where her marriage was concerned, but since that was already broken and being aired in public she felt there was more to be gained than lost.

Her sisters had pulled no punches when they gave her the sordid details the evening before. And now, in the light of day, she could see that they had known exactly what they were doing when they arrived at her door.

The three sisters were as close as they had ever been and this meant as much to her as it did to them and, of course, to their mother, Ivy. 'You have to *learn* to trust friends, Anna,' she murmured, 'but as sure as the moon will come and go family blood will always flow.' Her grandparents had passed away when she was a young girl but some of their old sayings, handed from one generation to another, drifted into her thoughts now and then. Lifting her eyes to the sky, she smiled to herself before silently asking her ancestors in the celestial world to give her the strength to carry through what she had set out to do: get her husband back on her side.

Chapter Three

Glancing up at puffy white clouds drifting across the light blue sunny sky, Anna slowed her pace as she neared the restaurant and remembered good times shared with Frank in the second half of the Swinging Sixties. That's when they had first met, at Tower Hill in his elder brothers' restaurant nightclub – the Lazy Blues. Being at an impressionable age, she had felt a rush of love whenever Frank had smiled at her from behind the bar where he mixed cocktails for customers. The spot had been a favourite of her sisters and it was they who had first taken her there to have a meal and then listen and dance to jazz in a fantastic atmosphere under subdued lighting. For Anna and Frank it had been love at first sight, and after a wonderful nine months of courting, a June wedding, and two years of glorious happiness, they had wanted the next good thing – to start a family.

Later on, once Anna was pregnant and had given up working in their small restaurant in Stratford East to stay at home with only herself for company, she had been thankful for the television and the radio because of the familiar voices of regular disc jockeys and newsreaders. She had often lain on the sofa in the evenings looking up at the ceiling, and the faint patterns cast across it from the rays of the street lamp, the old-fashioned street lamp that glowed through a small gap at the top of their William Morris patterned curtains.

For no reason that she could think of, Anna recalled the time when she had been trying for a baby. When their alarm clock had gone off at the crack of dawn one morning Frank had jumped out of bed in a rush because he had arranged to go early-morning fishing with a friend. Although only half awake at the time, Anna had tugged at his pyjama jacket and dragged him back beneath the covers to make love, because it was the right time of the month according to the chart she had been keeping. And this, of all the times they had followed the regime, was when she had successfully conceived. The one and only occasion when Frank had felt that he had to make love to order.

With all of this going through her mind, Anna willed herself not to weaken her resolve to save her marriage from complete collapse. She had every reason to be screwing her tissue into a tight twist because it did look as if she might have to bring her babies up as a single parent. The thought of being abandoned as her mother had been, terrified her. The day Anna's dad left for work one morning, with a wave and a smile, only to walk away carrying his suitcase and never be seen again was awful. This wasn't what she wanted for herself or for her boys, but she knew she couldn't take any more of Frank's excuses for being late, which had always been the same – the restaurant had been packed to overflowing with customers who wanted to drink and listen to music after time. The more Anna thought about it the more she berated herself for having let things go on the way they had for so long. Now, out in the real world, free from the confines of the four walls of her sitting room and her television serials, she could hardly believe that she had allowed Frank to get away with his lies time and time again.

When curled up in an armchair and watching television by herself, she had often wondered whether to tell her sisters how lonely and miserable she was. And now, because of them, she was going to give marching orders to the girl who loved to flirt. She recalled the day when there had been free drinks and canapés for the regulars at Prima as a kind of a leaving party for Anna. The toast given by Frank, though, had been to the promotion of Bridget from top waitress to his assistant manager, and this *had* hurt.

The regulars, men in particular, had been happy with Anna's replacement and who could blame them? Bridget loved to flirt with her naughty-girl smile and screw-me eyes when at the bar pouring drinks. The men knew that she was married to a decent guy, because Trevor was sometimes there during the evenings, eating pasta and enjoying a glass of wine while waiting for his lovely young wife. This was before Frank had insisted that he was duty bound, as Bridget's employer, to see she got home safe and sound at night and so a mini-cab was ordered especially unless Trevor called in unexpectedly to take his wife home.

Almost at Prima and knowing that Bridget would be there in her role as stand-in manager while Frank was elsewhere, Anna could now hardly wait to walk in unannounced. And why shouldn't she walk in out of the blue? This was her and Frank's restaurant, where they had once been happy to work side by side for hours on end, building Prima Pasta into one of the cool places to eat in the area – a bistro seating forty under subdued lighting and with the sound of love songs playing softly in the background.

At this time of the day it was normally a quiet spell, with mostly locals in for coffee and cakes, or simply lingering after a lunch of the pasta special chalked up on the blackboard as the meal of the day. Neither she nor Frank had set out to pretend that Prima was anything other than an atmospheric, small, family-run place. This had been their dream, something they had talked about for hours on end before they were married.

Anna wondered if her old friend, the palm reader Queenie Brown from Canning Town, had been bang on right when she had told her fortune and predicted that there was going to be a troublemaker in her life. At the time, Anna had laughed at the softly rounded woman with the big bleached white hairdo and old period fox fur coat, but now she wondered if it had been Bridget that Queenie had seen entering into her charts.

Her heart pounding faster the closer she got to the restaurant, Anna distracted herself by turning her attention to the oddballs around her – a singing drunk, a couple of touting prostitutes and the ordinary everyday folk. She knew that Frank was going to be livid with her for going behind his back, but still she was looking forward to it because the adrenaline was kicking in and she had never felt quite like this before. She arrived at the restaurant and pushed open the timber-framed glass entrance door of Prima Pasta to be welcomed by one of her and Frank's favourite records playing on the jukebox – the Kinks and 'Lola' – a song that had always made the couple chuckle whenever they heard it. Inside the small and cosy place, with its dark mustard and red décor, she saw the familiar faces of regulars and suddenly had no qualms about going behind Frank's back.

Nodding at the few relaxed lunchtime regulars, who were sipping coffee or something stronger, Anna showed a special smile to Detective Inspector George Blake, who looked a touch surprised to see her there at this time of the day. George was a warm and friendly guy in his mid-thirties, who also called into her sisters' salubrious home in old Bethnal Green on a regular basis. He, in his cheeky way, deliberately gave Anna the once-over and then winked and smiled at her.

'You're looking more gorgeous than ever, babe,' he said.

'I know I am,' she teased. 'You're not doing so bad either, all suited up and to die for.'

George chuckled as he watched her saunter, a touch sexily, through the restaurant, showing calm and decorum even though her heart was beginning to pound. She went into the small bar at the back and to the girl who she was about to send packing. A small burst of anger swept through her when she saw Bridget, who was dressed to kill. Anna's first thought was that she looked like a shop model except that she was pressing the keys of an adding machine and tilling up the takings. She was wearing a red silk dress with long tight sleeves and a full circle skirt, and her long ginger curly hair had been set to look as if it was tumbling naturally around her shoulders, perfectly dishevelled.

Anna stared at the back of her rival and so wanted to strangle her swan-like neck. 'You look glamorous today, Bridget,' she said, keeping her temper nicely in check while taking the girl by complete surprise. 'All dressed up with somewhere to go are we?'

The girl glanced sideways at her with an expression that was obviously meant to show that Anna looked like something the cat had dragged in. 'Oh, it's you, Anna. I didn't notice you come in.'

'Well, don't sound so surprised, I'm not a she-devil,' Anna laughed.

'You startled me, that's all.' Bridget spoke quietly and with a hint of practised superiority. 'Creeping about like Jesus himself. What brings you in today?'

'I wasn't creeping Bridget, I was arriving,' said Anna, and then, 'I'm not sensing a touch of dishonour am I? You didn't have your hand in the till perchance?'

With one eyebrow raised Bridet majestically turned her back to Anna and continued with the work in hand. 'I'll presume that was a joke,' she said, cool and calculating. This girl knew exactly how to put a person down.

'Presume away, sweetheart, but there's no need for you to look so anxious. It would come as no surprise to me. It's common practice, from what I've heard.' Enjoying herself now, Anna pushed her fingers through her soft blonde hair and then leaned on the bar. 'Quite a few of you temping staff steal a bit of cash from the till now and then, and who can blame you? Long hours and little reward. That can't be much fun.'

'You're probably right there, but I'm not temping, Anna. Let's not forget that I'm permanent staff. There's a huge difference. And in any case, I wouldn't touch a penny of Frank's money.'

'Permanent? Don't be *too* cocksure,' said Anna, her confidence rising by the second. 'You've not passed your apprenticeship yet. A year or so? That's nothing in the bigger picture, but don't worry. I'm not here to give you the sack today.'

'The thought hadn't crossed my mind.' Bridget looked far too cocksure for her own good. Throwing Anna a single look of derision, she turned back to the till. Speaking quietly so that she could only just be heard, she said, 'I think you're a little out of touch, Anna, and when I said you were creeping about – it wasn't meant as an insult. You're being far too sensitive and I'm not sure why. There's really no need for it.'

Allowing this to go above her head, Anna crossed her arms, narrowed her angry green eyes and looked intently at the cow. 'I told you, Bridget – I wasn't *creeping*, I was *arriving*. There's a big difference. But then you've got your mind on other things haven't you, and guilt is bound to fuck up your thinking.'

'My mind is on my work actually.' Bridget turned around yet again and looked directly into Anna's face saying, 'I can't say that I know what you mean by the word guilt?'

Anna laughed. 'I'm sure. And as for your mind being on your work – it's what you get paid for. And don't let's forget *who* it is that pays your wages.'

With the Cuban heel of her boot Anna then kicked

the bar door shut behind her. 'I think it's time that you and me had a little chat in private, don't you?'

'Really?' Bridget chuckled condescendingly. 'I hope you're not seriously going to try and give me the sack. I know that Frank likes to give the impression that this is a family-run business but he needs me more than even *he* realises, so if you're thinking of replacing me with a cousin or aunt or your own mother, I should forget it. And as for Frank, he's rubbish at keeping the books so as not to raise the eyebrows of the taxman. It takes a certain kind of a brain to keep this little business shipshape and looking as if it doesn't make too much profit.'

Then, just a touch too confident and a little too full of herself, she added, 'I wouldn't like to think of the state of the business if I were to leave it to Frank to keep the accounts.'

'Wouldn't you?' said Anna, smiling demurely. 'How generous you are with your loyalty towards your boss. And you don't have to tell me that my husband's not been keeping his mind on his work, Bridget, because I already know that. You'd be surprised just how many others know it as well. We'll have to run a few questions past him, won't we? Do you think he might have been messing with grubby little whores dressed in silk, satin and lace?'

'I hardly think so, Anna.' Bridget offered a patronising smile.

'Well, do you know what, Bridget? I couldn't give a toss what you think.'

'Oh dear, it's that time of the month is it? What we

81

women have to suffer. I can't imagine men putting up with the monthly curse, can you?'

'It's not *that* time of the month actually and you're not really listening. I *said* ... we'd have to run a few questions by Frank. And the question number one would be why does he come home from the restaurant at the end of the day much later than he should do? And why do his boxer shorts smell of perfume even after they've been in the soiled laundry bin for a day or so? I think you know the perfume, it's the one you're wearing now.'

'I can't imagine Frank going anywhere near a local whore, if this is what you're getting at. I can hardly believe you would think such a thing. But then hormones when all over the place *can* be a puzzle at times.'

Anna took a breath and folded her arms as she fixed her eyes on her rival's back. She was determined to make her stop what she was doing of her own accord. 'You don't think he's screwing some dirty little tart on the side then? That the rumour spreading about Frank treating himself to a whore in his and *my* flat upstairs is unfounded?'

'Frank? Going with a paid whore? I hardly think so.'

'I never said *paid* whore did I? But then what does a bottle of that perfume you're wearing cost these days?'

'Very amusing, Anna.' Bridget turned to face her, slightly curling her lip as she raised an eyebrow. 'If you don't mind my saying so, Frank isn't the sort to pay for his privileges. You're being a touch too hard on him. He's good with the customers because of his personality – they love him to bits, as we all do – but I can't see him wanting to touch the type of person you suggest. He's not like that. He runs this place as if he was born to it. He's hopeless with calculations and figures and keeping the books but that's what I'm here for. I was top of the class when it came to mathematics.'

'I bet you were,' Anna smiled. She then leaned forward and sniffed the air. 'Mmm. I think that's French perfume you've got on, isn't it?'

'It is French actually,' the girl said, lowering her eyes and focusing on her book-keeping. 'It was a gift.'

Anna laid a gentle hand on Bridget's silky soft padded shoulder and smiled at her, and she wasn't sure if it was an expression of fury that she saw in those soulless brown eyes or fear. Bridget, for most of the time, from what she had heard, behaved as if she was a simple girl up from the country, so it was hard to tell.

Carefully lifting thick strands of the girl's long ginger hair Anna twirled it around her fingers and held it tightly. Then, pushing her face up close to Bridget's said, 'You're nothing more than a tart really, but you set your sights high – I'll give you that. And you've got what you wanted. Frank. And he gets what he wants.'

The silence between the two of them for that split second could have been cut with a knife had it not been for the large, round, red wall clock ticking loudly. The clock which Anna had chosen, a bright and bold timepiece that was hung on the wall on the morning of the day that she and Frank opened for the first time. 'Pick up your handbag, Bridget,' Anna said quietly. 'Then lift your coat off the hanger and walk out of here with your head high if you want to save face.' She then let go of the girl's hair.

83

'I'll send your cards on and I'll leave it to you to tell that poor sucker of a husband of yours why you've been given the boot. You can tell him all about it yourself . . . how you've been sleeping with *my* husband in the afternoons, between lunch and evening shifts and then again around the midnight hour.'

Anna leaned closer as she whispered, 'Sleeping with Frank wasn't part of the job description. I know you've been sleeping with my husband and I know exactly how long it's been going on for. Frank's been giving you one while I've been in our house, our *home*, bottle-feeding one baby after the other. *Our* babies. *Mine* and *Frank's* twins. I wonder what your mother would say if she knew how disgracefully you, the good Christian girl, behaves? And what about your daddy, Bridget? Do you think he would be proud of his little girl?'

Bridget remained silent in the face of this onslaught, but Anna wasn't done yet.

'I suppose you do know,' she went on, 'that you're a running joke with the customers? My sisters tell me that the men have bets as to what colour silk knickers you'll flash when you're sitting on your favourite bar stool. You know, when you're in your teasing mood, and flippantly cross and uncross your legs while sipping a glass of white wine. You present yourself as the naive girl whose mouth wouldn't melt butter and then behave like a trollop. And you've been drinking too much white wine during working hours – or so I've heard. You've turned out to be a bit of a lush all round, really. Does that poor sod of a husband know what you get up to in mine and Frank's dirty old bed upstairs?

'I think you should talk to Frank, Anna. Not that he's going to be pleased about this. He won't be.'

'Go and get your coat and handbag, Bridget – and leave quietly. And don't ever cross this threshold again. I can't imagine what your family must think of you. I mean to say, you must have got some practice in back home for when you came to London for the big time. How many marriages did you wreck before you set your sights on Frank?'

Anna's angry green eyes bored into Bridget's dark brown ones as she said, 'Take your wages and get out of our lives.'

'But you've got it all wrong,' protested Bridget, determined to score a point. 'It wasn't me who did the chasing. It was Frank. I told him that it wasn't fair on you and he shouted at me, told me not to interfere in his private life.'

'You mean he's been horrible to you as well? Oh dear. That can't be right, can it?'

'Frank has *never* been horrible to me. But he wouldn't listen when I tried to tell him that we weren't being fair on you. You know what he's like once he digs his heels in over something—'

'There's no swaying the bastard is there.' Anna slowly shook her head as she said, 'You've been had, sweetheart. He's been using you.'

'Look, I know this is hard for you – but we are serious about each other. And you might as well know now that Frank wants the twins with us once we're settled into a new house . . . once they're old enough to go to a private nursery school.'

Anna raised her eyebrows in mock surprise. 'Really?

Well, he hasn't mentioned a word of this to me. And what about you? Once you're in this *new house* that you speak of? Will you want me to come and go? To visit my boys and their new mummy? Shall I be the one to baby-sit while you're in the restaurant working? Me and Frank by ourselves again and making love the way we used to? Me the rude girl and you the woman scorned? Of course – this is all presuming that you *want* my boys as part of the package?'

'God no! It's not what *I* want.' Bridget smiled as she raised a finely plucked eyebrow. 'I don't want to look after children thank you – my own *or* yours.'

'Oh, I see ... and Frank knows this, does he? That you've got no maternal instincts whatsoever?'

'Not yet. But who knows?'

Flabbergasted by the gall of the girl and with no thought of the consequences Anna took hold of Bridget's thick wiry hair again with her left hand and clenched her right hand into a fist. As she pulled her arm back ready to land an almighty blow on that pert little nose, the door behind her opened and a much stronger hand gripped hers. The hand of Detective Inspector George Blake.

'This isn't like you, Anna,' he said, smiling warmly at her. 'No one's worth bruising your knuckles for, darling. Leave it be, eh?'

'I appreciate your concern George,' said Anna, staring into his face, 'but this is between us two. No doubt you've got your reasons for not wanting her face in a mess but there are plenty more where this one comes from.'

George's face softened as he looked into Anna's.

'Don't be daft. She's a married woman. And her husband's a nice guy, a good and honest working man. So leave it be, eh?'

A few seconds ticked by as she stared at him. He was giving her a message with just one look. A message that she had seen before. One of honest-to-goodness respect. She had known him for a long while and not only trusted him but liked him a lot. Respecting his timing, she slowly nodded. 'All right, George ... I take your point. But leave us to sort this out for ourselves, eh?'

'Absolutely, babe – as long as you stop being silly and don't give me cause to have to call my boys in blue.' He gave her a friendly wink and went back to the lads at the table in the front of the restaurant. Bridget, still in Anna's grip, made the mistake of grinning slyly at her and it took Anna all her inner strength not to do what she wanted to do: slam Bridget's face down onto the bar.

'Lucky for me that our family friend George Blake stopped me from having to serve time because of you. And lucky old you that I've not splattered your feeble brains across the bar.'

She was about to slip down from the bar stall when Bridget pulled her arm back ready to punch Anna in the face. Had the girl not lost her footing an almighty blow would have landed between Anna's eyes, but wearing her red four-inch-stiletto-heeled shoes, it was hardly surprising that Bridget stumbled and fell. She crashed down awkwardly, her flailing arm catching a tray filled with empty wine glasses on the way just before her face hit the stone floor of the bar. Her scream mingled with the echoing sound of breaking glass as well as the song playing on the jukebox: Ray Charles singing 'Your Cheating Heart' – a record that George Blake had put on just for the hell of it.

As she leaned over the counter and looked down Anna saw blood trickling from Bridget's nose and, with false compassion, she asked her if she was okay. This could have been seen as a nice gesture had Anna not been smiling when she said it. 'That looks a bit serious to me,' she murmured. 'I hope you can find another over-sexed married man to bed you,' she added, 'because Frank won't want you with a crooked nose, sweetheart, trust me. He's a fussy fucker that husband of mine. You might be able to pick up one of his brothers though. They like a cheap Woolworths lipstick and powder whore now and then. I'd go for Johnny if I were you, not Alfie. Alfie has a penchant for pretty boys as well as girls. You might catch something you wouldn't want and pass it on to that poor sod of a husband of yours.'

Her head held high, her chin forward, Anna walked through the restaurant on her way out and gave Detective Inspector George Blake a wink and a smile and then blew him a kiss which he pretended to catch and put into his top pocket. He had been staring out of the window and looking the other way on purpose so as not to witness any bloodshed. He returned her smile with a look of gentle admonishment. He was a handsome sod and knew it. Handsome and sexy and someone who, for the cheek of it, had light-heartedly propositioned Anna more than once when she had served him at the table.

'Anna's a little cracker on the quiet,' said one cousin to the other. I wonder if she was one of them sixteen- and seventeen-year-old girls who wore no brassiere beneath their see-through blouses a few years back?'

'I very much doubt it,' said George, fed up with his younger cousin.

'Fancy one of your blokes arresting them girls for indecent behaviour. They brightened up our day, they did. I remember one in particular who worked on the forecourt of the Silverstone Garage in Finchley. I can't remember why I had gone to that area but a more beautiful girl you couldn't have wished to see. So what do we do about that little accident then?'

'Leave it be,' said George. 'Give her a bit of privacy to pick herself up. She's been humiliated.'

Exhilarated by having got rid of the tightness in her chest, Anna enjoyed the sense of being on top of things again. It was an incredible feeling. She didn't give a toss that George and his associates had heard all that had gone on. In fact she was revelling in it. She had known the small group since they were all rough kids on the street in and around Bethnal Green – a time when it was not unusual to see one of them with their arse hanging out of torn trousers. They were also the drinking partners of her sisters Hazel and Linda.

Once she was outside and walking away, George watched her through the window and then raised an eyebrow at one of his cousins who was grinning at him. 'What are you gonna do now, George? Strut out the back as if you're one of the Kray twins and warn Frank's lover off?'

'Do me a favour. One of the Krays? Neither of the twins would have known how to handle that little scene. They're not all they're cracked up to be you know.'

His cousin leaned back in his chair and laughed. 'You'd better not say that once they're out and about again.'

'I don't think they will be, David. They won't see the green green grass of home again. They were all right when they were kids on the street. They got too big for their boots, that was the trouble. They didn't live far from Mum and Dad once they moved to Valence Road – a three-up-two-down with an outside lavatory. Those back streets were a bit of a ghetto in them days for boxers, gamblers, hard drinkers and villains with one gang fighting another for competition. Mum and Dad moved out as soon as they could and got one of the first of those council flats to 'ave been built close to the Hackney Downs.'

'So you've said before. So what are you gonna do now, hero? Go and kiss the little tart out the back better?'

'Not yet. I know when to leave things be. I'll give her time to regain a bit of dignity.' He winked at the boys and lit a cigarette, a little more pleased with himself than he wanted to let on. It was Anna he was thinking about. He had just been her knight in shining armour and put a stop to something that could have seen her in trouble.

Once outside Anna drew in the fresh air and felt a tingling sensation in her spine ... one mission was over and another more pleasant one was about to begin. A bit of shopping therapy in the West End where she would treat herself to an outfit or two on her and Frank's account. She hadn't been one for expensive designer clothes in the past, but having seen the way that Bridget dressed these days, in stunning clothes, she quite fancied the idea of spending time and money on herself. Especially now that she felt sure Frank had been treating his lover to the latest fashionable outfits on the sly.

With the sun on her face and her adrenaline calming down, Anna had a change of heart about her shopping trip for now and decided to postpone it for another day. She went into a phone booth instead, to call her sisters. It was them she wanted to be with right now, not pushy saleswomen. She told herself that she could always go on a spending spree up West whenever the fancy took her. She had been so maternal and housewifely since she had got pregnant that she had almost forgotten the old Anna that was tucked away. The Anna who had always loved to have fun and follow the fashion. She smiled as she remembered the daring mini-skirts she once wore when her hair was long and straight, her fringe thick and covering her eyebrows. A time when she wore dark eye-shadow and lash-lengthening black mascara and pale apricot lipstick.

In the Sixties, when it was a case of anything goes, Anna had bought herself a 1930s fur coat from Oxfam and big floppy hats in the Portobello Road market. Just one trip to Biba in Kensington High Street and she would be right back there – in the thick of it and with a little more money to spend now than she had had when

91

she was a young and free single girl. She smiled as she remembered the times when she and her sisters enjoyed going to Sam Widges' coffee bar in Berwick Street, Soho, where senior citizens mixed with the new look beatniks who filled the place, all of them making a cup of coffee last a whole afternoon. It hadn't been a regular haunt of Anna's but it was a great place to pop into for a seat, a cigarette and a sandwich when her sisters had been in the mood to 'shop until you drop'. This had been a time when the upper-middle-class young were enjoying love-ins and burning joss sticks at Woburn Abbey and in Hyde Park. For a couple of years it seemed as if Flower Power and pop concerts were everywhere.

With these recollections floating in and out of her mind, as well as the vision of Bridget with a broken bleeding nose, Anna felt as if she was back to her old self again. And she had her adorable babies to love and care for. She had been shopping for her clothes locally, and mostly in markets, of late without a thought for fashion, but from now on she would use her and Frank's cheque book to equal the way he had been using it. She had been told more than once that she had a good dress sense and a flair for style and now she was going to make the most of it.

Her shoulder-length dark blonde hair, together with her big soft green eyes, gave her a kind of Swedish look and, even though she chose the new tailored style when going for a meal out, she was still comfortable in jeans and tops. She loved stiletto-heeled shoes as well as Cuban-heeled boots, especially the ones she was wearing right then, their heels tapping out a message as she walked – a message for Frank and his whore: Stuff you, stuff you, and stuff you.

Determined not to carry on trying so hard to be a mature woman but to get back to being a happy-go-lucky young lady, she was already on the road because she didn't really care what Frank was going to say once he had been told of the chaos that she had caused at the restaurant. As far as she was concerned Bridget deserved all she got.

'You've been a silly girl, darlin',' said George Blake as he kneeled on one leg behind the bar and briefly examined Bridget's damaged face, which was pale against the red blood trickling from her swollen nose. Handing her a second white glass-towel that he had soaked in warm water to wash away the blood from her face and neck, he did actually feel sorry for someone he had never been able to take to. Helping her up he spoke quietly, saying, 'I'm sure you must have been told before, sweetheart, to never take a leak on the boss's doorstep?' He then scooped her into his strong arms as if she were as light as a feather.

Her head flopped back and her long tresses soaked in blood, Bridget moaned as George carried her to a cosy corner out of sight of the lads in the restaurant and the harmless old tramp – also a regular – who had seen it all before during his lifetime in one place or another where he might have hung his battered hat. To George's way of thinking Bridget at least deserved privacy, and it would be too degrading for her if any fresh customers were to slip into the restaurant before the open sign on the door was turned around to show *Closed until seven p.m.*

Gently lowering Bridget to the floor, George grabbed a small bundle of clean white tea towels from behind the bar to place under her head. Carefully studying the damage to her face, he placed the fleshy part of his palms on either side of her nose and said, 'Think of your mother smiling at you, sweetheart.'

Then, with a tried and tested jerk and a click, he fixed her together again as her echoing scream resounded throughout the small restaurant. 'It might swell up like a pumpkin, darlin',' he said, 'but at least you won't have to go to hospital.'

With her head resting on the makeshift pillow, Bridget looked up at him pale and in pain. She could feel the throbbing and closed her eyes, wishing that she could start the day all over again. The next thing she knew, the man who she felt sure had the hots for Anna was laying his cool wet sparkling-white handkerchief over her injury. 'Do you want me to give Frank a call or should I send one of the boys to get your husband Trevor?' he said.

'Neither,' was all she managed to say – but her mind *was* ticking over. She was not only in pain and damaged but humilated, and even in this state she vowed that she would use George Blake, the bent detective inspector, as her counter-attack. She would tell Frank a little white lie – that George had been sniffing around Anna and been familiar with her when she just happened to drop in for a drink and a bite to eat at lunchtimes while he was at Tower Hill, and when George just happened to be there too. And she wouldn't stop there. She was a good and convincing liar and always had been. She would then say that one or two of the older generation who came in for their discounted spaghetti Bolognese on Thursdays had been placing bets as to who the baby twins looked most like, Frank or George. Lies, all lies ... but, helped by her pain, she was already thinking about revenge.

'How about if I get someone to drive you home where you can sleep this off in the quiet, Bridget?' George offered, not because he wanted to look after her welfare but because he was protecting the reputation of a woman who deserved better. Six years older than Anna, George hadn't played in the streets with her as a lad, but he had seen her out and about when he was a fresh young copper on the beat and she was only seventeen, and he'd sometimes advised her not to go down the same road as her sisters, that she was too soft for their world. She had known exactly what he meant of course and appreciated his brotherly kind of protection. George had also sat chatting to her now and then when off-duty and when she had been with her sisters in Frank's brothers' restaurant. But now of course, even though she was younger than him, she was a mature woman and the mother of twins. Even so he still felt duty bound to watch out for her as if she was family.

Waiting for Bridget to say what she wanted him to do next, George could see that she would be all right once she asked for a bucket. Throwing up was going to be painful but from all he had seen before, it was the best thing she could do so as to shift any forming blood clots. As far as he could tell there would be no permanent damage. Carefully lifting her into a sitting position, he gently propped her against the wall and went to collect a slop bucket from behind the bar to leave by her side. Without saying another word, he left her to it and strolled back through the restaurant to his table and his cousins, Jimmy and David, every bit the true gentleman. He knew that the delectable Bridget would not have wanted him to see her being sick. It was far too degrading for a lady who sometimes behaved like a tramp by sleeping in other people's beds.

'She all right?' said Jimmy, containing laughter but grinning like a schoolboy all the same.

'Will be now. She slipped on the wet floor, on slops from the coffee machine. Her nose was put out of joint but it's back – just like Humpty Dumpty. So ... to business.' He couldn't be bothered to fill in the gaps and nor did he wish to.

'Don't you need another scotch after that little incident?'

'You're like a big girl at times, Jimmy.'

'All right, all right,' said Jimmy, knowing he had gone too far with the banter. 'It was a joke. All right? No sense of humour, that's your trouble.'

It was hardly a side-splitting joke but then Jimmy, the juvenile of the three of them, wasn't all that bright. But he was a relative and he was reliable and could be trusted – and that was what mattered most because this little firm of smalltime friendly villains only worked with mates or members of their own family.

George leaned over the table and kept his voice low as he said, 'So it's Sam's removal van then?'

'Yep – and that was one of the best ideas you've 'ad

yet, George.' David grinned. 'My cousin the detective inspector. All brains *and* brawn, not to mention sex appeal . . .' Now it was his turn to torment their elder. 'Got that little bit of skirt from the Midlands tucked up nicely out the back 'ave yer?' He grinned. 'Gonna massage her pride once we've gone? A turn-on for you is it – a busted nose?'

'Watch your mouth,' said George, giving the fledgling one of his notorious icy stares. The lad had thoughts that could not be further from the truth. He had never taken to the girl and had had to bite his tongue once he realised that Frank was screwing her. He had seen her type before and kept at arm's length because of Anna being almost like family. George had had mistresses in his time, but if Bridget had come on to him he would have given her the cold shoulder. She reeked of trouble as far as he was concerned and now, if Anna wasn't careful, the tart would give her more grief than she could handle. He hadn't been far wrong of course, because when Anna finally gave up working in the restaurant, Bridget was straight in with not a trace of remorse in the way she calculatingly worked on Frank – the easy target. George and Anna had sometimes sat talking in the early afternoons when it was quiet in Prima Pasta and Frank was working at his brothers' restaurant or had gone upstairs to bed for a short nap, leaving her to run the place. His cousins Jimmy and David felt that they had picked up on stronger emotions than just friendship and liked to tease George a bit now and then. Giving him a knowing look David quietly chuckled.

'I know her out the back ain't your style. It's Anna

who's caught your eye.' He grinned, and thought he had managed to draw a guilty smile from George who he felt he knew inside out. They had after all played in the filthy back streets together as kids and were more like brothers than cousins. George raised one eyebrow and held his tongue.

'Right – back to business. The arrangements and expenses will cost us a grand but at least that includes the loan of the van as well,' said George, back on the subject of illicit business.

'More than worth it,' Jimmy replied, thoughtful and preoccupied. 'How many tea chests can you get into the van?'

'All four of them,' said Dave. 'You can leave the arrangements to me from now on. It's watertight. The gear will be in the loose tea leaves in the tea chests, nicely hidden should for any reason we get stopped en route. And each chest can take four gross, all nicely tucked away in the leaves. Two thousand, three hundred gold lighters at ten pounds a piece before expenses.' He sniffed and then raised an eyebrow. 'In a couple of days' time we'll be walking away with around five grand each I reckon. And that's why this will be my last involvement with you lot. You're younger than me. You can take over while I make the most of retirement.'

'Now when was the last time I heard that,' said Jimmy, chuckling. He slowly shook his head as a big smile spread across his face. 'Five fucking grand. I can't believe it. I could buy myself a little flat . . . fly off for a holiday in Hollywood. And still have a bit of spending money left.'

'Don't be fucking stupid,' said George. 'Do any of that and the old Bill will grab you by the collar. Put it under the floorboards for a year or so and don't be flash with it. I won't come anywhere near you if you attract attention by being flash. The days of greasing palms for silence are over. That's why I'm getting out of the Met ... before the major clean-up campaign starts.'

David quietly laughed now. 'How many times 'ave we heard that. You won't quit. You were born to make and break the law.'

'This time I mean it. I'm getting out of the force. While I'm still young enough to start up my own business. A legitimate business.'

'Such as?' said Dave.

'Not sure yet. But I've got a few ideas I'm mulling over which is for me to know and you to find out.'

'Each to their own.' David grinned and then said, 'I take it the old farmhouse close to the barn is still vacant and all right for two days' storage with no nosy parker about?'

'I should say so,' Jimmy cut in. 'That farmhouse ain't fit to live in. It was nigh on derelict, with rats running all over the fucking place last time I was there. It needs bulldozing.'

'Don't bet on it. Some of them old farms are being bought up and renovated for anyone with an eye for a bargain and a bit of money in the bank.' George looked from one to the other of his cousins. 'The living-off-the-land lot who want the good life in the country are snapping up all the little bargains from what I've heard. Then there are that lot who like to squat and them who fancy a bit of communal living and a bit of love, light and peace. Pain in the neck they are. Kent should be all right for a while though. And nobody's got any reason or right to go near the barn we're renting. That's where you lads should be investing your ill-gotten gains. Old neglected cottages in the sticks, before the property magnates pick up on it and buy everything that hasn't got legs or wheels.' He leaned back in his chair and went all thoughtful. 'I wouldn't mind a country farmhouse to do up and retire in,' he murmured. Anna was still shadowing his mind.

'You must be kidding,' said Jimmy. 'Nostalgia and romance with the gypsies in their wagons and us lot living in the huts in days gone by has gone to your head, mate. Shame, though, that them hop-picking days are well and truly over. More's the pity.

'It'll be good to have a look at them old brick huts again. It was like a spooky little village the last time we went ... that must have been a good year and a half ago. Even the old cookhouse was still standing. You remember that, George? Black corrugated iron roof and sides and a row of brick back-to-back fireplaces and shelter for cooking when it was pissing down with rain. All it needs is a young farmer to come along and plant the fields with vines and you'd 'ave plenty of London-ers more than ready to go hop-picking and fruit picking.'

'Never mind hop-picking. That's all in the past. I'm talking about the farmhouse and outbuildings,' said George. 'Maybe we should get in with an offer. We could take our time and turn it into a modest hotel once I've left the Met.'

'Whatever,' said David, a touch bored. 'The boys will pick up the tea chests from the barn and drop off the goods in Thetford. It can all be done and dusted within forty-eight hours and no trail left behind us.'

'And a brilliant bit of planning, even if I do say so myself.' Jimmy gave both men a wink. 'You won't find better brains than mine.'

'Keep your voice down, an' don't get too fucking loose with the tongue. And make sure the Thetford boys pay up on delivery. That, or no deal.'

Jimmy fell back in his chair and splayed his hands. 'What d'yer mean – loose with the tongue? There's no one in other than Tommy the tramp and he's too far gone on meths to make head or tail of us for fuck's sake. You're getting too paranoid, George. You never used to be so touchy. I think it must be time for you to get out and live with the carrot crunchers, my old son.'

'Your silly talk is getting on my fucking nerves, Jimmy. The slag's out the back don't forget, and she spells trouble.' George leaned back in his chair and rubbed his eyes. 'Anyway, this one will be a nice little earner and my last. You can all piss off to South Spain again for a couple of months while I stop behind and keep a straight face but then that's it. I'm packing it in. I can't go on working twelve or so hours a day on either side of the law.'

'Well, you would grow up to be a detective inspector,' Jimmy goaded.

George was in no mood for jest right then. He stubbed his cigarette out in the ashtray and checked his wristwatch. 'Right. I'm off to Tattler Street. Another midnight robbery to sort out.'

'Again?'

'Yeah. This is it though. Sammy isn't gonna get away with any more insurance claims. That's why he's made this the big one. Sly old fucker's gonna retire due to his heart complaint.'

'I'm sure,' said David. 'Nuffing wrong with 'is heart.'

'No. But there will be if he don't pack it in now.'

'Where's he gonna retire to then? Not fucking Spain I 'ope. Don't want the old fart out there chatting up the dolly birds in the beach bars. We'll all end up in nick.'

'No. He's off to Hawaii. It's been his dream for donkey's years and he can't wait to go. Give it two months and he'll probably drop dead from screwing every call girl going.' With that George got up and nodded towards the back. 'Stay until Bridget's okay. I'll drop in at Tower Hill and let Frank know there's been a fracas between the girls.' He winked at his cousins and left them to it.

All in all it had been a constructive afternoon and George had a good feeling inside, which he felt must be all down to the mention of the old farmhouse in Kent. He had always hankered after a place in the country, especially in that part of the world where as a kid he lived for five or six weeks of a year, picking hops and scrumping apples. He was more than ready to hand in his resignation and felt sure that now was the time to think seriously about making an investment for the future. He had had enough of living and working in London. On his way out of the restaurant, he slipped a five-pound note into the waiter's top pocket and told him to lock up and keep his mouth shut about the little dispute between the women. 'Bridget slipped on—'

'Sure, sure. I know. My fault,' the waiter cut in. 'I should've mopped up some drink I spilt behind the bar earlier.'

'Good man,' said George, squeezing the young waiter's shoulder. 'Keep the girls' conversation to yourself for now, okay? The little cat-fight's best forgotten.'

'Cat-fight?' the waiter smiled. 'Don't know what you're talking about.'

'Good man,' said George again, giving him a wink. 'Stay lucky.' Once outside in the street he glanced up at the sky to see clouds on their way over.

'Fucking weather,' he murmured. 'Fucking London.'

Chapter Four

Once she got out of the taxi at Victoria Park, Anna paid her fare and went through the large wrought-iron gates into the park gardens and boating lake. She was delaying the moment of going to pick up the twins from her mother's place so that she could have more time to herself to think things through. The echoing sound of stiletto heels tapping on the flagstones that was coming from the high-heeled shoes of three girls close by, reminded her of Bridget and the crack she had heard when the girl's face hit the floor in the restaurant. She felt a touch guilty at how painful it must have been but wasn't sorry that it had happened. She still felt sick inside but this was more to do with the reason she had had to go on her mission in the first place.

Ivy's flat was only a bus ride away from Victoria Park and Anna knew that her babies were being looked after properly, so she had no reason to worry or feel guilty and this comforting thought helped. All she wanted right now was to see her sisters and have them tell her that she had done the right thing. But she also felt the need for a stroll along a tree-lined parade, which brought back warm and comforting memories from her childhood. She wanted to be in Victoria Park and she wanted to sit on a bench overlooking the lake to watch the wildlife and the people she didn't know, coming and going.

She was calmer now, mainly because her anger and revenge had been spent at the restaurant face to face with the girl who Frank was possibly seeing as his future wife. Aware of her own footsteps now echoing on the pavement, she stopped to rest on a bench by the lake and, as she looked about her, she saw an old man walking slowly along with two sticks to help him and smiled hello. He smiled and nodded back and his efforts simply to get from one end of the park to the other made her feel humble. She began to think about the things that had been going wrong in her small world and how much of the blame might lie on her own shoulders. Questions began drifting through her mind: had she been so wrapped up in trying to get pregnant for all of those long months that she had killed off the passion Frank had once felt for her? And once the babies were born had she left him out in the cold? Or had she let herself go by always being in her dressing gown in the mornings before Frank left for work?

Her anger over her husband's affair now subdued, she was beginning to feel gutted inside. She only just managed to fight back tears as she tried to remember the last time Frank had hugged her lovingly. Her emotions all over the place, she measured his good points against his bad and a sense of fighting her corner for him was beginning to creep in. Ever since they had met as teenagers, she hadn't looked at another man — not before the ring was on her finger — or afterwards, when quite a few vain bastards had tried to win her over while she was working at the restaurant.

Of course she realised that she was young enough to marry again but this wasn't what she wanted. She and Frank had once been so happy and deeply in love that his indifference towards her still didn't seem possible. His loyalty and love towards her had all but come to a standstill since Bridget had stepped across their threshold to breeze her way into their world.

Leaving the park for her sisters' place, Anna strolled through the back streets into old Bethnal Green and passed boys kicking a football around. She tried to imagine a time when her twins would grow into lads and be doing the self-same thing. Now, with this peaceful time to herself, she began to relax more and more.

'It's partly your own fault, Anna,' she murmured. 'You should have read the signs earlier. You should have taken notice of the little warning bells in your head when you first saw the way she stood close, almost touching him, when they were having a conversation at the end of an evening shift at Prima and while a love song was played on the jukebox.'

Slowing down once she reached old Bethnal Green, she cleared her throat and braced herself for Hazel and Linda. They still looked upon her as the baby of the family, even though she was coming up to twenty-six. Just thinking about the way they were still over-protective brought a small warm glow to her heart. She of all people knew that, despite what others might think, they were good girls even though they loved the glamorous side of life, rubbing shoulders with the rich, the famous and a few carefully selected professional criminals. Criminals who paid for their pleasure out of the wealth they made on the backs of those richer than themselves.

The specially selected classy prostitutes on their virtuous list were not always from working-class backgrounds but came from all walks of life, and were chosen by Hazel and Linda for their beauty, intelligence and wit. They knew that most men liked or needed to escape from their humdrum lives and be pampered now and then and the girls were more than happy to fulfil their fantasies, weird or wonderful. Having been in this line of business for almost ten years Linda and Hazel had compiled quite a portfolio of men who totally trusted their integrity.

Nobody other than Anna's sisters got to see into the little red leatherbound book which held names and phone numbers of those gentlemen who wished to be fully protected from exposure: the titled, the famous, and one or two from the rich list in the Sunday newspapers. The reputation of Call A Girl Company was growing; it was becoming an exclusive gentleman's club in its own right for those who preferred to spend romantic nights in the house of assignation or in top-notch classy hotels in and around London. The company also catered for men who liked sleazy boarding rooms for their illicit nights of fantasy. It made no difference to Hazel and Linda so long as their clients treated the girls with respect and providing their wallets could allow them to be part of the exclusive club, which was now being praised in certain quarters, albeit in hushed whispers.

Hazel and Linda owned the detached building which

they had turned into a spacious, state-of-the-art Victorian house from a once dark sweatshop and boot-making factory. With a handsome loan as well as their savings, the girls had managed to see it renovated and refurbished until it resembled a palatial home which brought them considerable rewards. At the windows were beautiful drapes, which blended in perfectly with lighting and soft furnishings in all shades of soft gold and red, delivered mostly from Liberty's of London, or Harrods. So successful was their business that Anna's sisters had already cleared their loan and their bank balance was respectably in the black. They were going nowhere but upwards and onwards.

Ivy, choosing not to delve too deeply into what was going on in the house, was proud of her girls for having started up what she liked to refer to as their own dating company. It was a place that brought together lonely people. She thought of it as a kind of marriage bureau, where spinsters and bachelors met and found romance and a loving partner for life. All pie in the sky, but since this was the affectionate promise that the girls advertised in the Sunday newspapers, who was Ivy to question or to knock it?

Smiling to herself, Anna mused on the thought of becoming a hostess herself – to be driven around in a Mercedes or possibly a Rolls-Royce now and then. With all of this going around in her mind she told herself that she would be all right, that she wouldn't fall apart. In a feeble attempt to console herself she said, 'At least I won't have to put up with listening to you snoring in bed, Frank. Nor will I have to listen to your drawn-out drunken lies as to why you come home late at night.'

So deep in her changing thoughts and mood was she that the sound of urgent tooting from a car in the road that she was crossing brought her up with a jolt and her heart seemed to leap up from her chest. She nervously showed a hand and mouthed the word sorry. Sorry that she had almost caused him to kill her. Once safely across to the other side of the road, she burst into tears.

By the time Anna arrived at the wide stone steps leading up to the somewhat grand entrance door to the house that her sisters shared, Anna's mood had switched from melancholy to animated. She wasn't sure why this was the case other than it had slowly dawned on her exactly what she had done. She had been the cause of Bridget having had the accident. Not deliberately so, but it was because of her that she had ended up with her nose out of joint. She laughed inwardly at the memory of the expression on the girl's face just before she disappeared below the bar, as if she were a hand puppet in a Punch and Judy show.

Pulling at the old-fashioned and highly polished brass bell, Anna waited for the click-click of stiletto heels hitting the marble floor inside the wide hallway as one of the girls came to answer the door. She knew that it would be one of the so-called hostesses coming to greet someone she believed to be a client – who would no doubt have been furtively glancing from left to right had he been standing in Anna's place. A posh punter, hoping that there were no policemen or journalists around who might know this elegant building for what it was, a house of assignation. A brothel.

As predicted, it was one of the girls, a twenty-three-year-old known as Angelic who smiled broadly and waved her in with her long ivory and gold cigarette holder. 'The girls are out the back,' she said, happy that she didn't have to put on her mock upper-class accent. 'A right fucking pandemonium you've stirred up, madam.'

'You're kidding me,' said Anna, smiling. 'Word's not got through already has it?'

'Course it fucking well 'as,' said the girl as she closed the front door behind Anna. 'George Blake's bin in. You've only just missed 'im. His Mercedes pulled away not five minutes ago.'

'Oh. That's a shame.'

'He only stayed for five minutes. Lucky the woman who nails that handsome fucker, eh? There's nothing sexier than a man who works both sides of the law in order to fill his coffers – and a detective inspector at that. It's what sweet dreams are made of ... a handsome fucking bent copper who drives a Mercedes. Brilliant.'

'If you say so. So what mood are Linda and Hazel in?'

'Who knows?' said the girl splaying her hands. 'Those two still change wiv the wind.' The doorbell went again, and the tall slim prostitute wearing a slinky calf-length powder blue designer frock, with long, soft, leg-hugging high-heeled boots to match, went to answer it as Anna slipped into the shadows of the grand hallway and waited to see who was at the door. She liked the idea of it being George making a return visit because he would have seen her coming along while in his car. She cautiously listened unseen, but once she heard Angelic speaking in her pseudo upper-class accent she went through to the room at the back of the house where she knew she would find her sisters.

Unable to resist taking a peep at the gentleman whom the courtesan was leading up the beautiful staircase, she felt sure she recognised him – a blond, brightly dressed hippy in tight silk jeans and shirt with a few clashing neckties thrown in. She thought she might have seen him on the television but couldn't be certain. She went to join her sisters and saw that some of the other girls were there too. Attractive and fun-loving, these elegant young ladies sipped champagne one minute and cracked dirty jokes the next.

'Your ears must be burning, Anna,' said one of the girls who went by the trade name of Mimi. 'George's not long gone. We heard about your poor waitress slipping on her stiletto heel. Didn't push the bitch over did you, darling?'

'No,' said Anna, 'but I would like to have done though.'

'I take it that Mum's looking after our twins,' said Hazel. 'Your old next-door neighbour is a lovely woman, babe, but too old to baby-sit.'

'You know very well that I took them to Mum. I expect she's been on the phone half a dozen times asking if I'm back and giving you a running account of what she's doing with the boys?'

'You lot know each other too well,' laughed another

of the girls, who was quite new and who went by the name of Eliza.

'We're sisters. We should know what each other is thinking because as sure as snow is white we'll never get to the bottom of men.' Anna took a cigarette from a beautiful large silver case on the table and lit it with a matching silver table lighter.

'I didn't fink you smoked, Anna. You 'ave surprised me, gal.' This was Mary, who had her feet in an aromatic footbath ready for a pedicure from the resident beautician. Mary was another kettle of fish – a blowsy bleached blonde with a French pleat hairstyle and big gold earrings. She had been at the top of the tree in her time, but nowadays she was there mostly for the gossip and the old timers who had been her regulars for years, long before she joined Call A Girl Company. It was mostly the old boys with old money that she attracted. They couldn't get enough of her special massage.

'I don't smoke as a rule,' said Anna. 'But sometimes there are exceptions and today is one of them.'

'I should fink so. Slipped? Do me a favour.' Eliza pointed a finger at Anna and narrowed her eyes. 'I hope that nobody saw you push the little fucker over. Her sort would go to a poor man's solicitor and try and sue you for every penny you've got.'

Anna laughed out loud. 'So George really did fill you in then? You wait 'til I get my hands on him.'

'He'd love you to get your hands on 'im. I reckon he secretly fancies you, Anna. Why else would he come and tell us what had happened if you weren't always on 'is mind?'

'You mean he didn't pop upstairs with either of my sisters or one of the girls then.' Anna smiled.

Coming into the room, Anna's sister Linda topped up her own glass with some tonic. 'George never goes upstairs, sweetheart. He might have a favourite that he takes out for a drink and a bit of nooky without us knowing, but he's not a client. A very good friend but not a punter. And Mary obliges now and then with a rub to his shoulders when he's in this room.'

'I don't fink so,' cackled Mary. 'Not with all of you girls around to cramp my style.'

And so the jokes and the banter and the drinking and eating of crisps, salted mixed nuts and any amount of assorted cheese on the board, continued. This scene was one that Anna had been part of several times and always enjoyed. A little and often of being in these surroundings with these girls around and she was guaranteed to laugh. In some strange way this place reminded her more than it had done before that life *could* be fun and life *could* be a lot less serious. She loved the over-the-top plushness of the drapes, carpet and sofas. It was Eliza who brought the attention back to Anna and deliberately so. As far as she could tell, this lovely young woman was in need of a treat – big time.

'So ... my little cockney sparrow friend. What 'ave you planned for your birthday? Is it to be a show up West or knees up Mother Brown at your mother's flat?'

'I've not even thought about it, Eliza,' said Anna. 'And to be honest I'm not in the mood to plan anything.'

'Fair enough. But, if we was to get all the girls together and go out to the best restaurant in town,

you'd put a bit more lipstick and powder on for that –
wouldn't yer?'

Quietly laughing at this woman with the big heart
and lovely smile, Anna shrugged. 'How could I possibly
refuse?'

'Right well, that's that then. From what your sisters
said I gather it's only a few weeks away?'

'That's right. Just a few weeks away.'

'Well, there you are then. We've all got summink to
look forward to, haven't we? Now then, what restaurant is it to be? Chinese? Indian? Fish and chips? Or pie
and mash?'

'Chinese, but only at Silverlakes.'

'Job done. I couldn't 'ave suggested better myself.
Lovely old Chinese family and the best cooks in town.
Now – d'yer wanna go there and eat in style or have
them deliver in silver terrines?'

'I don't know. I'll tell you later. I don't really want to
think about it right now.'

'Say no more. I'll arrange it with you when you're in
the mood. And don't fink that I'll forget, because I
shan't. Birthdays are important. And your sisters who're
stinking rich can foot the bill.'

'Absolutely.' Anna laughed. She loved this place.
This was her sisters' day-to-day lifestyle where they
reigned supreme but behaved as if each and every one
of their girls was equal to themselves. Their spacious
sitting room had four luxurious feather-cushioned red
and gold brocade sofas which were set around a large
custom-made mahogany coffee table with polished
brass corners. Above the table and in the centre of this
magnificent room hung an exquisite Edwardian cut-

glass chandelier, and hanging majestically at the long sash window were midnight blue and gold brocade drapes. The ambience of this drawing room was a match for any exclusive Knightsbridge hotel. The girls had managed to create an atmosphere of an elite residence-cum-cosy nightclub-cum-home. And it would take a miserable sod to think that this was not a fun place to be, with its mix of banter, jokes and discussions. It wasn't the kind of place to be found anywhere else in the world.

Relaxing more and more into the scene, Anna enjoyed sipping red wine and then looking through the profile album of the so-called hostesses who were not always chosen for their figures but the expression in their eyes. Some of the girls preferred to stay anonymous and this was the reason for such names as Glorious, Lolita and Honey, to name a few. Others had little they needed to hide or worry over and so used their proper names. As for some of the clients, especially those with political leanings, they preferred the secrecy of the lovers' nest rooms above, while others were happy to be escorted in their own cars or by black taxi to luxury hotels or sleazy boarding houses – according to taste in the city or West End.

'You know what,' said Anna, closing the photo profile album and chuckling, 'I think I could get used to this kind of a lifestyle.'

'No, you couldn't sweetheart, because neither Linda nor I will let you,' said Hazel. 'You're the good sheep in the family – and you've got our twins to think of.' She flicked her long thick black hair off her beautiful face and smiled. 'But if you were to come into the business, you, unlike the slag Bridget, wouldn't have to advertise what's under your skirt with your eyes. You're not only a natural when it comes to looks, Anna, but you've got a lovely nature to go with it. That's why God gave you a sprinkling of freckles, sweetheart. Freckles show innocence is what our old gran used to say – remember? Frank's lost the plot that's all. Silly bastard. He'll be on his knees begging you to forgive him once he knows that you know and that he could lose you. And you've got two beautiful babies, never mind your warm radiant smile. And look at your eyes for Christ's sake . . . they're beautiful! Round and doleful and a soft green that could light up the coldest man's heart.'

'Comforting words,' said Anna, 'and definitely what I need – but I've got to go back and face the music. Frank is going to go bananas over this.'

Linda came in and joined them, having just said goodbye to a client of distinction. She was just in time to hear Hazel say, 'The tart from the Midlands knew exactly what she was doing. Frank must have been guided by his dick and not his brain if he didn't see through that shy little girl act.'

'Absolutely,' said Linda, who had a fair bit of experience behind her.

Studying Linda's face, Anna looked puzzled. 'But I thought that you thought that Frank was just as bad as Bridget? That he might not 'ave been doing the chasing but he was up for getting her into bed?'

'Did I say that? I don't remember. Anyway, as with all affairs, it's a bit of both,' she said and left it there.

'Whatever we hinted at, it worked, sweetheart,' Hazel

smiled. 'You finally got off of your bum and did something about it.'

Anna laughed. 'I should have known that's what you were up to. Crafty cows. Anyway, that was last night and this is today. I don't want to think about horrible things now that I'm here and in this fab company.'

After an hour or so enjoying herself with the girls, Anna knew that it was time for her to go back to the real world, her mother and her twins. Checking her appearance in the huge antique mirror above the rococo fireplace, she was almost ready to leave when the sound of the doorbell rang through the house. She felt a ray of sunshine filter into her heart when she heard the voice of George Blake as he made his way through from the hallway. He came into the room and she felt a warm glow when he smiled affectionately at her. George then looked from Anna to the girls and gave a friendly wink before turning to Anna and saying, 'A black cab just pulled up outside and I told him to leave it once he gave me the address where he was going. If you can give me five minutes with the girls, Anna, I'll give you a lift to your mum's place.'

With his genuine smile, George removed all doubts from Anna that he was there to bed one of the girls but had seen her earlier on when he was leaving this little corner of old Bethnal Green as she was arriving. Whether he had come back just so as to give her a lift she wasn't sure and wasn't going to question it. His timing was perfect. Whether she would let him take her and the twins on from her mother's flat to home was another matter. For all she knew, Frank might have gone straight there and she didn't want to drag George into her mess.

She had little doubt that Frank would have heard through the grapevine, if not from Bridget, that Anna had been into the restaurant and caused havoc. She knew that he was going to be furious but she wasn't bothered. She didn't even care if he went into one of his sulky, silent, spiteful moods that he knew she could hardly bear. She would take a leaf out of his book and not say anything unless she had to. She would keep him in the dark, wondering what she might do next. She knew that he would want his twin boys even if he didn't want her but, as far as Anna was concerned right then, if there was going to be a separation it had to be all or nothing. In other words, he had either to leave and only see the twins away from the family home, or he had to really want to stay with her as much as she wanted him to. She thought of the gentle smile that she had sometimes seen on Trevor's face and the lovely warm expression in his hazel eyes. Trevor, the poor sod who was married to the ghastly tease. 'Never you mind, Trevor,' she said to herself. 'You're worth a dozen of her type of person.'

Cutting right through her thoughts a familiar voice said, 'So if you want a lift home, Anna, babe, I'm your man.'

Quietly laughing at him she said, 'Well so be it, George – so be it.' She was glad to see him because she had had enough of the Frank and Bridget scenario. Never mind Trevor who was caught up in the centre of it all. She might not have been so unconcerned had she known that her sister Hazel had taken it upon herself to write to Trevor's dad, Arthur Plumb.

When a letter from Hazel dropped through the letter box and onto the doormat in the front sitting room of Arthur Plumb's small 1950s terraced council house, he was giving his working boots a quick buff. It was seven-thirty a.m. Not many people wrote letters to each other in his neck of the woods so it was always nice to see an envelope that wasn't a bill and was without a window. The gentle man was puzzled at first because he didn't recognise the handwriting as that of one of his family or close friends. Hazel had, in her own special way, managed to get hold of the man's address by asking George Blake to do a little bit of homework on the quiet, and without letting Anna know what she was up to.

George had told Hazel and Linda that he had crossed paths with Trevor's cousins who lived south of the river. And that even though, just like several people he knew, they didn't always walk the straight and narrow line and could be a bit violent when push came to shove, they were decent enough guys and very family-orientated. The letter from Hazel had been penned and posted to Trevor's dad just before the girls had breezed into Anna's house armed with Chinese takeaway and the determination to get Anna off her backside and doing something about Bridget before she lost Frank for good.

Short and to the point, Hazel's letter told Arthur about his daughter-in-law's affair with a married man who was the father of beautiful twin baby boys and the husband of her own youngest sister. She also wrote that a mutual friend had given her his address so that she could let him know what was going on before Bridget ruined her sister's marriage and caused Trevor to go into a deep depression.

Having read the letter for a second time, Trevor's dad remained seated at his yellow and gold Formica-topped kitchen table and stared out of the open doorway into his small and tidy back garden in which he grew wall-to-wall vegetables. He didn't like the tone of this letter and he certainly wasn't happy with the content. To his way of thinking this note, short and to the point, was telling him in the nicest way possible to get his son and daughter-in-law back to the Midlands so as to sort things out. This bit of advice actually suited Arthur down to the ground because he knew that, apart from fulfilling his own desires, it would make Trevor's mother a very happy woman to have her only son back in the fold. As for Bridget . . . they would both be more than pleased to see the back of her.

In his mind's eye Arthur could see his wife planning a new look for Trevor's old bedroom, where the walls were still decorated with his swimming certificates and awards. He wondered if his son realised that his attractive young wife was two-timing him. Knowing him better than most, Arthur felt sure that the lad would know what was going on and was most likely waiting for the affair to fizzle out. Waiting – and suffering alone and in silence no doubt. He popped the letter back in its envelope and into his back pocket, where it would remain until he found the right time to let his soft-hearted wife know what was going on.

The fifty-eight-year-old thought about the letter on and off throughout his day at the local furniture factory where he worked as chief turner in the leg-turning section. Chatting and laughing during tea and lunch break with his pals, he gave away nothing of his inner worry, but then Arthur had never been one to hang his dirty laundry on the line. By the time he was walking out of the factory gates early that evening on his way to catch the bus which would take him the four stops to his home, he had almost made up his mind as to what he would do once his temper over it had settled down.

Once by himself, he again sat, staring at nothing and picturing his son in the London flat that he and Bridget had taken once they were married. The cheap rent was the main reason for the couple putting up with what they saw as a depressing little place. But at least it gave Trevor a chance to save for a deposit on a flat of his own, which had been the intention. Sipping a drop of his tea, Arthur allowed a few tears to escape. 'Life's hard,' he murmured, 'but so long as family sticks together it won't be altogether too bad.'

He pushed from his mind the image of his son sitting alone night after night while his flighty young wife worked as a waitress and then bedded her lover. At last unable to think about it any more, he switched on his wireless, if for nothing else but to have voices coming into the room to take his mind off things. He knew that he was going to have to show Hazel's letter to Rose, his wife, but felt that there was no rush. He glanced at the clock and knew that she would shortly be home from her work at Marks and Spencer, her uniform on under her coat so as to have saved time getting out of the building. The less time this couple spent apart the better they liked it. To stop himself brooding over his son, Arthur took his special mixture of vinegar and salt and a clean cloth from the cupboard under the sink and set about cleaning the brass and copper knick-knacks. After doing that, he went outside and parked himself in his old green foldaway deckchair to think about life in general.

If his son was to lose his wife to another man he didn't think that would be such a bad thing. Trevor had top-notch qualifications and an excellent reputation when it came to expertise and style. He had been a natural-born swimmer from birth and had grown into a natural-born teacher too. Arthur had taken him to the local swimming pool when he was eighteen months old to get him used to the water from an early age. This had been back in North London before he and his small family moved out of the capital to take the more modern council house in which they now lived. They had always dreamt of living in a more countrified part of England, so it came as no shock when they exchanged their old-fashioned late Victorian rented house in North London for one on a small and brand-new housing estate on the outskirts of Northampton.

Both Arthur and Rose had had to hide their feelings when Trevor, their only child, had said that he wanted to go back to London to live and work. They had been gutted to the core. Taking him aside before he made his departure, Arthur had told his son that should he, having spent a year or so in the smoke, wish to return home to the Midlands, he must never let pride stand in his way and that he wouldn't be seen as a failure if this were to be the case.

Arthur's only real concern during his son's first term by himself in London and living in a furnished lodgings, had been the girl he had met in a local café while in the East End – Bridget. The girl who, when Trevor brought her home, was seen by close friends and family as somewhat vain and supercilious. Neither Arthur nor Rose had felt right about the person from day one. Deep down he had always suspected that if another man with more shekels in his coffers came along, she might well switch her affections with no sense of guilt.

To Arthur, Bridget's working-class family had done their utmost to become middle class, but had failed in their aspirations before they emigrated to Australia, taking only Bridget's brother with them. His mind working overtime, Arthur had another change of heart as one of his familiar warnings to himself swept across his mind: 'Don't put off until tomorrow what can be achieved today.' He decided there and then that he would suggest to his wife that she take a break and go to London to visit her son for a few days.

He heard the key turn in the front door. Rose was home. 'My feet are killing me,' she said as she entered the room. 'I've been shelf-filling all the day long. Two of the youngsters were off with the 'flu.'

'Well then, sit down and kick your shoes off.' Arthur grinned. 'I'll make a fresh pot of tea while you rest, and you can think about the nice break you're gonna have.'

'Break?' said Rose. 'What break?'

'I've just this minute decided to take you to London

so that you can stop with your son for a few days. And I want no discussion on it. We're not so poor that you can't take a few days off work.' He got up from his chair and made for the kitchen, saying, 'I'm not going in to work tomorrow myself either. I'll phone my apprentice later on and tell him to let the boss know in the morning. End of story.'

Rose laughed. She loved it when her husband came over all bossy like this. Anyone would think that what he had suggested hadn't ever crossed her own mind. But she was content to let him think that this much-longed-for suggestion hadn't been a seed that she had sown over the past few months. She was already mentally packing her weekend case. She could hardly wait to see her son again, even if it did mean having to put up with Bridget – his young and flirty wife whom she could not abide.

The next morning the middle-aged couple were up at the crack of dawn. After a full English breakfast at home to line their stomachs, and dressed in their Sunday best, they set off for London. Once they were halfway there, Arthur decided it was time to drop the little bombshell about Bridget in the way he felt best. With one hand on the steering wheel he eased Hazel's letter from the top pocket of his suit jacket and said, 'This came in the post yesterday. Don't start doing your nut over it. Just take it in your stride the way I did.'

'Oh?' said Rose as she took the envelope and peered at the handwriting. 'So who's it from then?'

'A woman called Hazel. She's the sister of a girl

called Anna who part owns the restaurant where Bridget works.'

'The sister of Bridget's boss? What the hell is she writing to you for? You've not applied for a job there or anything, have you?' Rose enquired.

'Don't talk daft. Just read it – and don't do your nut.'

Rose eased the letter out of the envelope. She read it once, and then again, and then a third time before she murmured, 'Wouldn't you just know it, eh? The little scrubber.'

'We don't know if it's true yet, Rose ...'

'Of course it's bloody true. You can tell from this. I'll strangle that skinny neck of 'ers, I swear to God I will.'

'You'll do no such thing. If you start shouting the odds you'll drive our son away from us. Never insult a man's woman, no matter what you've heard. You should know that by now. You stay quiet and you give your son a shoulder if he needs it. And if he does he'll make it clear to both of us.'

'I might have known you wouldn't come up with a sudden idea of a break for me for no good reason, Arthur.'

'What's that supposed to mean? You work because you want to. Always have done.'

'That's not what I meant. Think about it. How many times have I asked you to drive me to see Trevor? And all you can ever say is that there'll be too much traffic on the road. That he's younger than we are and should make his way to us. Well, from now on I'll take the train or a coach and visit him as and when I feel like it!'

'Finished?' said Arthur. 'Because if you are I

wouldn't mind a drop of tea from out of that flask. I'm parched.'

'You can't drink tea while you're driving. That's all Trevor needs is for you to have a crash and kill the pair of us.'

But Rose drew the flask from her shopping bag, unscrewed the lid and poured a little into a cup to hand to her husband the way she always did when they went out for a drive – after she had warned him in her own way to be careful with the steering wheel. They continued the journey in and out of silence, depending when either of them had anything of consequence to say. They knew each other inside out and both of them were upset by the contents of the letter, but pleased that the woman had written to them about it so that it could be dealt with.

When they finally arrived in Leytonstone and drove past the underground station, Rose took out the scribbled directions to the street where Trevor lived and read them to her husband. They had made this trip before of course, but it was always the last little bit with the many similar back turnings that had them confused in the past, leading to arguments as to who was right and who was wrong when it came to finding the way without getting lost. Today, though, they had little trouble because both minds were thinking as one. They couldn't wait to get to their son.

Once Arthur had parked in a back turning, they strolled towards the main road nearby and to the door to their son's flat, ready to use the spare key that Trevor had given them when he and Bridget first moved in. Their son had insisted they had this in case they fancied coming down to London on the spur of the moment when neither of them were home to let them in. Today they didn't quite know what to expect – whether he would be at work at the local school where he taught PE and sport or whether he might be teaching pupils at the local swimming pool. But after a couple of rings of the bell they heard footsteps from within as Trevor made his way down the staircase.

When he opened the door to them it wasn't his expression of shock, followed by a sigh of relief at seeing his parents, that caused each of them to want to weep. Their son looked awful. His face was drawn, he had lost weight, and it would have taken an idiot not to see that he was on the verge of tears. Hugging his mother first, Trevor held on tight to his emotions as his dad gripped his hand and squeezed it, saying, 'It's good to see you, son.'

They followed him up the narrow closed-in rickety staircase and when they arrived into his flat they were knocked for six at the state it was in. With the light shining through the window onto Trevor they couldn't help but notice the dark shadows around his eyes, or how unwashed his hair appeared to be – never mind the fact that he was unshaven and his clothes dishevelled. Clearly, he hadn't been to work that day and hadn't slept much during the night.

Looking half the man he was when they had last seen him, some three months since, they only just managed a smile. Rose was so taken aback at seeing her son looking like a vagrant that she could hardly speak, and all that Trevor was able to do was offer his open arms to his dad and hold him tighter than he had ever done before.

Feeling as if her heart was being squeezed to crushing point, Rose pushed from her mind the stuffy, narrow and dark rickety staircase they had climbed and looked around her, ready and willing to pull up her sleeves and get cracking. This wasn't the first time she had been to the flat so she knew where everything was kept; and she was used to the staircase, and the old three-storey building with another flat below Trevor's and an old-fashioned costermonger store on the ground floor. But now, inside this lonely-looking, furnished room, she had to summon every bit of her will not to weep. She was gutted to see that on the draining board in the tiny kitchen there was just one mug, one plate, one knife, one fork.

Looking from his mum to his dad, Trevor tried hard to stop his own tears from flowing. 'I'm sorry, Mum,' he just managed to say. 'I know this place looks a mess.'

'No it doesn't, son,' she said. 'It just needs a woman's touch that's all.' She immediately realised that she had said the wrong thing.

'I'll tell you what,' said Arthur, 'I'll put the kettle on and make a pot of tea and you sit down with your mother. We know about Bridget and what she's been up to so you don't 'ave to hold anything back to save our feelings.'

Dropping into one of the two old-fashioned and worn leather armchairs, Trevor sighed with relief and then covered his face with both hands. Once he had composed himself and had a cup of tea in his hand, he slowly started to tell them all that had been going on.

How lonely he had been and how heartbroken he was when he found out for sure that Bridget was having a full-on affair. 'I didn't want you to find out because I thought you'd be angry with me.'

'Don't be daft, son. Angry with you? How could we be? None of this is your fault, is it?'

'No. I've not strayed if that's what you mean. She's not just trying to get back at me or anything like that.'

'That's not what I meant, son,' said Arthur. 'You're not the type to two-time. So where is she living now? Because I don't see any signs of her lodging here.'

'She packed her suitcase two days ago and moved into the flat above the restaurant where she works. Anna – the wife of Bridget's lover, Frank, doesn't know this yet but no doubt she'll find out soon. Anna is part owner of the restaurant with her husband.'

'Yes, son, so we gather. One of her sisters wrote us a letter saying so. I don't know what she thought we could do about it but it certainly spurred me and your mother to come and see how you were coping.'

Trevor sighed with relief. 'I'm glad she did that, Dad. Really glad. It's much easier somehow now that it's out in the open.'

Leaving the men to talk in private, Rose wandered from the living room into the bedroom where the curtains were still drawn and it all seemed so dark and dingy. This room, just like the living room, was also dishevelled. Wandering back into the living room, she could hardly look into her son's eyes or his pained and tormented face in case she herself broke down.

Smiling faintly at him, she tried to ignore the half-empty mug of cold tea on a small grubby Formica coffee table by an old armchair, and the leftover cold fish and chips half wrapped in newspaper. She was so glad now that she had packed enough clothes for more than just a weekend because wild horses were not going to drag or chase her back home unless she was to take her son with her.

Sharing the fresh pot of tea as they made the best of the mangy sofa and armchair, Arthur and Rose learned just how much time Trevor had been spending in this ghastly flat by himself, with only a small black and white television set for company.

Chapter Five

Driving Anna from the girls' house to her mother's flat via the narrow backstreets of old Bethnal Green where the local whores hung out, George wasn't his usual self. The only reason for this that Anna could come up with was that he wasn't the flirt and womaniser that he had been made out to be. He really did seem quite shy now that he was alone with her in the car, and it was having a knock-on effect because she felt a little at a loss for making conversation. She didn't feel right about discussing the fracas in the restaurant between her and Bridget and yet it could hardly be ignored as if it hadn't happened.

'I didn't have any choice, George,' she finally murmured, right out of the blue. 'I had to find out for myself if Bridget was having an affair with Frank.'

'That's all right, babe,' he said. 'You don't have to explain anything to me. It's personal and private. I just didn't want you to go and cause bodily harm while I was in the restaurant. It could have been a bit tricky – to say the least.'

'Why?' Anna smiled. 'I wouldn't have been the first woman you'd have had to put the handcuffs on I don't suppose.'

George slowly shook his head and by the expression on his face he wasn't taking the incident lightly. 'You have to be more careful though, Anna. You've heard the expression *don't hang your dirty laundry on the line*. You'd be surprised how many people would put their hand up as a witness when a few ten-pound notes are skilfully shown.'

'I never touched the cow.'

'You had a grip on Ginger-nut's hair for Christ's sake. And if I hadn't have got the timing right you would have given her a right-hander. She ended up with her nose out of joint even though you let her go. It could have been a lot worse, with wineglasses flying and breaking. You could have been done for grievous, sweetheart.'

Anna found herself laughing. 'Did she break her nose then?'

'She pushed it out of joint and I clicked it back together again. But she could still have taken you to court for gbh.'

'And what about smh? Can I take *her* to court for that?'

'I'm not with you, sweetheart. Smh?'

'Shagging my husband.'

George laughed out loud and this in turn made Anna smile. 'I think the judge and jury might say that it takes two to tango, babe.'

'What about a jury of all women? They'd be on my side.'

'Listen,' said George, trying to pull this conversation back to facts. 'You've had your say and Bridget's come off worst. Leave it alone now and think about what you want. Either you want Frank back – and nobody's gonna argue with that – or you want a clean break.

You're a lovely girl and I can't see you being lonely for long.'

'It wouldn't make much difference if I were. I've been lonely for quite a while. I'd almost forgotten what it was like to be in company and laughing again. The girls at my sisters' place 'ave a great time, George, even apart from the different sorts of men they meet. The atmosphere there is fantastic. I feel as I've been stuck at home on my own for too long.'

George shrugged and then went quiet, concentrating on the route to Anna's mum's flat. Just as he turned into Ivy's street, he said, 'Listen . . . if you fancy a day out in Kent let me know. No strings attached. I want to go down and have a look at an old farmhouse that might be coming on the market.'

'At the place where you and your mum went hop-picking.' Anna smiled, all knowing. 'You want to claw back a bit of your childhood and the boy in you, and why not? Good for you.'

'It wasn't just me and Mum picking hops in Kent, Anna. My dad and two brothers were there as well.'

'I know, don't be so touchy. And yeah, if Mum will have the twins for me, I would love a day out. When?'

'This coming Sunday? I've already been on the phone and asked about it. Spoke to the owner in fact.'

'Amazing what a title does, eh, George. Detective Inspector.'

'It helps sometimes. The guy sounded distant at first but then once I said I wanted a place away from London to lay my hat he soon relaxed. So I take it that it's a yes then?'

'Providing Mum agrees to have the boys, it's a definite.'

'Good thing I stopped on the way to your sister's place and bought her a box of Milk Tray then.' George quietly chuckled, delight shining out through his eyes. 'And before the rumour gets up and running, my so-called wife is not around any more and it's come as no surprise to me. I gave her the freedom she wanted but kept it quiet. She's gone off to live God knows where. I don't know and I don't care, it's over between us. It was over months ago if I'm to be honest.'

'I'm sorry to hear that, but you won't be lonely for long. Or do you already know that? Have you got a sweetheart in the wings?'

Embarrassed by the question, George flushed. 'No I've not,' he said, and left it there. He then parked the car in silence.

Ivy was spooning some tinned peaches onto a layer of cold custard on top of the trifle she had made when Anna rang the doorbell. Knowing full well who it was, she asked her friend Gwen, who had been there all day and was now on her way out, if she would see them in as she left. Ivy had heard the car pull up and glanced through her net curtains to recognise George and his motor. She placed the trifle in the fridge, smoothed her skirt and quickly tidied her hair, speculating about the why and wherefore of George Blake. She liked him, and had known him a long while, but shadowing her youngest daughter and fetching her home made her think twice as to his motives. Men and their dicks spoke only one language in her opinion – but she was going to give him the benefit of the doubt because her other two daughters, who were experienced in the male species, were okay about him. If she found him to be a little too familiar with her youngest daughter she would give him one of her renowned black looks. She glanced through to the passage, and when he came in with a box of chocolates casually held out to her Ivy found herself blushing.

'You shouldn't have done that, George,' she said, all smiles. 'But they are my favourite so I won't tell you off for spoiling me.'

'You've never done so before, Ivy, when I've fetched you sweets – so why would you do so now?' He knew what was on her mind and wanted to clear the air.

She looked slyly at him while Anna attended to her twins and then moved closer to him. 'Don't you go and break her heart while she's on the rebound.'

'Come on, Ivy. Anna and I are old mates. Your daughters are more like my sisters than anything else.'

'If you say so, George. If you say so.' She checked that Anna was too preoccupied to take any notice of the pair of them and then whispered, 'What the fuck is Frank up to?'

'I'm not sure yet, Ivy. It might be a passing fling or something more serious. Time will tell.'

'That Bridget woman needs a bloody good spanking.'

'She'd probably enjoy that, Ivy.' George grinned at her.

'You're probably right. But seriously . . . why has she let herself be lured in like this by Frank when she's got a decent husband? I know what I would do if it were one of my girls behaving the way she is. I'd take the slipper to her arse.'

Slowly shaking his head, George quietly chuckled. 'Your Linda and Hazel are angels then are they?'

'I should say so! Look at the way they run their business. There's nothing shoddy about what they do. They provide a service for lonely men, young and old. You can't knock that.'

There was no answer that was going to appease Ivy so George kept his mouth shut. In any case, she had left him lost for words. Linda and Hazel were running a brothel after all was said and done. He crossed the room and looked out of the window, checking that there weren't any kids hanging around his treasured car. 'I was telling Anna about my hop-picking years on the way over. You never went down 'oppin' did you, Ivy?'

'No. We preferred fruit-picking in the summer time. Used similar huts to live in though. It was good but I wouldn't want to do it again. I like my home comforts too much.'

'I thought we might go for a drive this Sunday coming. A little nostalgia trip.'

'They don't do picking by hand any more though, do they?' said Ivy, quite fancying a day out herself. 'Machines are in full swing from what I hear and have been for a good few years.'

'That's right,' said George, keeping his eye on two lads admiring his motor. 'I'm kind of interested in a run-down farm near Tonbridge where we used to go as kids. The old farmhouse is a cracker but if left to itself it'll soon turn into a ruin. I think I could pick it up cheap.'

'What for? You wouldn't move out would you?'

'I might do. I was thinking of renovating it alongside a team of builders I know and turn it into a friendly type of small hotel and run it myself. Once I've packed in my job at the Met.'

'So you really do mean to leave the force, eh? Well, I don't blame you for getting out. London will end up like New York where crime's concerned according to a piece I read in the *News of the World*, never mind what goes on all around us.'

'Whoever wrote it wasn't too far out. But that's not the main reason, Ivy. I want out of the smoke. I want to live in the country and be stress free.'

'I can't knock that. So ... Anna wants me to have the twins for the day then, does she?'

'I don't know,' he said, all innocent. 'It would be good for her to get away for a few hours though – after what she's been through. It's not very nice is it, finding out that her husband's been sleeping with another woman.'

'Keep your voice down, George. She might hear you.'

'So what do yer think then? You reckon it'll be all right if she comes with me for a day out?'

'So long as you're back in time to take her and the twins home, I can't see any harm in it. Christ knows what Frank's gonna do.' She turned from the sink where she was rinsing teacups and slowly shook her head. 'What do you make of all this, George? Is he serious about the tart or what?'

'You'll have to ask him that, Ivy. It's been going on

for a while though. They act as if they're a couple when they're in the restaurant.'

Ivy slowly shook her head. 'I still can't take it in. And what about her husband? What's he making of all this?'

'I don't know. He's a quiet kind of a bloke. Comes and goes when he's picking up Bridget and doesn't really say much. I shouldn't worry too much over it. It'll all come out in the wash.'

'Famous last words, George,' murmured Ivy. 'Famous last words.' She was thinking of the day when her husband walked away from her and their three girls. 'My only worry now is what's gonna happen when Anna gets home. Will Frank be there and furious? Linda phoned and told me what happened. I hope to God that Anna didn't cause that accident, that's all.'

'Of course she didn't. Bridget wears stiletto-heeled shoes for work. It was an accident waiting to happen. She's gonna have a swollen bruised conk for a while.' He chuckled at the thought of it. 'Let's see what Frank makes of that. Anyway, your Anna won't be lonely any more. Not now we all know what she's been going through. I'll drop in and see 'er every now and then – if that's all right by you?'

'Of course it is, George. You're as good as family. Well, almost.'

A couple of evenings later, with the twins bathed and asleep in their cots, Anna, even though she was by herself again, for some strange reason was not feeling too lonely. She had had a good cry that afternoon and this had seemed to help. She still couldn't get over the fact that Frank would leave her for another woman, but he had slept at the flat above Prima the previous night and now she had no idea whether or not he would do the same thing again this coming night. She thought the reason that he was staying away was because he was full of guilt. But now she wasn't too sure if he intended to ever come back at all. At least she had Rachel next door to one side of her and the young couple on the other and this helped. Curled up in an armchair in the quiet cosy sitting room, she could hear the muted sound of Rachel's television, which was comforting, and now that she had put the twins to bed she had time to herself.

She had no regrets about going to see Bridget, and didn't know whether Frank was angry with her and showing it by sleeping in the flat above the restaurant, or whether he feared that if he was at home he might be pushed into a confession that would be the beginning of him leaving. Anna sipped her milky cocoa and glanced at the small brass carriage clock which was softly ticking on the mantelshelf. Nine-thirty. She wondered how Frank was managing to run the restaurant without Bridget, who was hiding away until the swelling to her nose had gone down. Relaxed, and in a pensive mood, she was startled at the sound of her doorbell piercing through the quiet, especially at this time of night. She got up to answer the door. For the first time, she felt nervous in her own home and switched on the outside light so that she could see the shape of whoever it was outside through the frosted-glass panes. From the shape of the man outside it looked to be Trevor Plumb, Bridget's husband.

Cautious, just in case it wasn't him but a stranger, she

slipped the safety chain on and opened the door to see through the gap that she had been right. Opening the door fully to him, she offered a weak, almost apologetic smile and then shrugged as she waved him inside, telling him to go through to the back sitting room. The reality of all that was happening was really hitting home now.

In the back room where the last of the setting sun was casting lovely burnt orange rays into the room, Anna smiled warmly at the sad young man. 'I'm sorry about what happened, Trevor,' she said, 'but it wasn't my fault that Bridget slipped—'

'I didn't come round for an apology, Anna,' he said. 'Is it all right if I take my mac off?'

'Of course it is.' She instinctively squeezed his arm and looked into his pale freckled face. Beads of sweat were breaking out on his forehead. 'I'm really pleased and grateful that you've come. And please ... feel free to visit whenever you want.'

'My parents are down for a day or so. I'm not by myself if that's what you think. I wanted to come and see you to ask what you thought of Bridget and Frank living together above your restaurant.'

'No, Trevor – they're not living there. I think that Frank's gonna move into his brother's flat above the restaurant at Tower Hill. Didn't Bridget stay at yours last night then?'

'No. Which was just as well because my parents arrived out of the blue and they're staying with me. It's a bit cramped, but Bridget wasn't there. She had already packed her bags and moved into your flat above Prima.'

'She did what! How dare she? Bloody cheek. I can't believe it. Are you sure?'

'It's what she said on the phone. I don't think she much cares what she does anymore so long as she gets her way.'

'And how long are your parents staying with you?'

'Only a short while – Dad goes back tomorrow because he can't take too many days off, but Mum is stopping on. I think she's worried about me.'

'Well I'll tell you what, Trev. Why don't you and your mum move into the flat above the restaurant? We'll shove Bridget out. She's definitely not going to stay there. No way.'

'I suppose she could nurse her nose back to being all right in our Leytonstone flat. If me and Mum did move into yours. If you really mean it.' He then broke into a soft and gentle laughter. 'You've got guts, Anna – I will say that.'

'She told you what happened then?'

'Yes. Over the phone. She said she couldn't stop herself falling in love with Frank. When I asked her if Frank felt the same she said that I was to ask him. That said it all really.'

'Yes, I suppose it did.' Anna felt a wave of pain grip her. 'I know she's a bit of a drama queen on the quiet, Trevor, but it all makes sense now. Frank's been walking about as if he's a hero in a romantic movie.'

'My mother once said that Bridget was the type who could become the village tart if we lived in a village. The marriage-breaker troublemaker.'

'Well, she's in a small corner of London now and one of a thousand of her type. I can't believe she's in my flat. Jesus. So what do you think? Will you want to move in? You can just turn up whenever you want and unpack your bags. I'll give you a key tonight. Then tell Bridget to move back into the so-called flea pit that she's always moaning about. She hates your flat from what she's said, so she can go and stew in it, can't she.'

Trevor laughed quietly again, and then said, 'Yes, she can. God, I'm glad that I came round, Anna. I feel better already.'

'Good. Now let's open a bottle of wine and celebrate your move in advance. It's hardly the end of the world is it? Sod the pair of 'em. Let's drink a toast to us, and others in the same boat! What d'yer fancy, a glass of red wine or something stronger? I've got some scotch.'

'That would be very nice. Scotch and water.' Trevor looked around himself and said, 'You've got a nice place here, Anna.'

'I know I have. And do you know what? I'm gonna hold onto it no matter what Frank tries to pull. Now then . . . are you hungry? It won't take a minute to make you a sandwich.'

'No, that's all right. For some reason I've lost my appetite.'

'Tell me about it,' said Anna. 'Sit yourself down and let's forget about my husband and your wife for five minutes. I'll get the drinks.' No sooner was she in the passage and going into the kitchen than the phone rang.

She hoped that it wouldn't be Frank's voice on the other end of the line. It was in fact Ivy, asking if she was all right. She told her that she was fine and made an excuse of having to go because she had just run a nice hot bath for herself. No sooner had she replaced the receiver than the phone rang again; this time it was George asking if she was still up for the day trip to Kent. She kept it short and told him she was. He then told her that he had booked off the day after the next. Sunday.

'I'll have to check with Mum,' she said. 'She'll baby-sit for me if she's got nothing else lined up.'

'I'll take that to be a yes, then, babe. Your mum would cancel a visit to the queen just so as to have her grandsons to watch over.'

'All right,' said Anna, 'take it as a yes – unless I phone to tell you that it's not.'

'Will do.'

'Sorry about that, Trevor,' said Anna, joining him again and handing him his glass of whisky and soda. 'Two phone calls in a row are out of the ordinary, but then the past couple of days have hardly been run of the mill.'

'You can say that again,' he said. They clinked glasses. 'Let's hope we'll come out of this happier than Bridget and Frank do,' Trevor went on. 'And if it's any consolation, I don't think they'll last five minutes.'

Looking into his soft hazel eyes, Anna shrugged. 'We'll see.'

'This isn't the first time she's slept with another man. It's happened twice before that I know of. And even though both affairs were a flash in the pan for the men involved, she languished over it for weeks. You're right, she's a drama queen on the quiet, is Bridget. But she also gets what she wants and doesn't much care who she hurts on the way.'

'Oh, well, that makes me feel better in a strange kind

of way. It couldn't have been easy for you to tell me that. I appreciate it, Trevor. And I do mean that.' She raised her glass and smiled. 'Here's to us.'

'Cheers. I hope she doesn't ruin your marriage that's all. She almost wrecked the two before yours, but the women saw the affairs as their husbands scoring with an easy woman who got off on having secret assignations with men who drove around in nice cars. One of her married men drove a brand new Range Rover and the other a red Jaguar. And from what each of the husbands told me, Bridget's preferred place to get screwed was in an expensive car.'

'She sounds as if she could do with seeing a psychiatrist.'

'She probably does need to but at least she gave the gossips something to talk about. They loved it.'

On the sofa now and drawing her legs up to be comfortable, Anna said, 'Will you take her back – if she gets down and crawls?'

'No. Would you take Frank back?'

'Probably. In fact – yes, I would. But I'll make him suffer for what he's done. I'll go out on a shopping spree.'

'Well, I wish I felt the same. But feeling as if your heart's been ripped out three times is not good. I'm finished with her this time. She can have her freedom and do what she wants with it.'

'Oh Trevor . . .' Anna reached out and took his hand. 'Don't go and do something you might regret for the rest of your life. You must love Bridget or you would have gone before now.'

'I *should* have done. I should have taken notice of the

hints being dropped here, there and everywhere by the parents of the children I teach.'

'Well, from now on you'll have a nice flat to live in. The one above Prima.'

'Mmm. But will I be able to deal with seeing her and Frank when I come and go?'

'Of course you will. It's got its own side entrance door don't forget.'

'Well, I don't want to leave London because of her. Because of Bridget. I'm not a bad swimming coach and my world is hardly empty is it? Not with all of those kids and their smiling faces. I taught beginners of around the age of six at local public baths until I'd cut my teeth. Then I was in charge of the more boisterous girls and boys from junior schools. After that I was moved on to the tough eleven- to sixteen-year-olds. Several of the youngsters that I coached swam in the area galas and won medals. My dream is to win the pools, buy a huge house in the country and turn it into a children's home and teach the underprivileged.'

'Oh, Trevor . . . that's such a lovely dream to have.'

'It won't happen, of course, but we all have to have a dream don't we? I *will* work for underprivileged children though. If I can.' Finishing his drink he stood up to leave.

'Let me know if you want to rent the flat. Once you've thought about it.'

'I have thought about. I would like to rent it.'

'Good for you!'

Anna could imagine Trevor and his mother living in the flat and looked forward to it. After all it would be a bit of a social life for the pair of them until his mother went home and then it would be his very own pad. No one expected Trevor to be full of the joys of spring, for obvious reasons, but this opportunity to live in a much nicer home in a livelier area had come at just the right time for him, Anna thought.

Anna stepped forward to give Trevor a sisterly hug. 'I'm so pleased that you took the trouble to come round to see me. Thank you.'

Blushing a little he said, 'I wanted to. And in a way I suppose I felt obliged as well. I hope it wasn't too encroaching.'

'No, of course it wasn't.' Anna gently laughed. 'You got it off your chest and you've helped me get some of it off mine. And don't think that you can't ring on that doorbell again because you can. But I would prefer you to phone and let me know if you're popping in. Just in case I'm in the bath or something.'

'I will next time. I promise.' He squeezed her arm and said that he would see himself out. Brief though their time together was, it left Anna feeling as if she had just made a friend.

Settling back on her sofa with the cushion for a pillow, Anna looked through the *TV Times* to see if there was anything worth watching that would take her mind off things. The one thing she was resisting was playing favourite love songs of hers and Frank's. She wanted to get through the next few days as coolly and calmly as she possibly could. She thought about her babies, fast asleep in their cots upstairs, and asked God to at least help her look after and protect them.

Then, closing her eyes, she tried not to think about anything else. She was ready for a long soak in a warm

Radox bath. The house had always held a peaceful and calm atmosphere and she appreciated this now more than she ever had. But there was another ring on her doorbell to pierce through the quiet. This time it was Jackie the Avon rep on her doorstep.

'What a sight for sore eyes you are,' said Anna, pleased to see the fresh young smiling face. 'Come on in and tease me into spending some of Frank's money.'

'I won't be stopping long, and sorry I didn't come the other day,' whispered Jackie, as if Anna's sleeping babies were within hearing distance. 'I've got the new catalogue with me and you'll love the range of eye makeup. Three shades of soft gold that'll bring out the little hazel specks that I've seen in your green eyes.'

'Oh God, don't tempt me . . .'

'You won't need persuasion, trust me. I'll leave you the catalogue and you can browse at your leisure if you want.'

'Good. That suits me fine. But come and take the weight off your feet for five minutes.'

'Now then, I've got two other clients to see this evening so no time to spare.' She smiled and her eyes lit up as she eased herself past Anna who was holding open the door. 'And one of them has a gorgeous young bloke for a son who loves the new range of products for men. Aftershave and the like.'

'They're the ones who'll spend the money, Jackie,' Anna laughed. 'Men love to pamper themselves on the quiet you know. More so than women I think.' Following Jackie through to the sitting room Anna listened to a running report on how well her sales were

147

going and how she had half a mind to take this work on full time and give up her job in the city.

'I think I'm more cut out for this,' she said, flicking her auburn hair off her face. 'I'm earning nearly as much as I get for my proper job.'

'I would give it another few months if I were you,' said Anna. 'This might just be a flash in the pan.'

'No, I don't think so.' Jackie settled herself on the settee and smiled broadly. 'I love this work and it would be great to do it full time soon. If my orders keep going as they are, I can earn a lot of money in this game. Hard work, patience, and long hours are what are needed. And I can do that for the next five years – no problem. I would love to do it full time.'

'Well then, far be it for me to advise you otherwise. You seem to know your own mind, Jackie, and that can't be bad, can it?' Anna stopped herself from relating what had happened over the past couple of days because she had had enough of discussing it.

So, instead of being miserable again this evening, she was pleased to sit and choose presents – a lipstick and a powder puff for Ivy, talcum powder for Gwen and some crème perfume in a lovely pink jar with a delicately printed flowery lid for herself. And all paid for by cheque from the joint account. Once the order was made, her young friend was up and away and on to the next client. Closing the door behind the entrepreneur, Anna climbed the stairs ready for that soak in the bath and then a much-needed sleep in her comfortable bed all to herself. But, just as she reached the top stair, the phone went again and she was in two minds whether to answer it. This time it was Frank, and when she heard his voice every muscle in her body seemed to go into a spasm.

'It's me,' he said, his voice quieter than usual. 'I think I had better stay at the flat at Tower Bridge again tonight, don't you.'

Her heartbeat quickening, Anna said, 'I thought that's what you were going to do in any case, Frank. After all, you can't stay at Prima because you've moved Bridget in. Her husband came and told me so.'

'Oh well, that drip would have, wouldn't he? I'll be back some time tomorrow to fetch some of my clothes.'

Angry that he dared to talk to her like this, she forced herself not to scream abuse at him down the line. 'No problem. I'll put them in bin bags for you.'

'Good. Leave them in the passage if you go out.'

'As it happens, I am going out tomorrow. Taking the boys over to see their aunts.' She guessed that this would put his back up.

'That's not clever, Anna. You know I don't want them anywhere near that brothel. Not now – not ever. And you should want the same thing.'

'It's not a brothel, it's a dating agency. The girls are not sluts and there is a big difference. But then you'd know all about sluts. You having turned our first little flat into your own private slutting place.'

Ignoring this he repeated himself. 'I don't want the boys in that house, Anna. They might catch something for one thing.'

Anna laughed at him. 'I think that you should be more worried over yourself. I should get down to the VD clinic if I were you. Bridget's been passed around

149

quite a bit from what I've heard. Ask her about it. And as for your clothes, you can take all of them while you're at it. Socks, pants, pyjamas, and the lot. I'll put them all in black bin bags, except for your underpants. I don't want to risk touching them. Not all bacteria come out in the wash you know.' She then gently replaced the receiver and felt so much better for the call. She liked the sense of getting back at him. She looked at the phone and said, 'You bastard.'

At least she had had the last word for a change and she had managed not to let him entice her into a row, which he could so easily do with just one of his timeworn sarcastic clichés such as, 'You need to get out a bit more with your friends,' or 'Why don't you get your mum to baby-sit while you go to a woman's evening class somewhere?' This was the kind of thing he would say when she had dared to ask why they couldn't go out together for an evening now and then. The worst of Frank's patronising suggestions was that he always spoke in a matter-of-fact tone while delivering them. And he usually delivered them while either watching the sport on the television or reading a newspaper. And now he was ducking out of a confrontation that he didn't want because he knew that he was as guilty as hell and Anna had dared to make it public knowledge. Whichever way it was viewed – this was the first step towards their separation.

Later on, once in her bed, as Anna had expected, she couldn't settle at all and didn't sleep well because she was crying on and off all night. Once dawn broke however, after hours of tossing and turning and fitful sleep, she dragged herself out of bed and went downstairs to make up the bottles for the twins, who would soon be letting her know that they were hungry. Looking out of the kitchen window and a little more alert, she could hear the beautiful sound of birds outside coming in through the small opening of the skylight. This was the time of the day that she loved most. The settling down of the wildlife after the first flush of activity from various town birds which followed the dawn chorus.

Lifting the white nursing chair, her first purchase of baby furniture from Mothercare in the early days, she carried it outside into the garden so as to be in the early morning sun and in the centre of nature itself – albeit in London's East End. After her first cup of coffee she went upstairs to the twins' room and found them awake and gurgling at each other through the bars of their cots. Had she left them waiting for five minutes or so longer, she knew that they would have been hollering for their feed.

Taking them below, one by one, she laid baby James on the settee and put on a clean paddy pad, then did the same with Oliver, and bottle-fed one after the other. She didn't feel anywhere near as lonely as she had done of late and appreciated the love and warmth exuding from her babies. Any leftover feelings of dread of the unknown and loathing towards Frank for all that he had done, simply melted away when she was holding either of her boys. She felt even better when she opened the drapes in the sitting room to let the morning sunshine flood in.

When she reopened the door leading out to the

garden after she had placed the boys in the playpen for a kick and a gurgle, she could smell grilled kippers coming from a neighbour's kitchen, which made her mouth water. Seeing that her babies were content enough in their playpen, she went into the kitchen again because she was hungry and ready for fried eggs and crispy bacon. Still in her pyjamas and dressing gown – her favourite pink and white candy stripe – she poured herself another cup of coffee when the sound of the front door opening struck through her as if she had touched a live wire. But then, as she drew breath, she told herself not to be stupid. If a burglar wanted to get in he would choose the dark of night to rob her and not broad daylight. It was now eight-thirty a.m. It had to be Frank.

Not knowing quite what she would say to him if he came anywhere near her, she peeled off two layers of bacon from the packet and laid them into the hot non-stick frying pan. Her heart beating nineteen to the dozen, she pretended she hadn't heard him and positioned herself at the cooker so that her back was to the open kitchen doorway. She didn't want to look at Frank. She didn't want him near her, and she could hardly credit that he was so thoughtless as to stay out all night after what had happened and then walk calmly back in through their door as if he had every right to come and go as he pleased. From his aura she knew that he was not here to apologise or explain. Old feelings of love had come and gone over and over again since the day before, but vanished when she pictured his expression of boredom whenever he had been in the same room as herself of late – when he could hardly wait to get out of the house, using any excuse possible. She moistened her dry lips with the tip of her tongue and braced herself for whatever was to come next.

Drawn perhaps by the smell of the frying bacon, Frank appeared at the open doorway of the kitchen, showing little other than a taut face – a defence tactic that she had seen before. He was as guilty as hell but not sorry for what he had done. She could read him like a book. She blanked her mind and thought of the birds, the bees and the flowers in her garden and ignored him. So as not to weaken, she reminded herself of what a self-centred, dour bastard he had turned into at home. Of course, once out at the restaurant or elsewhere, he was good old Frank, the easy-going, fun-loving decent guy who helped old ladies cross the road.

Glancing sideways at him, she could tell from his expression that he was going to carry on behaving as if he were the victim and not the *cause* of their marriage being blown apart. This was Frank playing the strong silent type, which was all bollocks as far as she was concerned. Once in the kitchen, he moved around in silence and opened the refrigerator to take out the milk and poured himself a glassful. He spoke not one word to Anna but she could tell that he was fuming inside.

He continued to behave as if she wasn't there and, because of this – not to mention his dark mood – she knew he was showing her what an ogre he could be when he was put out. She knew that he was waiting for her to come at him with questions and accusations. Having to be on the back foot was his problem. He didn't want her to question him as to what had been going on and for how long. She knew Frank inside out, whether he liked to believe it or not, and could tell that he had his rehearsed speech ready and waiting. Well, she wasn't going to oblige. Of course she wanted to hit him, to scream at him for being a selfish two-timing bastard but she was determined to keep control. Even though it was taking every bit of self control, she would not respond to his baiting tactic of silence. She had seen it too many times before, and in any case what did he think she would say? 'I'm sorry I upset Bridget. How is the poor dear soul? Did she break her nose or just put it out of joint?'

Gripping the wooden handle of the frying pan, Anna turned a slice of bacon over and wished that she had the guts to use the pan as a weapon and smack him round the face. Instead, just as if she were by herself, she opened the fridge, took out two eggs, and broke them into the sizzling bacon fat, humming a tune while doing so – a tune that Ivy had often sung to her when she was a child, 'Somewhere Over the Rainbow'. After all, it was Frank who had an apology to make and some explaining to do. She knew, of course, that this was not going to happen, because he was not the kind of man who could swallow his pride too easily, having been born with a stubborn streak. Inflexibility had always been one of his unpleasant traits.

What Frank didn't realise, or at least wouldn't admit to if challenged, was that he was transparent and not the deep and private man he liked to think he was. Even so, there was a side to him that she had never been quite sure about. If, for instance, she were to push him a little too far, would he give her a fierce slap around the face again? It had happened twice before within a year or so of them having been married. On both occasions, during an argument she had said things that had been a little too close to the bone when he had been in one of his dark and silent moods. And now he was there and in another one of them.

It seemed almost laughable that he was coming on with the strong and silent routine even though he surely knew that his sneak-around affair had been blown wide open and that people were now smiling behind his back. Since it had gone quiet in the sitting room, Anna knew that Oliver and James had fallen asleep in their playpen, so she went and collected them and took them upstairs to their cots. When she returned to the kitchen, Frank murmured, while opening his post, 'If you think you're being clever, Anna, you're making a very big mistake.'

He spoke as if he was talking to a business colleague and not his young and lovely wife. Taking no notice of him whatsoever, she spooned a little sizzling bacon fat over the yolks of her farm eggs. 'If Bridget decided to walk out on us after your little melodrama,' he continued, 'we'd be in real trouble. She practically runs Prima with me now.'

Still Anna didn't answer him or acknowledge his presence, even though it was filling the kitchen. She could hardly believe that he would dare to mention his lover's name within their four walls now that he knew that she had found him out. Even so, she wasn't going to let his patronising tone provoke her into losing her temper. He knew that she knew what had been going on and still he showed no signs of attempting to excuse or explain his behaviour. And of course no apology either. He and Bridget, according to what she had said to Anna, were making plans to buy a place together, weren't they?

'I'm gonna pack a few things in a bag and stay at my brother's flat until you come to your senses,' he said. 'You owe a member of our staff an apology, which I think, under the circumstances it would be better if you did in writing. You'd best not come to the restaurant until it all cools down. Bridget's not the type to bear a grudge but I think she might need some space for a while.'

Anna slowly turned to face him. She looked directly into his eyes and then, surprising herself, quietly laughed at the audacity of this man. '*What* did you just say? You want *me* ... to apologise ... to *her?*'

'I think you should, just to keep the peace.'

'Oh, do you?' said Anna, as she pushed her face up a little closer to his and spoke ever so quietly. 'Give me a break, Frank. The silly bitch buckled under her fuck-me four-inch stiletto heels. All I did was grip her hair a little while I was whispering that she ought to know that everyone's talking about her and the way she offers a shag with her eyes.' She raised one eyebrow and half smiled. 'I thought I was doing her a favour ... and you, come to that.'

'You're not funny, Anna. Don't you think I've got enough to think about – running from my restaurant to my brothers' and back again?'

'I'm *sorry*,' said Anna, now sporting a mock puzzled expression. 'But did you say *your* restaurant?'

'You know exactly what I said. What's with all the theatricals?'

Pausing for a moment, she looked him in the eye and could see that not only was his face taut but the little nervous tic that only showed now and then was going like the clappers. For a second or two, old feelings of love threatened to surface, but then he made the mistake of sporting his classic expression of patronising boredom. A look that told her that he wanted her to know that he couldn't wait to get out of the house and that he believed her to be incredibly thick.

She'd had enough. She moistened her dry lips with the tip of her tongue and said, 'Do us all a favour, Frank. Stop acting like Bridget's a brave soldier, it doesn't suit you. Fuck off and live with the girl if that's what you want. I don't need soiled goods around me and you have been reeking of stale scent for a long time.'

'What are you talking about? Soiled goods? Who've you been listening to?' Again Frank's anger broke through his matter-of-fact façade. The difference now though was that he was red in the face. She knew that he knew he was in the wrong, so why couldn't he just apologise and go?

'Everyone's been talking about you,' she finally said. 'I wasn't listening the way I should have been all of the time admittedly, but of course, now that I know everything, it all makes sense. I've smelled her perfume on your clothes and in your skin and hair. And *that* . . . is what *I* call soiled goods. Unlike you, I don't really need to listen to anyone else advising me what to do. I've discussed my worries with nobody. I didn't have to ask questions about what you were up to, Frank, because you talk in your sleep for one thing.'

Frank stared at her and she could tell that he was so filled with guilt that he had no choice other than to go on the attack. She now understood the saying, of not being able to change a leopard's spots. 'I'm not listening to this rubbish,' he said as he turned around and left the room. From the hallway he called over his shoulder: 'You should get out with the twins a bit more!' He then took the stairs two at a time and she knew that he was about to throw a change or two of clothes into his large, soft, tan leather holdall. This is what he had come for. A set or two of clean clothes and nothing else.

His high-handed tone infuriated her. He should have been full of apologies, of remorse. Fortunately, though, the melodramatic exit from the house that she knew he was about to make was adding fuel to her fire instead of bringing tears to her eyes. Taking a slow, deep breath, she brought Ivy to mind and could hear her quietly saying, 'Leave it be, darling ... leave it be. Stay silent. Say nothing.' The sad thing about all of this was that there was a time when Anna would have done anything for Frank, and he would have bent over backwards to make her happy. That Bridget had so influenced him beggared belief.

With her mother still in her thoughts, Anna dished up her eggs and bacon to take into the living room. She settled herself at the old pine table and began to eat as if nothing untoward was happening. Then, with all the nonchalance she could possibly muster, she drew the Avon brochure close, ready to flick through it once she knew that Frank was on his way down the stairs. Whether he came into the room or not didn't matter, because the door was open and he would not be able to ignore the fact that she was seemingly unruffled. She blanked her mind until he left the house without a word, slamming the street door hard behind him.

She knew that he would go straight to Bridget and fill her in as to the kind of reception he had received, but what she couldn't be sure of was whether or not he had found out that George had given her a lift home from Ivy's flat. Innocent though it was, she knew that he would use this as a counter-attack in an attempt to pass the buck. None of this really mattered in any case, because a clear-cut message had been given. He had packed his bags. He had left. Going to the front-room window, Anna watched as he drove away without so much as a backward glance.

'You cold-hearted bastard,' she murmured. She could hardly take in what was happening. She had done nothing to deserve this. She had done nothing wrong.

Back in the kitchen, she poured herself another cup of coffee, but this time she laced it with a little drop of brandy. Ivy's smiling face and voice came to mind again. *Purely medicinal, sweetheart. Purely medicinal.*

Just as she was about to sip her warming drink there was a knock on the front door. She hesitated before going to open it in case it was Frank back to collect something he had forgotten. But when she did open the door, to her relief it was only Rachel, who had seen the car come and then go again, and noticed Frank carrying his bulky leather holdall. Standing on the doorstep, her expression said it all: I'm here if you need an ear and a bit of comforting.

Anna waved her in and they went and sat at the table. Before she knew it, she was shedding bucket-loads of tears while Rachel held her hand and gave gentle advice, which was exactly what she needed – another voice in the room, a soft and gentle voice. Once she had stopped crying, the old woman said, 'Do you know what, darling? I think you are going to have to fight for your man. Fight with every weapon you have, even though it might go against the grain and make you feel sick inside. Once he's back in the fold, then you bide your time and you ask yourself do you want to spend the rest of your life with him? Give yourself the right to choose what *you* want. Don't be impulsive. Be clever and come out of this feeling that you are on top of it.'

'I don't know if I'm strong enough a person to do that, Rachel,' said Anna, drying her eyes. 'I don't even know if I want to be bothered. I think I would rather change the lock on the door so he doesn't come in here again.'

'Listen to me. You have the babies to think about even if you don't feel that *you* need Frank right now. Him coming and going this morning was a rotten thing for you to have to go through. Mean. He should have stayed a lot longer and talked to you before he left with his things packed in that silly bag. I'm disappointed in him and I'm surprised. I take it that he's sulking and is going to sleep in that little flat above his brother's restaurant to sort out his mind?'

'I think so. But really, I know as much as you do, Rachel. I think he said that he was going to his brother's flat in Tower Hill, but he's a clever liar so who knows whose bed he'll be sleeping in tonight? And do you know what – I don't think I care any more. One thing is for sure – he can't shack up with Bridget in our flat because I've let Trevor and his mum have the keys. They are going to move into it.'

'Well, that's no bad thing, is it? In fact I would say that this is a clever move.' The old woman smiled and her face lit up. 'And of course you care where your husband sleeps. But *you* won't lose any sleep over it. That's what you tell him should he ask. So, listen . . . I made some chicken soup first thing. You want that I should fetch it in around lunchtime? We could eat together.'

'No thank you, darling,' said Anna, squeezing the old lady's bony hand. 'It's enough to know that you're there for me. Right next door. But you mustn't worry – I will come through this, you'll see . . . even if it does take a while to adjust.'

'Well, that makes me feel better,' said the old neighbour. 'But also promise me that you'll knock on my door, no matter what time, if you suddenly need a shoulder to cry on or somebody to talk to, even.'

'I promise,' said Anna. 'And I do mean that.'

'Good. Then I shall love and leave you.' Rachel pulled herself up from the chair and looked around the room. 'You know, I think you would be just as happy here – with or without Frank – once you accept the idea of it. I loved my husband but he got in the bloody way all of the time, God rest his soul.'

Once she was by herself again, Anna ran through her mind what the old woman had said, and the more she thought about it the more it made sense. Rachel had been short and to the point when giving advice: 'Give yourself the right to choose what *you* want. Bide your time and don't be impulsive. Be clever and come out of this the best you possibly can.' These were words of wisdom that she was going to tuck at the back of her mind and not forget. Since it was quiet and her babies, by the sound of things, were still asleep, she felt as if she deserved to go back to bed herself for another hour or so to catch up on the sleep that she had missed during her restless night. The worst of this morning's fiasco was that Frank had walked away as if he was the pained victim. 'You can be a selfish bastard at times, Frank,' she murmured, as she filled a glass with water from the tap in the kitchen, hardly able to comprehend that her world had tumbled almost overnight.

'I should have known you would try and make it my fault,' she thought. 'Make me look like the trouble-maker. But that's all right – I'll be your scapegoat for a little while longer. Blame me all you want. I know I haven't done anything wrong and so do other people. Especially those who eat in our restaurant.'

With a heavy heart she tilted her head to heaven as salty tears trickled down her cheeks, and whispered, 'Please, God ... please look after me and my babies. Help me to take care of them and keep all of this dark and horrible stuff out of their innocent world. I do realise that I badly need your guidance. Amen.'

Then, just as if her prayer had been answered, there was a short ring on the doorbell. Dragging herself to answer it and not really caring who it was this time, her face lit up when she saw her sisters standing on the doorstep with a bunch of flowers in Linda's arms and a big box of chocolates in Hazel's. Slowly shaking her head and laughing, Anna said, 'If you two are not witches then my name's not Anna. Your timing is perfect. Come on in.'

After hugs all round, the three sisters flopped down in the living room, their shoes off, their legs curled under them as they sipped their freshly percolated coffee and smoked their cigarettes. Linda and Hazel were getting exactly what they came for. Their sister was talking ten to the dozen and they were all ears.

'I don't want to be seen in the same light as hundreds of other women who this has happened to. I don't want to be talked about as the spineless wife and mother of two who needs to get off her arse and be shaken out of domesticity. But I do want to still get on with taking care of my babies even if it does have to be by myself. And I will carry on doing the shopping, cooking and washing and ironing and housework. It's not a hobby – it's a fact of life. These things have to be done.'

'No one's knocking that, Anna. Why are you being a touch defensive?'

'I'm not. It's just that earlier on I read an article in a magazine about men and their affairs. Statistics show that the "other women" are mostly the ones who get the boot in the end. Once the sex bit has been done to death. That's when the men usually get down on their knees to the wife and beg to be taken back. And most do take them back. It made me angry, that's all.'

'Mum didn't take Dad back though, did she?' said Linda, sadly.

'Good for her is what I say.' Hazel gazed at the floor, thoughtfully. 'You know what Mum's like. Too proud and too self-sufficient to have let him come back in the door. Plenty of men have found themselves out in the cold with the locks changed.'

'But that's not what I want to happen, Hazel. I want things back the way they were. And I'll go about that in my own sweet way. After all, I am partly to blame for all of this.'

'Rubbish. It's the Bridgets of this world and men like Frank who can't resist a bit of oats on the side. And let's face it, Bridget's been like a heat rash all over him from the start.'

'I know. She behaves as if they're a couple at times and in front of me. I don't know how I've kept my fist out of her face for so long.'

'That's why we're here again, babe. To goad you back into the right action.' Hazel looked at Anna. 'Just make certain that you do really want Frank back before you make a decision.'

'Absolutely,' said Linda. 'You just might start to hate him later on in life when you're lying awake in the night and he's asleep beside you and it all comes flooding back. It might just dawn on you that you don't actually want him any more.'

'Exactly.' Hazel smiled. 'That's that out of the way. No more talk about the bitch that seems to be permanently on heat. She's wasted enough of our sister-time together. Fuck her. She's doomed now whichever way it goes.'

Anna stretched her shoulders and breathed a sigh of relief. 'I do feel better about things. And I can see it in a different light now. Any woman working at Frank's side for twelve hours a day and on a regular basis was bound to get on friendly terms. The difference is that Bridget was set on having it all from the minute she walked into Prima.'

'I think you might be right, Anna,' said Hazel, pleased that their little bit of brainwashing had worked.

'I knew all along that Frank had been too tired at night once he got in. I know how the busy spells can be murder at Prima from when I did my two-year stint. But before she came along exhaustion didn't affect Frank's passion or performance in the bedroom. We were always at it. So by not bothering to touch me I think he was giving me a message to keep my distance. He was acting as if I had done something wrong. And do you know what? I was beginning to believe that myself.'

Hazel and Linda looked from their innocent fair-haired sibling to each other and half smiled. They had achieved their goal. They had arrived at the point where their Anna was not only facing up to what was going on but voicing it as if she had got to this turning point by herself. They couldn't have wished for it to have gone better. It was true that tears were in her lovely green eyes and her hands were trembling and she was twisting her handkerchief into a knot, but this was something that they had seen before, when she was at school and facing end-of-term exams. So rather than talk to her about her husband's affair, they coaxed Anna into talking about the twins. They asked questions to do with the stage they were at and gradually, the more she talked the more Anna relaxed and the more she relaxed the more she talked. Both her sisters had to hold tight to their emotions as they listened to her giving pathetic reasons as to why Frank had been disloyal to her. They were happy enough, though, to be the patient listeners as they waited for her to talk herself out. When she did finally lapse into silence Linda was straight in.

'Frank's just a stupid sod that's been lured in by a tempting arse and fuck-me expression. Bridget's just another ambitious little cow who wants it all. And in this case it's the man, the restaurant and the money.'

'Absolutely. I should have known she wouldn't have been able to fool the pair of you, but I bet the customers think that she's just a lovely girl down from the country.'

'I don't know about that, babe, but fool us? No way. We saw from the start what she was up to. And Frank won't have been the first married man she's got her claws into. This one was born to break up good marriages.'

'So . . .' said Linda, having heard enough, 'do you want all of this to work its way into boredom, babe, or do you want one of the boys to bring Frank up sharp?'

'How about we send Bridget packing?' said Anna, more positive. 'Wouldn't that be the most logical thing to do?'

'It would be the best thing but maybe not logical. What's to say that Frank wouldn't take a drive to wherever she goes next so as to meet her secretly in some little pub or club somewhere? Men are turned on by the chase don't forget.'

'I don't think that he would go that far.' Anna looked from one sister to the other. 'Would he?'

'Oh, I think he might, Anna,' said Linda. 'He'll be just like the caveman pursuing the woman on heat. And let's not forget that Bridget hadn't been working there for a week before he was lured in by her little-girl smile when she posed in her flowing fuck-me frocks and high-heel shoes. The men could smell her from a mile off and Frank was only a few feet away.'

Anna's sister could be crude but she got to the point. 'You're right, Linda,' she responded. She *was* up for it. She was after Frank and only Frank. Frank the owner of the restaurant. The one with the money. If she wiggled her backside at any of the male customers it would have been to torment Frank and nobody else. It brings back a sickening picture in the mind – but it's true. It's all true.'

'Give her the fucking boot,' said Hazel. 'I can't see Frank going looking for her. She's just been a cheap thrill, that's all. I reckon he'll beg to have you back once this comes out into the open. And when this does happen, no more playing the perfect wife and mother. You're coming out with us now and then for a bit of fun. You're getting back out there again and shaking off the dust!'

A deep sigh of relief escaped from Anna. 'God! I think I might just be ready for that. Just one night a month would do. I want to rock and roll again.'

'Rock and roll? I don't think so.' Hazel turned to Linda. 'She's living in the fucking past.'

'You know what I mean,' Anna said. 'One of *your* haunts. A nightclub with a live band and lots of fantastic atmosphere.'

Quiet and thoughtful, Linda, out of the blue, said, 'Do you know what the most sickening thing of all is? Bridget never stopped talking to us about her husband when we were in there now and then for a quick bite at lunchtimes. Her Trevor. Her Trevor the swimming instructor. The poor bastard that she's been two-timing for God knows how many years. So what is that all about?'

'Ask a psychiatrist,' Anna said. 'As for me, I'm not all that sure what makes her tick and neither do I care. She's got our undivided attention and she's not even under our roof!' She looked from one to the other as she slowly shook her head and smiled at them, saying, 'I can't tell you how much I appreciate the pair of you coming round to give me another kick up the bum. I'll sleep better tonight having had it reaffirmed that I'm not on my own in all of this.'

'On your own? No way. And as for that girl getting her grip on the daddy of our twin nephews . . . forget it. Frank's been sucked in by someone who deserves a good slapping before she moves on, and if that's what it takes that's what she'll get.'

'Exactly,' said Hazel. 'Now let's get off the subject.' She leaned forward and brushed strands of hair off Anna's face affectionately. 'Would you like us to come back and sleep over tonight? Me on the sofa and Linda on the foldaway bed in the twins' room?'

'No. Thanks anyway, but I think I need to be by myself. I want to think how best to play this. If we're to get rid of Bridget for good it would be better if it was Frank's idea that she goes and not mine. I don't want to play it wrongly and kick myself for it later.'

'That sounds sensible,' said Hazel, even though she realised that there was a possibility that Frank might not choose Anna and the twins over Bridget. He had looked every bit the man in love when speaking intimately to the girl behind the bar at Prima.

'God,' said Anna quietly. 'I feel as if a weight's been lifted off my shoulders again by having you to share this with.'

Glancing at each other, Linda and Hazel knew that enough had been said all round. 'Well, don't forget that if you want to get out on a Saturday night with old friends, we'll be only too pleased to baby-sit.' Linda smiled.

'I won't forget and I'll be all right. I'll be more than all right.'

Happier now that their sister was in this frame of mind, the girls relaxed and stayed for a little longer, drinking coffee and tactfully filling her in as to just how much private time Frank had been spending with Bridget in the small cosy flat above Prima Pasta. Once they had said as much as they thought she could take in this second session of brain bashing, the girls promised every bit of their support before hugging their sister and then leaving her to herself.

With a glass of water in her hand, Anna slowly climbed the stairs as fatigue washed over her and a calm of sorts spread right through her body. She was tired, ready for her feather pillow and the quiet of her bedroom, where she doubted she would ever see Frank sleep again. Once beneath the covers, she drifted off into a light sleep feeling better for the fact that she had Rachel living next door. When she woke from her forty-minute nap she knew she had been dreaming of herself and George, in the thick of the Kent country-side by a river, with sheep in the background and hop vines all around her. She was looking forward to her day out in Kent while her mum, the doting grandmother, looked after the twins.

Chapter Six

Choosing to kick off with an early start, George had arranged to pick up Anna and the twins at eight o'clock on Sunday morning to drop the babies off at Ivy's flat before heading for Kent. Tonbridge not being that much of a distance, Anna knew that once they had got through the traffic leading into the Blackwall tunnel and out again, it wouldn't be much more than an hour or so before they were at their destination. From all that George had said, and had shown her on his map, the tiny village that they were heading for had only one shop and one pub. Up early as usual, Anna saw to the twins then got herself ready. Once dressed – in her favourite sandy-coloured corduroy flares with matching jacket and a soft multi-coloured blouse – she had time to spare.

In her hold-all she had packed a clean set of clothes for each of the twins as well as all the other paraphernalia that went with not just one baby but two. Now she had plenty of time to relax with a cup of coffee before George arrived and while the twins, dressed for outdoors, were asleep in their carry cots. Why her stomach was turning over at the thought of this outing she had little idea other than she hadn't had a day out in a long while and was excited by it. She realised that some people would see this as her going on a date with George, but this didn't bother her too much.

Checking her appearance in the mirror above the fireplace she smiled, then quietly laughed, at the image that greeted her. Her impromptu visit the day before to the new hairdresser's on the Mile End Road, with the twins in tow, had given her a new look. As suggested by the owner, a young woman of thirty, Anna had thrown caution to the wind and had one of the latest styles, referred to as the shaggy dog cut, which didn't alter the length of her hair but had changed it from one length to several layers – and she loved it. Adding to this sense of a new beginning and trying to sort out her life, she had accepted some of Rachel's old-fashioned herbal pills to help her relax.

Having been a family friend ever since she could remember, George was proving to be a tonic and she was seeing him in a slightly different light. Before now he had been one of the good guys who worked on both sides of the law and kept his private business to himself. Apart from the fact that he had lovely light blue eyes and a smile to die for, he was also six feet tall and attractive in a rugged sort of way. She wasn't sure what Frank was going to make of them having a day out together and wondered if, by doing so, she was making things worse between them. Even though he had treated her badly, she did still love him and still hoped that he would come to his senses and ask her forgiveness. From the way he had behaved when he came to collect his things, she could imagine him seeing her day out as revenge. She knew that Frank would have heard that George's wife had left him and so was now considered single and free. She didn't think for one minute that he was going to be happy with her being chauffeured around like this.

With this and other worries floating in and out of her mind, she sipped her coffee in the quiet until the bell rang and she opened the door to George. Standing on the front step dressed in his casual clothes she thought he looked more handsome and cuddly without the suit and tie. Cuddly – in a brotherly sort of way, of course.

Once they were settled in the car the couple chatted quietly as George drove the little family through the back turnings to Wilmot Street in Bethnal Green, and during a spell of comfortable silence, George had to admit that he rather liked this role of a father figure to the twins, which was how it felt to him right then. He was touched by the fact that the babies, who had woken up when he placed their carrycots into the back of the car, hadn't started to cry but had gurgled and smiled at him.

'What a lovely life, eh?' George smiled as he drove. 'Clean and warm and loved. I wouldn't mind swapping places with one of your twins.'

'Yes you would,' said Anna, smiling. 'Just think about having to start all over again . . . going to school for the first time; having to do homework; being told that you're too old to scramble about on old ruins or too young to play kiss chase . . .'

George chuckled. 'Fair enough. We've come this far in good nick, babe, so why turn the clock back?'

She looked sideways at him. 'Exactly. My marriage is on the rocks but look what I've got on the back seat. Not one carrycot with a baby sleeping soundly but two.'

George smiled warmly and continued on his way to Ivy's flat in a comfortable, placid kind of a mood. He and Anna were easy in each other's company and he put this down to the fact that they had known each other for a long time and so spells of silence were bound to be relaxed with no awkward moments.

Once they had dropped off the twins and were driving away from Ivy's, George said, 'Your mum's a good woman, Anna.' He then switched on the radio and tuned it, searching for some easy classical music on Three. 'She thinks the world of you girls.'

'And we think the world of her, George. She's a one-off who'd do anything for any one of us. But she's also a crafty cow.' Anna started to laugh as she remembered what Ivy had said as they were leaving her flat, *I wouldn't mind a little quiet drive out into the Kent countryside myself.* 'Mum reckons that she wouldn't mind moving out into the countryside. She reckons that by pulling the old terraced houses down to build blocks of flats in their place, the planning department are ripping the heart out of the East End.'

'She's probably right, Anna.'

'If you say so. She's gonna take you up on your offer to take her for a drive to Kent you know.'

'I don't mind if she does. I work long hours, Anna, and I work hard, so to sit in this driving seat and make for the countryside is a pleasure.' He smiled. 'In any case ... your mum and her mate, Gwen, are free entertainment and better than theatre comedy. They make me die.'

'I know. Gwen's funnier than Mum though ... the things she comes out with.'

'They play off each other just like any good comedy duo.' George laughed and then went quiet as he concentrated on his driving. Whether the two friends would have been so relaxed and in such a lighthearted mood had they known that Frank had arrived in Anna's turning some ten minutes or so before she and George left with the twins, was something else.

Frank's reason for being there was to pick up some more of his things but now, still in his car, he was seething. Having recognised George's car parked up outside the house on arrival, he had reversed until he was at a space that he had spotted on his way in. This had been an ideal spot because he was obscured between a lorry and a van and there he had sat and watched the pair of them. Frank had always seen George as a bit of a mate as well as a good customer at Prima, but now, still parked, he was wondering if perhaps George's car had been there all night.

Sitting back and watching for any sign of action, he had been in two minds as to what to do next when the front door had opened and George had come out with the handles of a carrycot gripped in his hand. Once he placed this on the back seat of his car, Anna had followed him out with his other baby son, in his makeshift bed. Frank had been livid when he saw Anna get into the front seat to be driven away. A little happy family scene was what it had looked like.

Still parked in the same spot and seething, Frank was having a one-sided conversation with himself. 'What a fucking bastard. What does he think he's up to? The shit-faced turncoat! The two-faced bastard.' His mouth dry, his anger burning deep, Frank could hardly believe that he had watched the car pull away with his family aboard and George the bent copper in the driving seat. 'Well, it didn't take *you* long, did it Anna?' he fumed. 'It didn't take you long.'

Filled with rage and what could possibly have passed for jealousy, Frank couldn't quite bring himself to get out of his car and go into his house to make a cup of tea which he badly needed. He also wanted to sit down in his living room and have a cigarette in the quiet. He was so put out that he was trembling with what he believed to be fury. Shock and dejection, of course, were furthest from his mind. He wasn't the kind of guy to be jealous and never had been. At least this is what he was telling himself. The worst thing of all as far as he was concerned was that both Anna and George had been laughing. There were no signs of heartache coming from his wife over their impending separation, only laughter. He now wondered if they had been seeing each other and if so, for how long?

George, from what he could tell, had been sharing a joke with his Anna. Sharing a joke after possibly sharing a bed. His bed. He felt sick. He didn't know what to do next. After a few minutes of sitting in the car with not much going through his mind he badly needed some fresh air. Getting out of the car, he leaned over as he rested a hand on the bonnet and drew in long slow breaths of fresh air that tasted sweeter than it had ever done before. This done, he collected himself, locked the car door and crossed the narrow road to unlatch the little gate that led into his tiny front garden. Seeing Rachel, their neighbour, snipping and clipping bits off her tall neat privet, he nodded and just about managed to say a civil hello. Rachel had in fact come out of her house once she had seen, from her upstairs window, George pulling away in his car just after she had spotted Frank manoeuvring his so as to park and watch the comings and goings.

Pretending she knew nothing, Rachel smiled at Frank. 'What have you forgotten this time, scatter-brain?' she said.

'Oh you know me, Rachel, I'd forget my head if it wasn't screwed on. I didn't see you there when I just came out from inside the house,' he said, testing to see if she had any inkling of what was what. She was old and senile after all. 'Gardening already, are you? You'll get green fingers ...' he gently teased as he just managed a smile. 'I forgot to take this week's menu list that I worked out last night before bedtime,' he said.

'You men,' she said, 'you're all the same.' With that Rachel smiled and gave a little wave as she went back inside her house and closed the door.

'Well, well, well,' she murmured. 'What next? He is prepared to tell a lie so as not to fall out with me. So? What can this mean?' She laughed quietly to herself and went to put the kettle on the stove. 'He'll be back, Anna ... but you must make him suffer first if you take him back. As I think you will. But who knows?'

Frank let himself into his house with a very strange feeling inside – it was almost as if he didn't belong there any more. When he picked up on the awesome silence with no sound of the radio, TV or stereo and worse still, no sound of Anna or his twins, James and Oliver, tears came into his eyes. Drawing a deep breath, he told himself to get a grip before strolling along the passage and into the kitchen. His intention had been to come in and collect the rest of his clothes and let Anna work it out for herself that he was leaving her. But now, he was having second thoughts. He was in a bit of turmoil. He felt as if he was going from a dream into a nightmare. The dream was of he and Bridget living in their fantasy world, and the nightmare was Anna letting him go without so much as a goodbye. Never mind that she was already out there with George Blake ...

He poured himself some lime juice and added water from the tap and felt as if he was doing all of this in slow motion. Then, when he strolled into the living room and saw a tiny sock on the floor close to the twins' playpen, reality kicked in. He looked from this to the window and into his small lovely back garden where washing was hanging out on the line to dry. Some of Anna's laundry, some Babygros and nappies. Nothing of his was out there blowing in the warm breeze. Then, catching a glimpse of Rachel clipping dead leaves off her climbing ivy and clematis, he realised what he had done — and what he had been slowly doing for a year or so. He shook his head and swallowed against the lump in his throat as he murmured, 'You stupid bastard, Frank.'

Anna and George's outing from the East End to the countryside seemed to be taking no time at all because the friends were so comfortable in each other's company and could chat about this, that or the other without touching on the more serious side of life. George had freely opened up with his reasons why he was looking for a place in the countryside to restore and renovate as a going concern for the future.

Consumed by his dream, he opened up to her more and more. 'To be honest with you, babe,' he said, after a short spell of silence, 'a little bit of work on the side that me and the boys were recently involved in is the last as far as I'm concerned. I want out of the Met as well . . . while the going's good. We did have a nice little earner from the gold lighters, which I think you might have picked up on in the restaurant when you were in—'

'I did as it happens,' said Anna cutting in. 'One of your cousins needs to realise that even his *hushed* voice is loud enough for anyone in the close vicinity to hear. I did think about mentioning it to you but thought better of it. Male pride and all that.' She smiled.

'So long as I've got my male pride, that suits me fine,' said George. 'We delivered the goods and we've been paid out, but there are still a few loose ends to tie up.'

'Such as?'

'Paying off one or two people who played a small part. There's a grand in my pocket right now – believe it or not. And yes, I had already arranged to go to Kent to sort that little bit of business out before you ask. But you weren't an afterthought, Anna. When I made the arrangements over the phone you came to mind. I thought a day in the countryside and the fresh air would do you good.'

'Well, we're not even there yet and I already feel good. I'm in a nice comfortable car, sitting next to a handsome man. What more could a girl wish for?'

He smiled as he looked sideways at her and seemed a bit shy as he said, 'Thank you for that. But I do need to be in Tonbridge at one point, babe, and so I'm gonna have to nip off by myself. To see two guys in a pub. It shouldn't take long and there are some nice little tea rooms in Kent where you can wait for me.'

'Sounds idyllic. Afternoon cream tea. Lovely.'

'Good. That's settled then. I was worried that you might get the 'ump over it.'

'Don't be daft. And I'm pleased that you're getting out of the Met. And I think that your idea of buying a cheap rundown old mansion to do up is brilliant. Enough said?'

'Absolutely, babe. Spot on. I want to do something completely different that's all above board. I'm not the type to go into the protection racket lark that some coppers who've got out of the force have done. It's not only the Kray twins who went down that road. Although as well as making money from their protection racket, the Krays must have been running over thirty different clubs and pubs all around London. It's a shame that they went from lads who loved the sport of boxing to lads who thrived on terror and risk. But there you go. They fell into the trap of needing to sleep with guns under their pillows.'

'It's their parents I feel sorry for. What must it have been like to see their baby twin boys growing into evil criminals?'

'Don't even think about it, Anna. There was something wrong with the pair of them. There had to be. I just wonder if their mother was actually pleased when they moved out of their family home in the mid-

Sixties to a lavish apartment in Clapton. From what I heard they did it up as if it was a wing in Buckingham Palace. And then of course, in time, Reggie got married ... and didn't we all pity that poor cow. She didn't know what she was letting herself in for.'

'George ... don't talk about it any more. It makes me feel sick to think about the underworld not that far away from where I'm living. Don't let's spoil our day out.'

'Sorry, babe. I do go on a bit.'

'It's understandable. You knew the Krays before and after their stroll into crime.'

'But we'll change the subject. Tell me about your dad and what you remember of 'im.'

'I would rather tell you about my gran and granddad before they died, if that's all right. They were like second parents to us girls.'

'Fair enough. Off you go.'

Anna began to voice her favourite recollections during the rest of their journey. They laughed and joked and discussed all kinds of things – except each of their failing marriages. On the last stint of the ride to the small and old-fashioned village of Hunston, George was reminiscing about when he was a lad and had come down to this neck of the woods for hop-picking.

'The little butcher's shop is still there and run by the same family can you believe?' He spoke as if it were a miracle.

'I think that might be the case with most butchers and fishmongers, George,' she said. 'They tend to be passed from father to son, don't they? Even in the East End. But it's lovely that you can come back after ten years or so and still see the same name above the shops.'

'They're not really shops though, Anna, are they,' he said, steering his car around the tree-lined narrow and curling lanes. 'Not the way we know shops in London in any case. In Hunston was the post office and store that was the bottom half of a cottage with living space above.' He slowly shook his head as he recalled it all. 'Do you know what I used to love as a kid? The bare floorboards in the village store. Varnished ... but bare floorboards all the same. I loved the sound our boots made on 'em. Daft things you remember ...' he murmured, and then went quiet.

'When was the last time you paid a visit to the farm?' Anna asked, touched by the sensitivity of this man who dealt with hardened criminals every week of the year. He was one of the few who enjoyed the thrill of keeping law and order one week and bending the rules the next to meet his own ends, and he was not the only officer within his realm or outside it to do so. To some, it was all part and parcel of the job when working in major cities where life was fast and risky and the workload heavy.

'I was down nigh on twelve months ago to the day as it happens – to see to a little bit of business with some gear we had stored in the barn that we've been renting at a cheap price for a few years. I just go along with them, or by myself come to that, for the ride every now and then when needs must, but only when I think the cousins need the boss to hold their hands.' George chuckled.

'Oh, so you're their boss then, are you?' Anna teased.

'It was meant to be a joke, Anna.'

'I know it was, George.'

He glanced sideways at her and smiled, and as she smiled back at him he felt his heart beat a little faster. Drawing breath, he spoke to her as if she was a mate and not the woman that he thought he was in love with. 'Once we're in Tonbridge, I'll leave you in a lovely little tea room for fifteen minutes, enjoying the best fruit and malt bread going and the best pot of tea you'll find anywhere.'

'Oh ... and will this be after we've visited your old farm where you picked hops or before?'

'Afterwards, babe. But it won't take me much more than twenty minutes or so. I've got to see a man about a dog. You won't mind sitting by yourself will you?'

'No, I don't think so. So long as I'm not stuck there for hours waiting for you to come back.'

'I wouldn't do that to you, Anna,' he said, as he turned into a long winding lane. 'And now ... I'll show you the huts we used to live in and then, if we've got time, we'll go and 'ave a look at the farmhouse that's up for grabs.'

'How did you know about it in the first place?' said Anna.

'I put some feelers out months ago and it turns out that the wealthy landowner's gonna move to Ireland where he's bought acres of land, and an entire little village by the sound of it.'

'And you fancy the idea of living in Kent, then? Or would you just come down for nice weekends?'

'I don't know. It's not cut and dried. And it'll take a couple of years to get the place into shape from what I hear. But it's a fantastic house. Must have about eight double bedrooms. Colonel John Knight and his wife had all kinds of staff living in, and there was a small family who lived in a little cottage that went with the job that was a part of the estate. It's an old titled family that goes back years and you couldn't wish to meet nicer aristocrats who are nowhere near as wealthy as some people think. They were good to us hop-pickers. Treated us as if we were no different to them. Well, almost.'

'Do they still grow hops on the farm?' said Anna enjoying this little outing that had been mentioned in passing one minute and was happening the next.

'I'll tell you what,' said George, smiling, 'if they did still have pickers coming down I would sign up.'

'Oh, shut up.' Anna laughed. 'You're too used to home comforts just like the rest of us now. You wouldn't live in a tiny hut and sleep on straw. Give me a break.'

'Well, maybe you don't know me as well as you think you do because I think I would.' To the sound of Anna's soft laughter, he turned into a narrow lane just wide enough for two cars but not a car and a tractor should one happen along. He remembered it well.

'And to answer your question, no they don't grow hops anymore. The farmer turned all of that in once picking by hand was done and dusted. Once mechanisation and modernisation found its way on to the hop fields.'

Going all quiet and thoughtful as he drove slowly and soaked in the silence of the gentle countryside, George saw in his mind's eye another way to try and resurrect that style of living – without the hop-picking. A holiday place that had more to offer than just camping out in tents or huts but still with the great communal way of life. 'Do you know what I reckon, Anna,' he murmured. 'I reckon that the farmhouse, which is more of a rambling mansion, would make a fantastic up-market bed-and-breakfast place for holidays. That's what I can see – a brilliant place in the thick of the Kent countryside, with one section rigged out for the wealthy to luxuriate in and another part for the not so highly paid townies. A little bit of country living and an escape from the mad world in the fast lane. I reckon me and the lads could pick up that rundown estate cheap. It was in a dire condition when I last came down.'

Anna slowly shook her head. 'You've got great ideas, George, but if you wanted to do what you've just said you'd need a huge loan from the bank for the development.'

'Yeah ... and so did Mr Taylor and Mr Woodrow. The market boys who grafted their way to success from running a stall selling any end-of-the-line goods they got their hands on in the Roman Road and became property developers. Little acorns and big oak trees, Anna. Little acorns and big oaks.'

Turning into yet another long and winding lane, George smiled and slowly shook his head. 'I love this bit of the journey. It takes me right back to when we were kids on the back of the lorry. Happy as Larry we were once we finally arrived, belting out old-fashioned songs with the older generation.'

'I can remember the kids around our way getting

excited when September came round,' said Anna. 'We never went hop-picking ... I don't know why not though. A lot of our neighbours did. Even if Dad hadn't left Mum when we were little, I don't think he would have taken us. We all went to a holiday camp once a year up until I was about eight or nine.'

'That's odd,' said George, a puzzled expression on his face. 'That's *really* odd. I can see smoke which I can only imagine is coming out of the chimney of the old cookhouse on the common.'

'Maybe some squatters have moved in,' Anna said. 'And who would blame them in this little bit of heaven.'

'No one. Tramps have been doing the self-same thing for donkey's years. They get away with murder if they have a mind to,' said George. 'The boys in blue leave them alone in and around London. Long may that last.'

The closer they got to the common and the row upon row of brick huts with black tin rooftops glinting in the sunlight, the more excited George became and he didn't mind showing it. He was like a boy who had gone looking for a lost shilling and found a pound note. He could hardly believe what he was looking at. People were living on the site, which now resembled a medieval village, and were meandering around campfires on which they were cooking their Sunday dinners.

'Bloody hell ...' said George, steering with one hand and running the other through his hair. 'They've knocked two huts into one in every row and turned 'em into little country cottages. I don't believe what I'm looking at.'

'I wonder why David and Jimmy didn't tell you. You said they came down recently.'

'Not to this part, sweetheart,' said George, still a touch dumbfounded by it all. 'The barn we're renting is on the acreage around the old farmhouse that I was telling you about.'

Overwhelmed by all he saw, he drove slowly and in silence towards a nearby oak tree and parked beneath it without saying a word. He then got out of the driver's seat and looked around him as he went to open the passenger door for Anna and found his voice again.

'I can't believe that the farmer would 'ave sold off the huts to Londoners, Anna. It would only have been for peanuts if he had've done. I would 'ave been in like a shot and bought the lot of 'em.'

Looking from the little commune to George's face, Anna hoped she wasn't about to discover a side of him that she had not seen before – greed. 'Maybe the fact that you would 'ave bought them in a job-lot was the reason why it was kept a tight secret? Maybe those that have bought a little bit of nostalgic heaven for themselves didn't want someone like you to approach the farmer.'

George looked sideways at Anna, frowning slightly. 'I'm not a developer, babe,' he quietly said.

'But you would 'ave been ... if you had bought up the job-lot though, wouldn't you? You would have been just as bad as those who would want it all for themselves with nothing other than profit on their minds.'

'Point taken.' He looked into her lovely face and those big soft green eyes and drew a breath. He then spoke with a touch of shame in his voice. 'Seeing all of this brings back memories, Anna, and yes, you're right; if I'm honest I would 'ave loved to have been the creator of the scene we're looking at as well as being part of it now and then.'

Sorry now that she had doubted his integrity, Anna slipped her arm into his and smiled. 'Come on then, Mister Amazed-Man. Let's go and get a slice of nostalgia for you to take back as a nice memory to tuck under your pillow tonight.'

George peered under his hand to see that just across the field, which had been patterned by nature with wild flowers and weeds, there were well-kept vegetable beds. 'Jesus Christ,' he murmured, 'they're growing Mary Jane, Anna.'

'What are you talking about?' Anna laughed. 'Mary Jane?'

'Just another name for the obvious, sweetheart – marijuana.' He glanced at her, his eyes twinkling with amusement. 'It's in the herb garden – the patch that's closest to us.' He then burst out laughing. 'All neat and tidy like Hampton Court and nurturing drugs among it all. Brilliant.'

'Well, it wouldn't be the first time I've heard that, George. According to my mum – and you can ask her yourself – her gran, just like other housewives, used to grow something similar in their herb bed. For soups and stews.'

George looked sideways at Anna and waited for her to say that she was only kidding, but she simply laughed at him. 'Don't tell me that you've never heard that before?'

'I've not as it happens,' he said. 'I suppose none of them knew what it was?'

'Oh of course they did! It was a herb they used in cooking and by the look of things still do. They made nice hot bedtime drinks with it as well. But mostly it was used to lift someone's spirits if they were down in the dumps or in shock over something or the other.'

'Pull the other leg, Anna ... please.'

'I'm not making it up! You must know about the old herbalists? Mum used to go over to Wapping to Mary Reeder, who was married to a lovely West Indian guy. They grew all kind of things in her back yard. We used to have hot peppermint tea, spearmint tea ... something to make you go if you were constipated ... and something else if you had the runs.'

'Yeah, all right, babe, point taken.'

He shook his head slowly and then nodded towards the campsite. 'We'd best go and let them know who we are. I'll avert my eyes from the herb garden that's smack bang in the centre in this nostalgic little universe where pensioners grow cannabis.'

'Stop calling it that,' said Anna. 'Let's go and see who it is that's peering at you peering at him.'

George nodded and then went and locked his car out of habit. 'I hardly expected this, on my life. I can't tell you how much it means to me to see people living in the huts again. Amazing.'

She took his hand in hers and they walked along a dirt and gravel track towards the homesteaders – just two good friends from the old days. He was enjoying a bit of childhood nostalgia and Anna was relishing this little bit of freedom.

Coming towards the couple from the village-like scene was an old-fashioned chap in his seventies, who was peering at them under his hand even though he was wearing a docker's cap on his head to shade his eyes and his bald patch. George, still smiling, said, 'If this is a picker from the old days that I know, Anna, get your hanky out because I'll need that as well as my own.'

'You old softie,' she said. 'Men are worse than women, I swear it.' She liked the way he sometimes showed the feminine side of himself – whether he knew he was doing it or not.

As they drew closer to the old man he stopped shielding his eyes and looked at George as if for a split second he recognised him. He then straightened, placed his hands on his hips and said, 'Are you visiting family or just being nosy parkers?'

'I'm not visiting any of my family and, to be honest, I'm still a bit too overwhelmed by all of this to recognise who you might be.' He offered his hand saying, 'My name is George Blake.'

The old man rubbed his chin thoughtfully and then shook his head. 'That name rings a bell.' He then looked George straight in the eye. 'Did your family used to come to this farm to pick hops in the old days?'

'For nigh on ten years or so. Probably further back if you start to think about great-grandparents.'

'Oh ... right ... well, I probably will 'ave known them then. The memory ain't all it used to be but it'll come to me soon. Course it will. Now come and meet the missus. The kettle's on the stove so you're just in time for a mug of tea.'

They followed him to a row of brick huts – one which George had shared as a bedroom with his two brothers when they were kids. His emotions all over the place, he looked at Anna with tears coming into his eyes and murmured, 'You're gonna have to help me out here, babe.'

Anna took hold of his hand again and gave it an encouraging squeeze. The gentleman, who was clearly one of the governors of the commune, showed his importance in his stride, which was not as stable as the old boy would have liked to think, and since it was too early in the day for beer, George assumed – correctly – that it was the old boy's hunched back that was a little incapacitating. Even so, he was wiry enough, and a bent back for the older generation from the East End or south of the river was not unusual because they had either worked in the docks or the markets, from boy to man, carrying heavy loads.

'We don't keep coffee in the hut because we're tea drinkers in the main,' said the man as he glanced over his shoulder at them. 'But if you like you could buy a bottle of Camp coffee from our little on-site shop.'

'Tea's fine by me,' said Anna, secretly amused at this comical sight of someone who made her think of a favourite television programme – *The Beverly Hillbillies*.

'Tea sounds lovely,' said George, also stifling a giggle.

'It's all right, our little shop. It does us nicely. We all take turns to serve on a kind of a rota system.' He stopped in his tracks and almost had Anna and George bumping into him. Staring down at the ground he shook his head. 'Now, what was I about to do?' He nudged his cap back a little and scratched his head. 'I'll be blowed if I can remember.' He turned and stared at Anna. 'Just remind me, ducks ... do I know you?'

'No,' said Anna, warming to this old boy. 'But your family or one or two of your friends might know George. He used to stay in these huts when he was a kid – at hop-picking time.'

'That was it! That's what he said, wasn't it? Bloody memory's playing up today.' He held out his hand to George and clicked his false teeth. 'Welcome back, son. Welcome back. The name's Ernie.' Then, chuckling to himself, he turned around and continued leading them to his hut in one of ten rows. 'Yes,' he said, 'having our own little shop saves us walking up to the village every time we need something. And it saves us 'aving to listen to the plumber who's always going on about how much it costs in petrol just to turn on the engine of his car. You can't blame him though. This lot would have him running about like a delivery boy on wheels if he didn't put his foot down now and then.'

Then, as if he had somewhere important to go, the old boy stepped up his pace, swinging his arms like a man in a hurry to get to the pub before it closed. Doing their best to keep up, Anna and George glanced at each other while the old-timer stopped again to have a think. 'A lad comes on a pushbike with the newspapers most days,' he murmured, 'and sometimes fetches a choice of damaged paperbacks for us to buy. I mostly use the library in Tonbridge myself – when I can get someone to give me a lift there. That's where my favourite pub is – the Gudgeon. We all go together in Willy's converted ice-cream van every fortnight on a Tuesday. He's put wooden benches in and his wife Rosie made some lovely long cushions to fit the length of 'em.'

'You seem to have thought of everything,' said Anna. 'You've created your own tiny village by the sound of it.'

'Oh yes, we don't want for much. It was our resident plumber's idea to convert two huts into a launderette. He fetched down a van filled with six second-hand machines that he'd rebuilt. It makes a decent laundry room, that conversion. I made the surface for the washing machines to go beneath. Lovely bit of old pine that was.'

Walking on again, he continued his running commentary. 'I'm the resident carpenter. We used to do our washing by hand years ago in one of the old tin baby baths. We've still got one hanging up somewhere that one of the Romany gypsies painted for us the last time they set up camp in the field. Beautiful it is – with lovely flowers all over it. Laura Leigh, who married out and settled in the village, comes around the huts with 'er basket every other month selling pegs and that. Sight for sore eyes she is. She can tell fortunes so they tell me, but I don't believe in all of that.' He stopped again and stretched his back. 'Now whatever made me tell you all of this?'

'A bit of local history's no bad thing,' said Anna, wishing this man would not keep on stopping short.

Setting off again he said, 'We only used paraffin lamps and lanterns at first. And candles of course. But then we got electric lines connected. We had to give up our little council house for this way of living, but fair exchange is no robbery is the way I see it.'

'Did you honestly do that?' said Anna.

'Oh yes ... and it was the best thing we ever did do. The borough council of Hackney and Poplar paid for the renovations of the huts by all accounts. The farmer wouldn't 'ave made a loss, you can bet your life on that. But the point is we *own* the huts, you see. Oh yes ... we're all property owners now. We each privately own two and joint own the communal building where the washing machines and that are. Some chose to 'ave back-to-back huts knocked into one and some, like me, took a pair next to each other. The Stepney Council wanted us out of our old tenement houses so they could sell on or knock them down for new estates ... or, as my missus would say, rabbit warrens. It was a nice little deal that's paid off all round, you could say.'

Ernie's wife, Betty, a nicely rounded woman with soft grey curly hair showing beneath her knotted paisley turban which matched her wrap-over pinafore, was checking her pot roast over the open fire. Once her husband had seen to the introductions in his own muddled way, she said, 'When I heard your car I thought it was the postman. I look forward to Paul coming down the track in his little red van. He's from the village. His father used to come onto the common, and his father before him, with the letters and little parcels when we were down here for the hop-picking.'

'Betty's the presser,' said her husband proudly, placing an arm around his wife's shoulders. 'Trouble is, she prefers pressing the men's trousers if you know what I mean?' This brought a small burst of polite laughter.

'I'm in charge of the laundry rota, thank you very

194

much! I do most of the ironing because I *love* ironing,' laughed Betty. 'But I make them all pay me. It's a nice bit of pocket money for the piggy bank. I usually take somewhere around four to five pounds a week, which is very good money for doing something that you enjoy.'

'Hard work brings its rewards,' said Ernie. 'Mind you, standing outside in the sunshine and ironing? That's more of a leisurely thing to do if you ask me. Mind you, I don't do so badly – I get a free ride *and* my ticket for the pictures in Tonbridge paid once a week for organising the work rota and that.'

It was fun listening to these folk, who clearly were in their seventh heaven in what seemed to have become a retirement home in the country, camping style. Others soon gathered around Anna and George, and the more Anna heard the more impressed she was. When a nice fresh cup of tea was offered to her she took it gladly. The folk then told of how they went fruit- and pea-picking during the seasons and how, other than potatoes and most root vegetables, which were delivered in sacks from a local farm at a knockdown price, the men mucked in and grew most of their vegetables and salads. An acre of a ploughed field had been given to them when the huts were sold off.

'We all muck in, this is the point. Some of the work is a bit too much for some of the men.' The woman lowered her voice saying, 'It's hard work for Ernie but we don't let on that we think so.' She winked and smiled at George. 'Pride is important – so long as it doesn't come before a fall.'

'I couldn't agree more,' said George, wishing that he

had been in on this little project. He hadn't been slow in clocking that some of the residents had built little brick extensions onto their huts and planted climbers in pots here and there. The once plain brick constructions were already beginning to resemble little cottages and, from what they had gleaned so far, the settlers spent most of their time outside, often until dark unless there was something worthwhile on the television – each of them had a set inside their own cosy dwelling.

Looking around her, Anna quietly said, 'George . . . this scenery is incredible. I feel as if I'm in the centre of a landscape painting.'

'I know what you mean. Can you imagine what it's like when the sun's setting? What the evenings are like? With this lot sitting round their campfires? I can just picture it . . . and it takes me right back to the old days.'

'I could stop here for ever.' Anna sighed.

'I know, but we're gonna have to make a move to Tonbridge, sweetheart, and to that café I was telling you about. I don't want the bubble to burst either but business is business.'

'I know. And anyway, we could come back another time, couldn't we?'

'I don't see why not, babe.' A touch moved by the whole scene he said, 'I'm just gonna have a quick nostalgic wander around the huts – I won't be more than a few minutes.'

Anna watched him go, guessing that he would be looking to see if there was an old unused building that he could lay his hands on so as to be part of this little world at weekends. He was looking across to a field in the distance. She followed his gaze and could see a small herd of cows that looked so perfect in the setting. She loved it. She was in the centre of a medley of old-fashioned Londoners enjoying their little bit of this old-fashioned heavenly place. Coming along the dirt track was an old boy who was red in the face as he struggled to push his bike. Blowing and puffing, it was clear that he needed to rest, so Anna walked over to him and took hold of the bike while his wife saw him into their hut and sat him down on an old feather-cushioned armchair. None of the others seemed too concerned, and Anna gleaned that the old boy frequently returned exhausted. Sitting down on a simple wooden chair by the campfire with a few of the women, Anna felt happier and more relaxed than she had in a very long time.

Content just to let the heart-to-heart chinwag go above her head, she thought about Frank and the twins, and how lovely it would have been for them to spend a bit of leisure time in such a place as this every now and then. There didn't seem to be any one of the folk who didn't bring something to the table – or in this case the fire. Each had something to offer in the running of this little commune of Londoners.

One of the men had been an electrician, man and boy, and another could boast a plumber's certificate. A couple of the women, who weren't old enough to get a state pension, worked in a biscuit factory in the small town of Yalding and fetched back bags of assorted broken biscuits. Broken, but as fresh as the day they were baked. And another woman told Anna that she loved housework and did a bit of cleaning for most of the others as her way of making a little spare cash.

'I love housework so much that I would clean and polish for nothing,' she said. 'But they will insist on paying me, which suits me fine because I put it all away for Christmas and that way I've got a nice little bit to spend in London.'

'So you do go back to your roots from time to time then?' said Anna, finding this little oasis pulling her further in by the minute.

'Oh yes, we all do. It makes a lovely day out. My son comes and fetches me now and then. Lee's a carpet fitter. He fitted out most of our cottages with carpet or lino. Well, when I say cottages, really and truly they're only huts. But then we don't spend many days indoors in any case.' The bright and breezy woman looked at Anna, a knowing twinkle in her eye. 'I can see that you wouldn't mind one of these places,' she said. 'And I don't blame you. But I don't think there's any going spare now.'

'Oh, I'm just soaking it all in really. I love to hear the birds singing and cows lowing in the distance. I love it.'

'It is a good way of life, and we get to go to the pictures and to see shows in village halls around and about us. I couldn't ask for anything more really. Except coming up on the blooming pools!' She suddenly burst with laughter. 'Now that *would* be lovely, because you know what I would do? I'd have a really nice long hut built for my son and his wife to use at weekends. That's what I would do. That'd be lovely!'

Picking up on her contagious laughter, Anna only just managed to say, 'How do you get your washing dry on wet days?'

'We don't do washing on wet days. It's as simple as

that. But if it's dry weather but cold and damp we use one of the two dryers in the laundry shed.'

'And do you know, we nearly always get to go and see the West End Christmas lights by train, even though there's plenty to entertain us around this way. And we go along to the local little chapel of a Sunday *if* the sun's out. The church is a bit of a long walk for most of us but we do go sometimes for a bit of a sing-song. We all love to sing, whether it's by the campfire or in the church. The best times are when the Girl Guides or Boy Scouts come all dressed in their uniforms to kick us off. That's smashing, that is. They volunteer to do little jobs for us and they're good company.' The woman became thoughtful. 'You see, there always someone to chat to. This is my point. And I s'pose that's what keeps our brains alert.' She smiled sweetly at Anna. 'I'm sixty-seven but do I feel it? Course I don't!

'Now some might call this little place a retirement home, but so what if it is? We can all tell each other our little problems, and if a row breaks out it's usually forgotten within the hour unless someone is really put out over something, then it takes a bit longer.'

Her face broke into a lovely warm smile again as she lowered her voice and looked cautiously around. 'There has been a few romances between widows or divorcees and one or two have knocked dividing walls down between huts and set up home together. Happy as larks they are. But don't let on that I told you so.'

This was wonderful. The older generation were behaving worse than the so-called promiscuous young. Anna said, 'So you never get bored then?'

'Bored? No dear. There's always something to do or something happening. And I'll tell you what else ... we've got a doctor that will come out if we're not up to going to the surgery. We've even got a resident healer as well. Can you believe that?'

'I can,' said Anna. 'I can believe anything in this place.'

'She lays a hand on top of your head and she can tell if there's anything wrong, and I'll tell you what – she's never far out. You get a lovely warm glow going right down your spine when she lays a hand on you. She's got rid of a migraine for me more than once. She's got the gift, and you can't bottle that, can yer? She can bring a temperature down quicker than medicine will.'

Anna nodded attentively, even though she was now caught up in her own thoughts. She felt as though the ancestors were showing the twentieth century how things could be without all the trappings of the modern world. She wondered if it was feasible for her to bring up her twins in the countryside. She could just see them when they were older – running around on the grass and laughing.

'I would never go back to the way I was living before this,' continued the woman, bringing Anna back to the here and now. 'I can't imagine living back in our old turning in Hackney with all of the traffic and the markets and crowds of people everywhere. London born and bred until you're dead?' She slowly shook her head. 'No ... I realise now that you can easily pull up your roots and start all over again.' She grew pensive again. 'It's been a wonderful new beginning.'

'I'm sure it has,' said Anna, her heart sinking a little.

She was thinking of her own predicament. Then, pushing her troubles from her mind, she drew a slightly trembling breath and said, 'You know what you've done? You've created your own little village by the river. Just like the first settlers who came from overseas.'

'Yes – I suppose in a way we have, dear. I can't say that we're totally self-sufficient mind you, but we don't go short of much. We go to the village fetes in the summer and that's lovely. And then there might be a Country-and-Western dance on in the village hall that we'll attend. My husband used to play in a band years ago, so he gets to have a go on his saxophone now and then.

'He also teaches music part-time to the children at the home just outside of Hunston. We helped to run a fete in the gardens last year when we saw the piece asking for volunteers in the local paper. And we've been doing our bit one way or another ever since. We must have had about thirty children here on Guy Fawkes last year. Most of the villagers came too. It was lovely. A lovely big bonfire and a little firework display.'

'I bet the orphans loved that.'

'It was a joy to see the expression on their little faces. I don't know how many sausages and beef burgers we cooked on a grill over the embers. They loved it – and so did we.'

'And they go to the local school do they?' said Anna.

'No ducks. No. The home has its own little school ... a proper school with desks and that. I suppose in a way it's like a private boarding school except that it's not full of the posh children with wealthy parents going in to visit with hampers and that.'

Trevor immediately came into Anna's mind. She could imagine him here – resident PE teacher and swimming coach – which was his lifelong dream. To work with underprivileged children.

'I think there are a few such places spread around the country. Few and far between but at least they've not all been closed down.' The woman glanced at Anna. 'There's another site similar to this one if you're thinking of moving out of London. I don't think they would let you have it as a weekend kind of holiday home though.'

'No, I wasn't thinking of that,' Anna smiled. 'I've got twin babies. But I can see my mum and her friend Gwen living here. They would love it. But wild horses wouldn't drag either of them from the East End. London's in their blood. No, it was the children's home that made me think. I know someone who might just be interested in being a resident sports and swimming coach.'

'Well, remind me to give you one of their leaflets before you go. You can give that to your friend as food for thought.' The woman then nodded in the direction of George, who was making his way back. 'Your husband looks as if he likes it here as well.'

This made Anna laugh. 'We're not married. We're old mates from when we were kids on the street.'

'Oh, now you *have* surprised me,' said the woman, as she watched George looking into the open-fronted bike shed. 'You seem like the ideal couple. But do you know what? A good friend is often better than a mediocre husband – but don't repeat that or some around here will get the hump over it.' She laughed.

'You could be right there,' said Anna. 'I think that George has been turned on by the bikes and the thought of riding along a gravel lane. Look at him. Miles away in dreamland.'

The woman glanced at her watch. 'Oh look! It's time for my programme. *Crossroads*. I must love and leave you.' With that she was away, back inside her hut. Staring after her, Anna couldn't resist the urge to follow and take a peep inside her home.

Standing in the doorway she spoke quietly, saying, 'I don't suppose I can have a little look inside can I?' She smiled apologetically for intruding.

'Of course you can, dear! It's only two huts knocked into one at the end of the day, but you can go through and have a look at our bedroom, bathroom and kitchenette if you like. But you must excuse me if I don't show you around because I never miss an episode. Go on – go and steal a look at my kitchen with all its mod cons. It might be small but it's functional.'

Anna accepted and crept past to the kitchen; she was impressed at how neat and tidy and yet homely it was, with enough room to take a fridge, electric cooker, sink and floor cupboards with work space above. Through the small window she could see a view of the wooden bridge over the river and black and white cows in the background chewing the cud.

The small double bedroom reminded her of the old people's ground-floor flats that had been purpose built on the new council estates in and around Stepney and Bethnal Green. There was enough room for a bed for two people, a double wardrobe and a chest of drawers – and just enough space to walk from one bit of furniture to the other.

Her lightning view over, Anna was back into the cosy living room with its small three-piece suite and an old-fashioned dresser holding an accumulation of china. In the corner of the room was a pre-war oak dining table for two that could be extended to sit four. The walls had been decorated with a floral wallpaper which went with the old-fashioned mustard gloss paintwork. And on the walls hung an assortment of framed family photographs, going back a decade and coming to the present day. This little home was lovely. It was welcoming. And it was a sight for a townie's sore eyes. A bit of old-fashioned London life in the heart of the countryside, in the middle of a field by the river. And there was George, tall, broad and handsome, chatting to the old boy who had struggled home on his bike. She felt like weeping and didn't know why. But it was time for her and George to leave and head for Tonbridge, where she was to wait while he conducted his little bit of business.

Chapter Seven

Anna, relaxing in the quaint little tea rooms in Tonbridge while waiting for George to return, was enjoying her afternoon tea which consisted of delicate sandwiches, home-made cakes and a fresh pot of tea. Her table for one was at the front of the Elizabethan building and in these surroundings she felt as if time had stood still. She watched through a small leaded glass window as a young couple on the opposite side of the cobbled street fussed over their baby in a pram. She could picture Ivy, with her twin grandsons, in the same place loving the life and the fresh air.

The difference between Anna and the young mother, of course, was that the girl had her husband beside her and he was holding firmly on to the handle of the pram. Smiling at him, his wife was pointing out a nice summer dress displayed in the shop window. Nodding agreeably at her, the man looked so relaxed that Anna, for the first time in her life, knew what it was like to feel envy. This is what she so wanted and yet it was just a simple everyday family scene, nothing out of the ordinary but certainly no longer within her realm – not where she and Frank were concerned in any case.

Out in the real world, away from the comfort of her four walls hugging her like a big security blanket, and with more time to think, it was becoming clearer that during the past year or so she had cut herself off from almost everything. She wondered again if she had been so wrapped up with trying to get pregnant that, once she had finally achieved her dream and delivered her babies, she had built invisible walls around herself and them.

She had done everything she possibly could to protect the twins from the dangers of the outside and all of the germs on planet earth. But had she, without realising it, cut the babies off from Frank too? Guilt swept over her like a fierce heat rash. Guilt, mixed with a fear of the unknown that she was facing.

Shaking off this mild panic attack, she reminded herself that earlier on at the converted huts she had realised that this outing with George had restored some of her self-esteem, so all was not lost. She didn't know why it had but she wasn't going to question it. She turned her attention back to the couple across the street and watched as they happily sauntered off together. They had reminded Anna how she had imagined that she and Frank would be once the twins were born, but he hadn't once gone for a walk with her when she took the babies out in their pram. Not once. Not even on his days off from the restaurant, preferring to watch sport all afternoon of a Saturday and play golf on Sundays in order to unwind.

Frank, having gone from his house to the flat above Prima and then to his brothers' restaurant at Tower Hill, was now on his way to Ivy's with every intention of collecting his baby boys. After what could only be described as a fit of rage coming from bruised pride he was still in a sorry state. He had wanted to be in his brothers' restaurant, which opened on Sundays, so that he could sit for a while in a place that was familiar but which meant nothing much to him, but he hadn't been able to settle. Having driven through the back streets, a touch too fast, he arrived in Ivy's turning and parked just around the corner, out of sight of her kitchen window in case she happened to be looking out. He didn't want her to see him pulling up in his car because he knew that if she did, by the time he was inside her flat, she would be ready with a bit of rehearsed preaching about right and wrong. He wasn't in the mood for it and, apart from this, he couldn't be sure if George was inside with Anna and the twins, or if they had gone out for a nice lunch somewhere. In short, he didn't know what the fuck was going on and this didn't sit right with him. Frank wasn't used to being on the back foot like this.

He could hardly believe that George would be straight in with his wife before his own side of the bed had gone cold. He rang the doorbell, aware that he was grinding his back teeth, a dead giveaway that he was angry, but even so he couldn't stop himself. His face set, his mood dark, he listened for the sound of his wife's voice from inside. When Ivy opened the door she gave him a kind of all-knowing, all-scolding look, as if he were still a boy, but she stood aside to let him in.

'I was hoping you'd come round to see me for a chat,' she said, as she pulled the door wide open. 'Go on – in you go. Into the kitchen. I'll put the kettle on.'

'I'm not stopping for tea and a chat, Ivy. I've come to pick up my boys.'

'And what makes you think they're with me?' she said, as she filled the kettle. She then told him to sit down for five minutes and, surprising her, he did so in a quiet, humble kind of way which didn't square up to the fierce expression in his eyes. She knew him from old and could tell that he was in what she would call a bit of a rage.

'Rachel told me that Anna and George were on their way over to you,' said Frank. 'She was quite casual about it as well. Almost as if it was an everyday occurrence. She said that your place was where I might find Anna and that she was dropping our twins off here. I take it that she's gone out for the afternoon with an old friend of mine.'

'George? An old friend of yours? I didn't know that. Of course Anna's known him since his arse hung out of his trousers and he searched for pennies in the gutter with the other kids his age.'

Settled on a kitchen chair and leaning back with his legs stretched and crossed he said, 'I don't know what they think they're playing at, Ivy, and I'm not all that bothered, but I don't like the idea of my wife and my best friend going out behind my back.'

'I don't think they're playing at anything, Frank. But I do think that you're being a bit of a drama queen, if you don't mind my saying so. George is a close friend of our family. We all go back a long way, son. So what is your problem?'

'Oh right ... so they've done this before then, have they? Gone on an outing and left my boys with a baby-sitter?'

'Baby-sitter? I'm their grandmother! And those

babies are safer with me looking after them than they would be with you. You wouldn't even know how to change a fucking napkin. And before you ask, they're upstairs, sound asleep.'

'You know what I'm getting at, Ivy. Stop trying to be funny because you're not amusing me and I am very annoyed over this.'

'No, as it just so happens, Frank, I *don't* know what you're getting at! If you're asking me if Anna has gone for a nice day out the answer is yes, she has, and good luck to 'er. If you're wondering if she's made a habit of it the answer is no. If you ask me if I think it's a good thing – again the answer is yes, it most definitely is a good thing. She deserves an outing, which is more than I can say for you. How's the little tart managing without you pandering to her every whim? Are 'er knickers in a twist – or didn't you stop to 'ave a look before you left her to come round here?'

Pushing his hands into his face and rubbing his eyes, Frank spoke in a tired voice. 'I work bloody long hours, Ivy, and I get a bit exhausted now and then. All right? So stop having a go at me.'

'I should think you would be exhausted.' She poured boiling water into her brown teapot and then said, 'Did you know that statistically men are known to 'ave less energy than women even though they are all brawn and body? So I should think that's why you're tired ... working all day long and then shagging your waitresses for hours on end once you've bolted the door.'

'Oh right. So Anna's been telling you pork pies has she? Your baby daughter's been laying it on your shoulders again. You're gonna have to let go of your girls, Ivy. They're all grown women now.'

Ivy turned her back to him as she took a bag of sugar out of the kitchen cupboard and topped up the sugar bowl. She couldn't stop the smile that was spreading across her face and had to will herself not to laugh at Frank. He was on the attack, which was a first. From what she had seen in the past, if even a tiny bit of criticism was fired at him he would go quiet and walk out of the room.

'I don't think my Anna does tell lies. And I thank God for it because do you know what, a lie is the lowest form of defence and often used simply to score cheap points.'

Turning to face him, her smile now dissolved, she said, 'Frank ... don't ask me all the ins and outs. Go and see our Hazel and Linda and ask them what's what. All I can tell you is that Anna's none too pleased with that girl you took on. The one who's married to that lovely feller called Trevor.'

'She's been listening to silly gossip, Ivy.'

'I don't think so, son. And if you don't mind my saying, it's a bit too late to deny anything. If you want her back you're gonna have to play your hand honestly, and with more than just a little bit of discretion if you don't want to be left the joker. I saw the look in Anna's lovely eyes this morning and it wasn't green for envy, sweetheart. There was a relaxed expression that I haven't seen for a while. I won't say it didn't please me because it did. And do you know why? Because my girl is back in there – and in her own calm way, she's fighting fit.'

'Well, I hope she finds a battle then because I don't know what you're going on about. And if you all think that I'm having an affair with my waitress—'

'Assistant manager. And as for me ... it's hear no evil, see no evil, and speak no evil. That's me, sweetheart. Always has been. Always will be.' She spooned three sugars into his tea because she knew this was how he liked it.

Having got nowhere with Ivy, and once back at his and Anna's house having almost crashed into another car when he had gone through a red light, Frank couldn't wait to get comfortable and chill out. He poured himself a glass of red wine, and then opened the door from the sitting room into the garden and welcomed the sound of the birds calling to each other, with the only other noise coming from the distant hum of traffic.

Easing himself down into the cushioned armchair where he had a better view of the garden, he soaked up the sunshine coming in through the windows. He glanced at the brick barbecue that he had built when they first moved in and remembered the dinner parties they had thrown. He could almost hear the sound of his and Anna's friends laughing and talking as the wine flowed and records played – friends who had slowly dropped off over the past year or so since he had spent ever more time at the restaurant.

Trying for the umpteenth time to think what to do for the best, which he had been doing since the moment Bridget dropped the bombshell just a couple of weeks ago that she was pregnant, he could come up with nothing. Nothing other than to let other people toss the whole thing up in the air and see which way the cards fell. Then he would make a decision whether to stay with Anna, who he thought that he probably did love, deep down, or move in with Bridget, who really did know how to make a man feel like a king in the bedroom. The excitement and secrecy of their affair had been intoxicating, and better than anything he had experienced before. Bridget could be a very naughty, rude lady when she felt like it and brilliant at taking the piss out of morons when they frequented his restaurant. She made him laugh, and laughter as far as Frank was concerned was all-important – one of life's best tonics.

Shaking his head as if trying to bring himself out of a drug-induced state, it dawned on him that the girl had actually been like a drug . . . one that he had tried just for the fun of it and then found himself hooked. Bridget made him feel like a prince among ordinary men, especially when they were between the sheets. But then his Anna could sometimes melt his heart with just a smile. What would be perfect, he thought, would be to have the two of them rolled into one. He tried to think which of the two he was going to have to let go. Weighing it all up, and especially when it came to this house that he loved and that he knew he would have to sign over to Anna for her and the boys, he felt himself go cold. If push came to shove and a divorce was on the cards he stood to lose a lot more than he would gain. A hell of a lot more. He could hardly bear the thought of it.

He was so deep in his self-inflicted troubles, he was pulled up sharply when the shrill sound of the doorbell broke through the peace and quiet. Rising from his chair, he surprised himself at how eager he was to see who was on the doorstep. He was half wishing it would be one of their old friends dropping in after a long gap. But it wasn't an old friend – quite the reverse in fact – it was Bridget's husband, Trevor, standing there. The two young men stood looking at each other in silence until Frank stepped back and opened the door wide. A touch sheepishly he said, 'You'd best come in, Trevor.'

'No, I don't think I will thanks. I wasn't expecting you to be here. I came to see if Anna was all right. And to ask if she knows that Bridget's carrying your baby. She told me so this morning. Bridget that is. I'll be in touch with her through my solicitor from now on. You're welcome to the whore.' This said, he turned away and got into his second-hand light blue Anglia that meant even more to him now, and drove off.

'Fucking hell,' said Frank, as he shut the door and leaned on it. 'What the fuck 'ave you done, Frank?' Feeling as if he had just woken from a long sleep he went into the back room and withdrew a favourite bottle of his Scotch whisky, that was thankfully still a quarter full. He felt as if his brain needed a quick zap. Apart from anything else, two men had come to his house today, one for a little tête-à-tête with his wife and the other to take her for a drive into the countryside. He wondered what the hell he'd done to deserve all of this.

Later that day, when George pulled up outside Ivy's flat and went inside with Anna for a cup of tea, Ivy was only too pleased to be able to pass over her treasured grandsons to their mother. Her cheeks flushed and her pulse racing a little faster than usual, she fancied she was starting to go through her second menopause. 'I've loved having my grandsons, Anna darlin', don't get me wrong, but Christ Almighty; I'd forgotten what a full-time job looking after babies is.'

'Tell me about it!' said Anna, with feeling. 'Feed, bathe, change, play, sleep, feed, change, get their wind up again ...'

'Yeah, all right, don't remind. I'm dog tired, and I'm supposed to look my best tomorrow. I shall have to have an early night with my curlers in, that's for sure.'

'And why have you got to look your best?' asked Anna, looking from one of her sleeping babies to the other while George filled the kettle from the kitchen tap. 'Going to Buckingham Palace to get your OBE are you? Your award for being the top best grandma in the world?'

'And pigs might fly ...' Ivy sighed. 'No, I'm going on a blind date, that's why. A blind date at my age must be the best one to go in for with no reason to explain, I shouldn't think.' She quietly chuckled at her own joke.

Anna smiled, and nodded knowingly. 'So ... you are gonna go and see those old boys of Gwen's then, are you?'

'Not so much of the old, young lady. The chap's only in his early sixties. That's not old these days.' She turned her back on Anna to mouth the words to George: 'Frank's fuming!'

Then, turning back to Anna, she said, 'Oh and by the way, love ... our twins' daddy came round to see me earlier on. By all accounts he went home to pack a few more of his things and Rachel from next door told him that you and George had gone for a ride and that I was baby-minding.'

'And?' said Anna, looking up at her mum. 'What else is new?'

'No more than this as far as I know. He came round to ask if he could be of any help in looking after them and I said I was coping all right. I told him that the pair of you had gone to Kent for the day.'

'And?' said Anna. 'Come on, spit it out, Mum. I can tell by your face that there's more to it than this.'

'Well ... he wasn't any too pleased—'

'Oh really? He wasn't any too pleased because I was having a few hours off for a change and going for a ride into the countryside? He begrudges me that after all he's done?'

'No, I don't think that was it. I would say, if anything, that it was more from jealousy than anger that he chewed the inside of his cheek and went pale ... when I told him that the pair of you had gone out for the day.'

'Can you believe that man?' said George. 'What a nerve! After all he's been getting up to? And then he's got the nerve to play up because she took a day off, Ivy?' George went quiet and thoughtful and then said, 'I'll go and see him face to face and just let him try and throw a wobbly. We've had a lovely day out and he wants to cast aspersions because of his own guilt? No way!'

'Oh shut up, George,' said Ivy, wearily. 'Carry on like that and you'll have me thinking there's more to it than you and Anna being just good friends.'

'Come on, Ivy, even you've got to see that he's taking a liberty coming here to check up on her after what he's done.'

'Oh, stop it, you two. This is daft,' said Anna. 'You're letting him do it again. Here we are – the three of us having enjoyed a lovely day, one way or another – and even though he's been and he's gone he's left something behind for us to feel bad about.'

'Maybe you feel bad, Anna, but I don't,' said George. 'No way, sweetheart.'

Ivy slowly nodded because they were both bang on right and she knew it. Frank had come into her little domain where she was happy as Larry with her baby grandsons to look after, and he had managed to pull her down and make her feel a touch sad instead of angry with him by the time he left. She had enjoyed her day though, before he arrived, and once he had gone again. 'It's strange how just one person can, without meaning to, change the mood in a room whether he's present or not,' she said.

She then remembered the look on Frank's face when he left and it made her stomach turn over. 'The silly man is all at odds with himself – and with the rest of the world I should think.'

Pushing it from her mind, Ivy looked from George to Anna and said, 'Well you can love and leave me, now. I'm gonna put my curlers in and set my hair ready for my day out with my chap tomorrow.'

The look on her daughter's face made Ivy smile. 'Good for me, eh, love? Bloody well good for me. I'm looking forward to my blind date.'

'Definitely good for you, Mum. And you should be

looking forward to it.' Whether it would go well or not really didn't matter too much. A day out was what Ivy needed – a change of scenery, a change of people, with a little bit of romance thrown in as a wild card.

That evening, tired after the travelling, Anna was only too pleased to be back home, relaxing on the sofa after putting her babies to bed. Appreciating the silence and her own company, she had no desire to watch television or listen to music; she just wanted to enjoy the peace and quiet. Sipping a glass of sherry, she kicked off her shoes with a sigh of relief and pulled up her legs to recline full length. She was tired but not yet ready for her bed. She had so enjoyed her time with George and had got to know him better. She thought about the people she had met who lived in the huts – it all seemed so unreal. But her contented solitude was not to last because the sound of the street door opening told her that this was Frank who, clearly from what her mother had told her, was confused as to what he wanted or what he expected of her.

Coming into the doorway he looked around almost as if he was checking to see if anybody else might be in the house. He tried to seem casual as he said, 'I take it that my boys are asleep in their cots?'

'No, Frank, they're not. They're out in the garden pulling up the flowers.'

'Very funny, Anna. So ... you've told your mother that I'm having an affair with Bridget, so I might as well fucking have one, mightn't I? Because she is very attractive. So I'll take it that I've been given free rein, and – if she still wants me – I'll move out of our house for good and in with her to the apartment above my brothers' restaurant in Tower Hill. Okay?'

'It's up to you, Frank. I don't think I much care one way or the other now. Sadly.' She wasn't going to let him know that she had found out from Trevor that Bridget had moved into their flat. And neither was she going to mention the fact that she had said that Trevor and his mother could move in there.

'And actually, Anna – you're hardly ever in the restaurant to see what's what. So if it's not the gossips that have lined up at our front door to fill you in then it must be Hazel and Linda that's been poisoning your mind. Or George of course . . . just so that he could get his end away. Some men are like that. They like to fuck a woman who's not long delivered a baby – or in your case, two babies. Maybe the hero George is a bit of a perv on the quiet, eh? I mean – if you're so close to each other for him to be taking you out for a day in Kent while your mother baby-sits – the little love affair can't only just be starting, can it?'

'If I didn't know you better, Frank, I would say that you've got a sick mind. I think you're letting your imagination fly a bit *too* fast. How dare you tar me with the same brush as Bridget and, as for George, he is a lovely man. He doesn't seem to mind what he does for any one of us girls. But then, of course, he knew all three of us long before you did so I s'pose we're like close family really. Not that I'm suggesting that you never was like family. You were – once.'

'Was?' said Frank. 'Were? So I'm past tense now, am I?'

'You tell me,' said Anna sipping her drink. 'You tell

me what your plans are because I don't know you any more. Are you going to buy a house with Bridget? Because this is what she said. Or was she just being nasty to me? And if she was – why? I've not done anything wrong. She has.'

'If she said that to you, Anna ... *if* she did ... then she was getting carried away. I've flirted with her a bit, I admit that, and I shouldn't have done because she's gone and got a crush on me.'

'Oh really?' said Anna. 'So you've not been having an affair with her? You've not been having sex in our old flat above Prima?'

'It was a fling, not an affair.'

'Well, that's not the way she told it. She's a liar as well then? But then again – what about the gossip that's been up and running that I've only just picked up on? Is she spreading poison everywhere? Telling people in the restaurant that you're leaving me for her? If so, we had better give her the sack. And if you're not careful, she'll be the cause of you losing access to your sons. But then maybe that won't bother you now? Now that there's another rumour floating in the breeze. And if you don't know what that is, I'm not gonna tell you.'

'Who has been told what and what has she told them, Anna?'

Looking at him, she almost felt a touch of sympathy when she saw that he was chewing on the inside of his cheek, a habit from childhood according to his mother. She had to be strong though and get him to do the talking if she was to find out just how serious the affair was.

'Well, she laid her cards on the table and told me everything when I popped in for a little chat with her.'

'Told you what?'

'I think that you should ask Bridget that. It was a shame she went and twisted her ankle, but what could she expect wearing those high-heeled shoes for work. Anyone would think that she was employed there to model the dishes rather than deliver them to the tables. How is she now? I think her nose must be black and blue and swollen. Was she on her feet or on her back when you last saw her?'

'You're not funny, Anna,' said Frank. 'What exactly did she tell you?'

'Oh . . . far be it for me to interfere between lover and mistress. You must ask Bridget. But don't you go and fret over this because of me. I'll be all right. I'll be fine. In fact I'll be more than that. I've come through all the lonely nights by myself, never mind the sleep I've lost for months on end. I was stupid to suffer in silence but that's over now. My sisters know about you shagging Bridget and so do most of our customers, so don't worry if you want to go off and buy that house that Bridget mentioned – you carry on, Frank. I've got my family and I've got my friends. I'm thinking of throwing a party. A kind of a get-together of all my old mates that I've neglected since I got pregnant.'

'And what's all this with you and George? How long's that been going on for?'

'Me and George? Oh years. I thought you knew how close we were. He took me for a lovely drive to the countryside today. We had a fantastic time. And of course – as you've probably heard – he's split with his wife, so really . . . we're both in a nice little rowing boat at the moment, me and George.'

Frank leaned back against the wall and folded his arms as he stared at Anna, trying to face her down. But he saw a different expression on her face than the usual compliance. He saw guts and determination. 'I don't know what you said to your mother but she seems to think that we're gonna get divorced.'

'Well . . . Mum, as you know, does form her own opinion at times, and especially now that she thinks you've treated me like a toe-rag for God knows how long. She can forgive a little bit of steering off the road now and then but you've taken liberties. You've gone too far. Shagging that silly cow in our flat that we first lived in? Even I think you should be ashamed of yourself, never mind the older generation.'

'So I'm being seen as a bastard all round then, am I?'

Anna shrugged and showed an expression of uncertainty. 'I'm sorry that I can't fight your corner, Frank. You have been a rotten bastard and it's gonna take a lot on your part to gain your respect back. I'm easy-going as everyone knows, but you've rocked our boat a little too much and do you know what – I can be more stubborn than my sisters when something just doesn't sit right with me.'

'So what am I supposed to think about you going off for a day to the countryside with George? For all I know you could have been at it in a haystack for hours. Some men love that kind of thing.'

'No. No, we didn't do anything like that. We had a lovely day out. To Kent. To where George and his

221

family used to go hop-picking. He wanted to show me what he loved about it when he was a boy.'

'Anna – you're not clever. Stop talking about the prick.'

'But you asked me,' said Anna, all innocent. 'And it was a lovely day. Our family never went hop-picking, but we did go fruit-picking, but then that was only for two weeks of the year whereas hop-picking—'

'All right, Anna! You've made your point!' Frank glared at her. 'You were sharing a bit of romantic nostalgia. I don't need a chapter from one of those romance books you've always got your nose into.'

'I suppose . . .' said Anna, gazing up at the ceiling and ignoring the jibe, 'that it was a kind of a romantic place. Hops are a kind of herb that goes into making the best beer . . . and you can't beat a river and fields and cows. I think nature couldn't have made a better setting for romance.'

Frank knew that she was reeling him in like a fish on a line and it grated. He didn't like this new Anna, even though he knew she was acting. 'I want to spend a day or so with the twins,' he said.

'Oh . . . that's nice. Just let me know when you want to take over and I'll make sure I'm out for the day. And if you get stuck you can always call Mum. She'll give you all the advice you need as to how to feed two babies when they're both crying from hunger and thirst. I'll leave a list for you on how to make the bottles up with the Cow and Gate and how to test the heat just before you feed. You drip a little onto the back of your hand and only feed them the milk when it's blood-warm. And once you've winded 'em, give 'em twenty minutes or so in their playpen to have a kick around before you change their napkins, so they'll have filled them up good and proper before you put them down. And don't throw the paddy pads down the lavatory whatever you do, no matter how much they smell. You wrap them in newspaper and then put 'em in a plastic carrier bag tied up so that flies can't get in. If you get stuck, just ask Rachel next door what to do. She may be long in the tooth, but she knows all the tricks in the book. She'll help you out if you can't cope.'

'You've made your point, Anna. You keep the boys under your wing.' Clearly gutted, Frank turned to leave and then turned around again. 'I didn't want this, Anna. This isn't what I wanted. I've always known what Bridget's been up to – what she's after. But if you force my hand I won't have any choice but to leave you.'

'And why's that?' said Anna.

'Because Bridget stopped taking the pill. She's missed a period and if she is pregnant it won't be Trevor's baby but mine in there.'

'Well, that *is* a fine mess you've got yourself into. A fine old mess,' said Anna, longing to get up off the couch and slam her fist in his face.

'It's my own fault for trusting that she wouldn't forget to take a pill. I was careful, doubling up by using a condom, but Bridget couldn't see the point in using both, so we decided to stick with the pill.'

'Close the door after you, Frank. The street door, that is. And all I'm gonna say about your little bit of news is that you're one hell of a stupid bastard. You've fallen for the oldest trick in the book, she's got you right where she wants you. And don't slam the front door.' Frank looked at Anna, and realised again just how stupid he had been. He drew air in through his nostrils and then slowly exhaled, and looked to be on the edge of shedding a tear or two. He then quietly turned and left Anna to herself.

The house suddenly seemed too quiet. She was alone again, but for some reason that she couldn't be bothered to fathom she didn't feel lonely. And the fact that Bridget was pregnant with Frank's baby left her cold. Whether he realised it or not, Frank had just damaged their marriage beyond repair. She wasn't angry. She wasn't even sad. She felt nothing. But strangely enough it was George who came to mind. She felt like phoning him and saying that she and Frank were over, but she knew that this was not the right thing to do.

Chapter Eight

The following day, Monday, Ivy and Gwen set off on their arranged outing into the West End, wearing their best frocks and summer coats and a little more lipstick and powder than usual. And while they were changing from one bus to another on their journey, their dates were waiting in the spacious sitting room of Horace Travers-James' flat, which was crammed with old-fashioned furniture, antiques, and several Persian rugs on the polished oak floorboards. This flat, just off Tottenham Court Road, was absolutely charming, though it couldn't have been in a more archaic Victorian building. The gentlemen waited patiently for the girls to arrive for afternoon tea. Horace, an upright man of around six feet had thick silver-grey hair and light blue eyes, and what Ivy would term a Roman nose – long and straight. He had chosen to wear his black and gold 1930s silk smoking jacket, while Gwen's chap was in his usual smart attire, except that he had treated himself to a new navy and white spotted tie for the occasion and had left off the cap which usually covered his thinning hair.

Horace, sitting on a faded red velvet sofa with a carved mahogany frame, was idly thumbing through a weekly journal taken from the neat pile of magazines on a low table in a corner of the room. He stopped at the astrology page, about to read aloud to the annoyance of his friend. 'I am correct in my assumption that you are a Gemini, Wilfred dear boy, am I not?'

'You are,' said Wilfred, 'and you know it. Don't start reading that bloody rubbish to me. I'm not interested in what's to come and you're not interested in what's been and gone. So why torment me now with star signs and predictions?'

'I wouldn't dream of tormenting you, dear boy,' said Horace, giving his friend a sly look. 'Although I must say that this week's is rather interesting. It says that we Leos are in for a bit of an illuminating few days. Maybe this woman friend you are introducing me to is not a born and bred Cockney after all, and we may have at least something in common. Anything in common would help.' He shuddered melodramatically. 'But how rude of me to read out my own horoscope. Now then, let's see ... Gemini ...'

'I would rather you didn't read out mine, thank you very much. I don't want to know what is gonna happen to me, as I've said a thousand times before.'

'How can you possibly mean this, my dear Wilfred, when you've no idea what is in your stars for this coming week? What if they were to tell you that you're in for a windfall? I presume that you did fill in your football coupons, as usual – wouldn't you like to know if you are to become a millionaire overnight? Or do you already know this? Have you already taken a little peek at the horoscope?'

'You realise that the horoscope you're reading is a year or so out of date,' was Wilfred's response.

'Well, it matters not one iota. It is the day of the

226

week in which it is read that counts – in my humble opinion, that is.'

Continuing to read, but barely audibly now, Horace glanced over his spectacles at Wilfred. '"Immediate developments when you will embrace romance are not far away . . . but conflicting loyalties leave you uncertain of what to do . . . for the best. You have the time to learn more about those around you so—"'

'The ladies will be here soon,' interrupted Wilfred, stopping his friend in mid-flow. 'Read your horoscope in bed tonight before you go to sleep when nobody else is around for you to bore to death.'

'If I must, then so be it.' Closing the magazine, Horace sighed loudly. 'We don't get anywhere near enough visitors coming into this building – this is the problem. Not that it surprises me in the least when you consider the sort of people you normally find in abodes such as this decrepit Victorian prison-like place. I mean to say . . . it's bound to put some people off, is it not? Do you not agree with this one tiny observation, Wilfred? I mean to say, the others who live here do tend to offer only false smiles, and false promises of neighbourliness before disappearing into their lavish apartments. It is all a perfect setting for a murder mystery – I would have thought. What we could all do with from time to time is a visitor or two for afternoon tea who, out of good manners and a gesture of good will, would bring a fresh Victoria sponge from the food hall at Harrods.'

'You're harping on about your two cousins from the country I presume?'

'Yes, I suppose in a way I am. They were more like

sisters to me when I was a boy. I lived with them for a while once Mother ran off with her fancy man. Then I came back to London, to be with Father, of course, but mostly so that I could work in the best of our British theatres. I was terribly lonely at first, what with my father getting on with his own full social life and letters from my aunt and cousins not arriving as often as had been promised. None of the family wanted me to go on the stage, you know.'

'So you've said.'

'It was hard to know what to do for the best at times ... follow my heart or the well-meant advice. I don't suppose I would want to live anywhere else if I am to be honest with myself. I've been happy enough in this modest abode.' He withdrew a beautiful old gold fob watch from his waistcoat and sighed theatrically.

'Where on earth could your lady friends have got to?' He glanced wistfully at his chum. 'Let us hope that the exterior of this place has not unnerved this blind date of mine. This female who comes to me straight from the very heart of Charles Dickens territory.'

'Dickens never did live in the East End, Horace.'

Ignoring the interruption as he was apt to do, Horace continued his flow. 'They are, nevertheless, from the poorer parts of London, are they not? In such parts where only the Cockney will survive. Where thieves and rogues continue to kill each other in dark alleyways ...'

'You had better not start all of that acting malarkey once they are here. We'll go out for a walk if the pair of you finds that you can't fill a silence.'

'If my blind date and I have little or nothing in

common, you mean? This of course could very well be a problem.'

'You might be like chalk and cheese but you've got nothing to lose. It's just a bit of fun, that's all. If it doesn't work out, we'll stroll to the park and then see them to the bus stop. Nothing lost, nothing gained, and there are seven days to a week and fifty-two weeks to a year.'

'Indeed. So what are a few hours of discomfort in one's somewhat lonely life? Although I will say that I have always got on with the Cockneys. This is probably because of the war, when we all rubbed along together regardless of creed or breed.'

'You've been on your own for too long, Horace, that's your trouble. You've got used to the solitary life and that's not good for anyone. You've been lonely I expect. You need a good woman to help you enjoy your money.'

'That is as may be my dear friend, but I think I would rather be lonely than risk being miserable with somebody else. Did I tell you that two out of the three of my fiancées were also in the theatre?'

'Many times, Horace, many times.'

'Oh . . . well, then, do please forgive me for being so tiresome!'

'Just don't go and mention your fiancées once the ladies are here.'

'I'm not a complete fool, dear boy. But there – we shall see what we shall see. Maybe this woman whom you seem to think is a match for me will get little dicky rearing its head again to see what is what?' He glanced at Wilfred and raised an eyebrow. 'I've put on a clean shirt, clean socks and brand new underwear that my sister gave to me several Christmases ago. I do believe they are called Y-fronts these days and not short Johns.'

'Short Johns?'

'Yes, dear boy. Long Johns cut down.'

'And that's what you usually wear is it?'

'In the summer it is. I have four pairs of the originals for the winter, and five pairs of the older originals cut down for the summer so as to let air into one's private parts that never get to see the sunshine. And each garment is still as white as the day it was purchased. Bleach and cotton go hand in hand, dear boy, hand in hand. I have always said so and shall continue to say it.'

'Fascinating,' said Wilfred as he gazed out of a window. 'That kind of talk should turn the girls on.'

Horace chuckled as he looked out of another of the grimy, almost ceiling to floor windows fringed by fading, dusty red velvet drapes. 'Do you know, if either of us were a cat or a dog, I do believe we would have been put down by now.'

'Don't start all that again.' Wilfred looked across at his friend and smiled. 'You look handsome in your Somerset Maugham attire. Quite the gentleman. So try not to be too Jack Blunt when the women arrive, eh?'

'I? Jack Blunt? Dear boy . . . you surely confuse me with some other person. I have always prided myself on being discretion itself.' He straightened the perfectly pressed white handkerchief that just showed above the top pocket of his quilted silk smoking jacket. 'I was brought up by a wonderful nanny, you know.'

'I do know. You told me already. You're always telling me. You should have stayed on stage. You're a good actor.' Wilfred wandered about the room and then went back to the window and looked out to the pretty back garden below. 'If you didn't live on this top floor we could 'ave 'ad our tea outside.'

'We'll save that for another time, old chap. Not tea though, it would be far too much trouble having to take down a tray et cetera. Cold beer and cut sandwiches would be the ticket – should it all go well this afternoon, that is.'

'At least it's a nice quiet afternoon. I like it when it's quiet. That's why I suggested the women come on a Monday.'

'Not for long will it be quiet,' said Horace. 'I do believe I can hear footsteps in the corridor, Wilfred. Our visitors have arrived. We are about to have female company, dear boy.'

The tapping on the big heavy mahogany door confirmed his supposition. With a theatrical wave of the hand, Horace urged Wilfred to open the door while he stood up and glanced at his reflection in his ornate, if rather tarnished, mirror above the white marble fireplace. He felt that he still cut a dash, and winked at himself before breathing deeply and arranging a pose next to his high-backed armchair. He clasped his hands together, and waited demurely to see whether it was to be a beauty or a beast entering his lonely yet quite contented world.

'Bloody tourists . . .' moaned Ivy, as she came into the room. 'I've never known the roads in the West End to be so packed, or so many of the bloody things on the road all at once. I would 'ave like to have jumped off our double decker and got onto one of them open-topped sightseeing buses and gone on a little tour myself on our way here.'

Having cut right through the silence, she looked straight at Horace and smiled broadly. 'You look very smart, sir, I must say.'

'Really? How very good of you to pay such a compliment to an old veteran.' He smiled. 'And you look a picture in what I can only describe as a *powder blue* costume that matches your lovely eyes.'

'I've seen you on the telly, haven't I?' said Ivy, a twinkle in her eye.

'Possibly,' said Horace, smiling back at her. 'I have been in one or two of Harold Pinter's plays, to name just one playwright.'

'Well, I'm proud to be in your company, sir,' she said, offering her hand to shake his with the elegance befitting an actor of standing. She was lying through her back teeth about having seen him before, but wanted to cut to the chase so as to break the ice and soften the atmosphere. Gwen's chap Wilfred knew exactly what she was up to. He turned a blind eye and helped Gwen take off her lovely lightweight primrose summer coat.

Looking about the room, Ivy said, 'Do you know I feel sure that I've been in this building before, years back, when I used to clean and disinfect telephones for a company called Micro Clean. We mostly went round offices, but the company had a few contracts for these big types of residential places as well.' She crossed the room to look out of the long sash window at the grounds below and the gate which led out to a small

232

garden, and silently told herself that she could live in such surroundings.

'This is a lovely place,' she said, turning to find that Horace had quietly moved and was standing behind and quite close to her. 'The name's Ivy, by the way.'

'And mine is Horace, I am sorry to say. I can't imagine what my parents could have been thinking. Please, do sit down.'

'Thank you very much – I will take the weight off my feet.' She looked around the room again and felt comfortable in her surroundings. 'It's a nice flat,' she said. 'Very nice.' She sank into a faded armchair and looked at Gwen, waiting for her to say something.

'Yes, I suppose it's not a bad place you've got here,' said Gwen, picking up on her friend's unspoken request. 'You know, you could bring that old Persian rug up a treat if you were to grate two raw potatoes into a basin of cold water and let it stand for a few minutes—'

'Oh here we go,' said Wilfred, cutting in. 'Another of her old-fashioned ideas she won't let go of. Well go on then, get it over and done wiv.'

'It might be out of date but it bloody well works.' She gave Wilfred a look of remonstration and then continued. 'Once you've strained off the liquid, Horace, you dip a dry old rag into it and rub the rug all over. Then go over it again with a cloth that has been wrung out in clean water.'

'And it really works?' said Horace, sounding truly fascinated.

'Indeed it does. And if you can be bothered to clean your cut-glass decanters, when they're empty, cut up potato into small bits and drop this into the top of the bottle and then swish it around in a little cold water. Or you could cover some eggshells with lemon juice and stand for forty-eight hours. The eggshells should have dissolved by then and so you pour the liquid into the decanter and shake occasionally.'

'Shake what?' said Wilfred. 'Himself or the mixture?'

Ivy found this amusing, as did Horace, but she saw Gwen giving her man friend another dirty look. 'The mixture, Wilfred, the mixture.'

'Actually,' said Horace, 'I do sometimes use such old receipts myself, which are far cheaper than those in the supermarkets and far more efficient if you were to ask my opinion. For instance, did you know, ladies, that to look after leather upholstery as it should be looked after, one boils a half-pint of linseed oil for one minute and then have it go cold before adding a half pint of vinegar? All that is then required is to give it a thoroughly good stir. Then one takes a clean piece of rag to rub it into the leather – another soft piece of rag is then required to polish it up – and this will also prevent cracking.'

'So you kill two birds with one stone? Very good. I would definitely try that if I had leather furniture, but mine's mostly Dralon covers that come off and go in the washing machine.' Ivy smiled fondly at him. 'But I shall remember that and pass it on to my daughters.'

A touch put out at just how Ivy was sailing through all of this, Gwen sniffed and, turning to her friend, said, 'You look very much at home, Ivy, I must say.'

'I feel very much at home as it just so happens.' She glanced at Horace, who politely nodded to acknowledge

234

the compliment, and she couldn't help feeling a slight tingle in the crevice of her womanhood.

'My father was rather a wise man,' said Horace. 'Being a sporting gambler, he took a chance when purchasing this lavish apartment – a very long time ago. He dealt mostly in stocks and shares during the weekdays and gambled at Newmarket and such race-courses at weekends – when he wasn't playing golf. He would have been so proud of our Tony Jacklin for winning the British Open Championship in '68 and then the US Open in 1970.'

'A sporting man as well as someone who kept his eye on the property market? That's no bad thing, is it, Horace.'

'Indeed not, Ivy. Had he not have purchased one or two properties such as this one, he might well have been penniless when he passed on to the world beyond. But he could die with dignity because he had left to me, his favourite child, this apartment, which I believe would now fetch a pretty penny or two. I can't imagine what he would have made of the many changes we have seen.

'It is now a case of anything goes, with the scruffy young wearing old fur coats and animal skins when they sit in one of my favourite little coffee shops in Berwick Street, where we seniors are now made to feel as if we are strangers. The so-called new-style beatniks fill the place, all of them making one cup of coffee last a whole day. And the only thing one hears when it comes to conversation is talk of legalising marijuana. Not that I'm old-fashioned mind you. I have always prided myself on moving with the times.'

Ivy was surprising herself. This tall and handsome gentleman in his early sixties certainly was warming parts of her where the sunbeams hadn't shone in a very long time. She liked him. She liked him a lot. 'You must be very happy living here,' she said.

'As a matter of fact I am,' he said, looking into Ivy's smiling eyes. 'We do have a communal garden at the rear of the property with a gate that leads into a small grassy square, which has benches and beautiful shrubs. It is a small public park of sorts, which not many seem to know about, thankfully.'

'Now then,' said Wilfred, 'what's it to be? We've bought some cakes and I've set a tray with a china tea set, so who's for a cuppa?'

'Smashing,' said Gwen, easing off her shoes as she rested back in her armchair. 'I didn't know there was a gate leading into a park. I shall 'ave to investigate that, Horace.'

'You do surprise me, Gwendolyn,' said Horace. 'I would have thought that our mutual friend here would have taken you for a stroll around by now. There used to be a mass of bluebells out there but the children would pick them and so they eventually gave up I'm afraid. As a matter of fact, my father planted two beautiful shrubs in the little green and now they are quite established. So we have red berries in the winter and white flowers in the summertime. And do you know what I love the very most of all, Ivy?'

'No, but I would like to know, Horace,' she said.

'The smell of rain on warm damp earth.'

'Yes. Yes, I know what you mean. Has your father

been dead long?' Ivy was giving him her complete attention.

'Oh, about six or seven years ... Ivy,' he said, his voice dropping to a whisper.

'And what about your mother?' she continued.

'Mother? Why, she left long before Father passed away. Ran off with her titled lover I'm afraid. I've not heard a whisper from her since. She may not even know that her husband, my father, is no more. It was I who looked after him towards the end, you see. We lived here together in this apartment.'

Ivy was surprised at how easy it was to talk to this lovely gentleman, who she would have thought to be snooty had she met him outside in the street. She smiled at the thought and silently berated herself for being more of a snob in her own way than he was.

She was just about to ask if he had been given help with looking after his father when he said, 'Death is not so bad, you know, if getting to it isn't too unbearable. If there is someone there to assist ... if you get my drift.'

'I do, Horace, and I agree wholeheartedly. I was by my mother's side for the last three weeks of her life and, do you know, I can't remember her being sad even though she knew she was going. She seemed ready for it – as if it was all part of her travels – if that makes sense.'

'Oh, indeed it does, Ivy. Indeed.' Horace was clearing enjoying himself and was in full flow as if he were behind the footlights. 'Sadly, Father was incontinent towards the end,' he continued, 'but even that wasn't anywhere near as bad as I imagined it to be.'

He replaced his handkerchief and drew a quivering

breath before letting out a long sigh. 'I can see it now as if it were yesterday. My father would be in his bed and I would roll him against the wall, ease out the soiled sheet, and then let him roll back onto the rubber. Get a dry sheet, push him towards the wall again, hold him there, and get the dry one on as best I could. He would then roll back and rest, and I would sit on a chair by his bed and he would look at me and only just manage to whisper the words, "Thank you my boy." I truly never minded one bit. And the good thing about it all was that he knew I wanted to be there doing this for him. It went fairly well, all things considered. When the weather was fine I managed to get his wheelchair into the lift and out into the garden. He adored the sunshine in the summer and coal fires in the winter. Sometimes he sat by the fire with his legs stretched out so that his feet almost touched the flames.'

'And you say that he was a gambling man?' Ivy smiled. 'Did you manage to place a bet for him while he was bedridden?'

Horace became thoughtful and then slowly shook his head, saying, 'Do you know, he never ever asked this of me. It was as if that part of his life had already gone on to the ever after. I expect he imagined that there would be a racecourse in heaven awaiting him.'

Tenderly laughing, Ivy felt more and more relaxed in his company, as if she had known him for years. 'You paint a lovely picture, Horace. A kind of a watercolour painting of a heavenly place that we'll all go to one day.'

'Do I really?' He looked pleased. 'Well, that's very sweet of you to say so, Ivy.'

'He never 'ad a bad life though, your old man, did

he?' said Wilfred, feeling a touch left out. 'I mean to say, he drove around in an old type of a car, right up until he was in his mid-eighties. He was dead within a year of knowing, wasn't he, Horace?'

'I should think it was about a year, yes.' Gazing down at the floor he slowly shook his head. 'It takes a year for any of us as a baby to learn how to walk and feed ourselves and it takes a year to forget again. At least, that's how long it was with my father. A year to the day almost. Until the body, mind and soul finally slept for the last time.'

Touched by this, and a little saddened, Ivy crossed herself and whispered, 'May he rest in peace.'

'Oh he will, my dear, don't you fret. My father was ready to meet his maker. My father was everything to me. Perhaps this was because I never married and so therefore had no offspring of my own to worry over. Who knows?'

'And why was that, do you think?'

'Why was what?' said Horace, a glazed look in his eyes. 'I'm so sorry I've lost the thread ...'

'I asked why it was that you never married.'

'Oh, I'm not entirely sure if you want the honest answer.' He smiled ruefully and shrugged. 'Always the best man but never the groom.'

'Were you ever engaged?'

'Yes. Three times as a matter of fact. But I could never quite take that next and final step. The trust wasn't there you see. I couldn't trust that a woman wouldn't do to me as my mother had done to my father. He wouldn't have admitted it to anyone, but I saw what a broken man he was once she left. He spent a very long and lonely time on his own ... before he went out and about again. Then he made up for lost time and became a bit of a playboy.'

'Well, all I can say to you, Horace, even though I've not known you for five minutes, you're a lovely gentleman. And I expect that your mother was a fool to walk away from your father. You can take me to the pictures any night of the week. We'll try our hand at courting and see how it goes – if you would like to, that is.'

Breaking into a lovely smile and then a laugh, Horace slowly nodded. 'I think I would enjoy that very much – but you'd have to show me the ropes.'

'I'll do my best,' said Ivy. 'I can't say more than that.'

'I can,' said Gwen. 'You're a bloody fast worker!'

Chapter Nine

Anna, while her mother was being entertained in Horace's West End apartment, was making the most of the time while her twins were contentedly asleep. Her eyes were closed and she was enjoying the warm sun on her face as she lay on one of a matching pair of foldaway sunbeds, almost drifting off into a light doze. In her back garden at this time of the afternoon it was usually quiet. Almost asleep, she hadn't heard Frank come into the house, and her heart felt as if it had leapt out of her chest and back again when, from the open door and right out of the blue, he said, 'If you're thinking about George, Anna, you're wasting your dreams. He'll go back to 'is wife again. They're like yo-yos, that pair. So I would stop fantasising if I were you.'

Willing herself to stay right where she was and not respond, Anna put into practice a relaxation exercise she remembered from her afternoons at the ante-natal clinic. 'What is it you want, Frank?' she finally said, her best bored tone to the fore.

'A cup of strong coffee would be good. But don't get up, I'll make it myself.' He went to the kitchen, leaving her to marvel at his audacity. He had moved all of his things out and into the flat at Tower Hill where he was now living with Bridget, and yet he had the nerve to walk in as if nothing had changed, as if he had been nowhere. She so wanted to tell him to fuck off, but her inner voice was telling her not yet, that it made sense for her to remain silent, keep her eyes shut and wait to see what it was that he wanted. What he had to say. She knew that he would be able to see her through the kitchen window, but he couldn't see inside her mind and this was what would be getting to him more than anything else. She had learned to imitate him by giving little or nothing away.

'I know you're not asleep, Anna,' he said, once he was back with a mug of coffee in his hand. 'So you can stop play-acting because it doesn't wash.' He spoke in a softer tone than usual. She realised of course that he had previously been covering his guilt by playing the sometimes angry, sometimes silent man who had a load on his mind and on his shoulders. Turning her head ever so slightly she peered lazily at him and said again, 'What do you want, Frank? Why are you standing there? Bridget gone off with an older and wealthier man, has she?'

'No. Why do you ask?'

'Just curious, that's all. Take whatever it is you've come back for and go. I really don't want any horrible discussions today. Go away and live your life the way you want to and leave me to lead mine.'

'This is still my house and my home, Anna, as well as yours. I suppose you think that you're clever letting Trevor and his mother move into our flat?'

Anna did her level best not to smile. She was proud of just how easily she had been able to slip back into her nice relaxed mood again, even though he was still there. She kept her face to the sun and her eyes closed, and spoke calmly to him. 'When you say *our* flat, Frank, what exactly do you mean? Because, as far as I'm concerned, until Trev's whitewashed all the walls and ripped up the carpets and torn out the curtains, it's yours and Bridget's shagging place. The sheets on the bed reeked of the pair of you. They'll make good dusters though, now that they've been ripped to shreds.'

'I don't remember signing a contract to say that the drip and his mother could rent the flat,' Frank retorted. 'I want any signs of Trevor out of there so that I can move back in when I'm good and ready. Tower Hill is all right as a place of work – but to live? No. It doesn't entirely suit me.'

'There isn't a contract, Frank. I'm letting him and his mother stay there for the time being. Do anything daft or cruel, like chucking their things out, and the law will be down on you like a ton of bricks. Even squatters have rights these days and Trevor and his mum are my guests. So forget trying to stir up trouble and go back to your little sex den at Tower Hill with your little whore. Or is she too busy with other clients now that she's in that rich tourist area?'

'Very funny, Anna. I'll tell her you said that. And what about George, who you seem to have taken a fancy to all of a sudden? Don't forget that he's my friend as well as yours. I can read him like a book and I'm telling you – he'll drop you like a hot potato should another free fanny come by. You'll soon be yesterday's fish and chip paper.'

Ignoring his crude and insulting remarks, Anna sighed loudly and pretended to shut him out. She knew that he was using George to bait her, but since they had been more like cousins than friends even when they were kids on the street he was wasting his breath.

'Stop making up stories about people, Frank. And before you go on about his wife, she's on a world cruise.'

'Well then, she must have decided to cut it short and jump ship, mustn't she, because she's back in his realm.'

'George would have told me if this was the case. We're good friends. I played with him and his brother when I was a kid – as did my sisters – so if his wife is back on the scene I would have heard. Go away, Frank. Back to Tower Hill. The tourists will be about and Bridget's on the loose. You've got to keep an eye on girls like her. *She'll* be coming home in the wee hours next, smelling of aftershave.'

Anna heard his deliberate angry sigh but she was enjoying this new experience of speaking up for herself, of baiting him for a change. It was fun. 'If I'd thought that you were gonna come in and out disturbing my new way of life,' she said, 'which doesn't include grief, I would have changed the lock on the street door.'

Frank's silence proved that she really had got to him this time. A few seconds passed before he said, 'I came to see my twins. But before I go up and take a peep I'm gonna make myself another cup of coffee in my kitchen. All right?' He then stepped out onto the small crazy-paved patio to inspect an old-fashioned, overgrown rose bush which he had never pruned in his life. Anna was the one with the green fingers. 'This is in a bit of a state,' he said. 'You're letting the garden go to pot as well now are you? Too busy going for outings in the country and leaving our babies with one baby-sitter or another. Is this what it's come to?'

'So far I've only left them with their grandma and I've only had one trip to Kent, Frank. Although more are planned. Jackie along the turning has offered to have them for a few hours whenever I want. And she said she'll baby-sit in the evenings for me as well. She's a lovely girl. And she does seem to love the twins. She could easily get work as a freelance nanny to release young housewives who don't want to give up work once married.'

'Well, that's something at least. Jackie could have them for, say, three days a week, and you could go back to work as a telephonist part-time. Put a few quid in the joint account for a change instead of taking it out. I might go and have a chat to her about that.'

'Don't bother ...' Anna yawned. 'I shan't be going back to work until the boys are at school. In five years' time. Now, I just want to drift off for ten minutes, I'm tired. Both our babies are teething and I was awake half the night. But you don't wanna hear boring old stuff like that.'

'So you don't want a coffee then?'

'No.'

'Or a cup of tea with a drop of brandy in it might be better. You seem a little uptight.'

She wasn't uptight and he knew it. She didn't want him there, especially not if he had come to try and woo her back into his good books for his own selfish reasons. She just wanted him to go. 'Just do me a favour and leave me to catch up on a little bit of sleep.

And don't slam the front door of the house when you leave, the way you've slammed it on our marriage.'

He was getting on her nerves but she was now going to hold her tongue to put a stop to any further dialogue. He had come around because he realised what a fool he was making of himself. Gossip spread quickly in their close-knit world. She knew him like the back of her hand and could tell at a glance that he wanted her to feel sorry for him. But this was Frank all over and he was too far gone to change.

She had been hurt by him many times during the past year or so, and she knew what he was like when he was sorry and wanted to make up. But this was different. Much different. He was now living with another woman.

'I'm all right, Frank,' she finally said. 'And the boys are fine apart from the teething. Mum's being a brick and my sisters fantastic. And I *have* phoned your mum, before you ask, and I've told her that I'll take them over to visit soon. She was all right about it. She apologised for you of course but, as I said to her, we can't be responsible for the way our children turn out. She and Mum are keeping a little bit at arm's length for a while until we've sorted things out between us ... you and me that is. They agree that this is for the best. It won't be long though, until they're back having pie and mash together with Gwen and John from next door to Mum.'

'John?' Frank sniggered. 'You'll be linking arms with 'im next and strolling along the Bethnal Green market or going to Columbia Road to buy some pretty flowers.'

'Yeah, that's a nice thought. We get on well. Always have done. I might even go out with him and his chums one night. They have a fantastic time when they're out dancing from what I've heard.' She turned her face to the sun and away from him.

'I don't suppose there's any point in us talking?' he said, after several seconds of silence. 'I'm not really bothered one way or the other what either of our mothers do or don't do. It's my twins I'm thinking about – especially once you go clubbing with the "boys who will be girls."'

'Us talking about what, Frank?' she said, ignoring his sarcasm. 'Divorce?'

'No. Not divorce. Us. Just talking . . . about what's best for the babies for instance. Or don't their welfare come into it?'

'Don't you mean what's absolutely the best for you, Frank? That's what you'll be saying next, and do you know what? All I'm thinking about right now is what's best for me, because I'm not completely off the page am I? I *am* still breathing.'

'Stop trying to make this harder than what it is, Anna. I meant . . . is there any point in us trying again? And before you ask – and in case you've not heard – Bridget's definitely not pregnant. She just missed a couple of periods, apparently.'

'I couldn't give a monkey's what she is or what she isn't. I don't even want her name around me. All right? So just take it, put it in your trouser pocket, and fuck off.'

'Oh, right. So you're not pleased then?'

'Pleased? Because that silly cow all of a sudden isn't having a baby?' She let out an exasperated sigh. 'Give me a break, Frank. And to be honest, I really couldn't care less one way or the other now. Pregnant? That's the oldest trick in the book. Go away Frank, I don't wanna hear any more. I can hardly believe that anyone would try that these days – even that sly cow. And before you start to defend Bridget, what exactly do you mean by us trying again? I don't remember having to *try* before she arrived on our doorstep fluttering her eyelashes. I thought that we were in love. No sorry, not "in love" – that we loved each other. There's a difference. So I don't go for "trying again".' Anna was delivering her words with no hint of sentiment but, inside, in the pit of her stomach, she felt as though there was a ball of fire.

'What I'm trying to say is – is it worth us wiping the slate clean, Anna?'

'You make our marriage sound like a dish chalked up on our menu board, Frank. One that hasn't been all that tasty.'

'And you sound as if you've been around your sisters too much.'

'So what?' said Anna, yawning again. 'I'm sorry, but I was just sinking into a lovely doze when you arrived.'

'I'm not finding this easy, you know. I'm trying to patch things up, here. We've got our sons to think of.'

'Well, that's really good of you, Frank, but I shouldn't bother yourself. It's far too soon – and possibly far too late as well.' This was her leaving the door ajar, and if he picked up on it fine; if not, enough was enough. She had flogged her emotions to death and all he was serving to do was to remind her of how drained she was, and how fed up with him and his self-pity. She wondered if he had forgotten that he

248

had telephoned a few nights earlier when his speech was slurred from drinking. Missing the point she had made about it being too soon, he continued with his usual rhetoric.

'I'm not stretching your brain too much am I, Anna? It's not as if I'm trying to have an intellectual conversation or anything. I'm just asking if you want us to try again. It's up to you.'

'I'm tired, Frank,' she said a touch condescendingly. 'Go away and leave me in peace.'

Frank pulled a packet of cigarettes from his trouser pocket and lit one with what looked like a new slimline gold lighter. 'I'm gonna make myself another cup of coffee. Do you want one or not?'

Anna knew that this was a very big step for Frank. He was eating humble pie. She just wanted him to leave; grief was building up again and she was too drained to cry any more. Her pillow had been soaked with tears too many times.

'I don't want anything to drink, Frank. And I'm not in the right mood to discuss us, I need time and I need space.' She could smell the familiar scent of his aftershave, and this of all things almost had her break her resolve as she felt tears welling again. 'Please go away now, Frank. Leave me be.'

'I need to know if you want me to move out permanently. If you want your freedom, I can't say I think much of your choice, but I s'pose that George is a good-looking bloke even if he is a bent copper.'

Placing her hands over her face as if she were shielding it from the sun in order to hide her expression from Frank, she forced herself not to let his galling attempt at patching up their marriage make her scream. Right then, she didn't think that she could forgive or love him the way she used to. The daft thing about it all was that Frank was focusing on George when it was she and Trevor who, without saying it aloud, were perhaps having to keep a check on their emotions. Of course she loved being in George's company because he was fun and he was attractive in every sense of the word, and this alone had told her to be on her guard from the very beginning of her break-up with Frank. She wasn't made of stone and she didn't want to be hurt again.

And as for Trevor ... she didn't think she would ever forget how awful it was when she had seen the state of the poor sod when the muck had hit the fan.

'You're gonna have to accept that this is all going to take time, Frank,' she finally murmured, hoping this might be the end of it and he would go back to Tower Hill. 'I need time here in the house by myself with my babies to get over what you've done. You've not only been sleeping with another woman, but someone who everyone knows. Even my own mother. How do you think this makes me feel? I've got my pride, if that's all I've got, and I'm protecting that in the same way as I would protect my babies. Go and stay with your mum if Bridget is getting on your nerves.'

'Why would I want to do that when I've got the flat at Tower Hill that you seem to think is good enough for me? And Bridget's *not* getting on my nerves.'

'If you needed to get away from Bridget, is what I meant. You owe your mother a bit of time as it happens. You can take the twins to visit her whenever you want.'

Appearing not to have heard the suggestion, Frank sighed loudly and then said, 'So what's this little whisper I've heard about you and Trevor being all matey then?'

'Exactly that, Frank. So leave him alone and let him stay in the flat with his mum for a while and let's see how it all pans out. If it wasn't for his mother coming down to stay with him I think the poor sod might have topped himself. Bridget's a selfish, self-centred bitch for leaving him like that.' She adjusted the cushion under her head. 'I don't want to talk or think about any of it any more. I'll phone you.'

Waiting for him to start up again, Anna breathed a sigh of relief when, after a short spell of silence, she heard the front door open and close again. He had gone. 'Don't you dare let go, Anna,' she murmured as tears filled her eyes and her throat seemed to close up. 'Don't you dare let go.' She was determined not to let his intrusive arrival upset her because, as far as she could tell, the only reason he was behaving like this was because his precious Bridget wasn't the be-all and end-all as he had first thought. Well, that was his tough luck. If anyone was going to get her sympathy it was Trevor who, unlike Frank, didn't show any signs of self-pity whatsoever. He was gutted over Bridget behaving like a slag, but he had kept his feelings to himself. His wife had trampled all over him and the pain sometimes showed in his eyes – but that was all.

She and Trevor had something in common – their partners had shacked up together and they had both been humiliated. Somehow she felt responsible for the poor sod, and when she had mentioned this to Linda and Hazel, they had applauded her suggestion that Trevor move into the flat above the restaurant. Anna had already slipped in the side door of Prima on the quiet to see Rose. She was received with warmth and the two women had got on like a house on fire. She liked his mother a lot. And as for Frank, she knew that he would have to let things stand or else be seen in a very bad light by everyone if he turned Trevor and his mother out.

Closing her eyes again, content on her lounger with the comforting early summer sunshine on her face and a soft rug over her legs, Anna, within seconds of closing her eyes, was drifting off to the distant sound of the birds as a lovely familiar background. As far as she was concerned right then, even though her marriage was falling apart at the seams, the song of the birds would always be there, no matter where she lived. And if Frank thought that it was always going to be the East End of London he was mistaken. She was beginning to think that she might let her house to her eldest sister, Linda, who had now touched on the subject more than once; she was looking for a two-bedroom place like Anna's nearby so that she didn't have to live above the shop any more. The shop of course being the grand House of Assignation. So, not only did Anna have a ready-made tenant in the wings, but her home would be kept in the family and she would be able to come home and visit and stay whenever she chose to.

She had no real plans yet, of course, but she hadn't been able to get out of her mind the little commune in

Kent where huts had been turned into homes. She had loved the sense of the ex-Londoners living as if they were on a permanent holiday. Nor had she forgotten the quaint tea rooms where she had enjoyed watching people through the window – especially the happy young couple who were out for the afternoon with their baby.

She wondered what Frank's motives were. Had he expected her to fall into his arms? One thing was clear – he was not too surly over Trevor and his mother moving into the flat. Even though he didn't know what was going to happen next, he wasn't as angry as he should have been. The plan was for Rose to stay for two weeks or so to keep her son company, and Anna was more than happy with the arrangement of cash in hand of forty pounds a month to include electric, gas and water bills.

Holding the image of Trevor and his mother living in Frank's secret sex den, Anna drifted in and out of a light sleep with a smile on her face. She was turning the tables on the bastard and she was relishing it as she luxuriated in the peace and the sunshine. How long this mood would last was another matter, but she intended to make the most of it. She hadn't felt this light inside in a very long time – no longer the downtrodden victim, tossed aside like a bundle of old clothes for the ragman any more, and she so welcomed the new feeling.

She could imagine Rose and Trevor living in the flat and possibly making new friends. No one expected Trevor to be full of the joys of spring, but this opportunity to live in a much nicer home in a livelier area was his just reward.

Rose, having ignited the old spark of home decorating, had inspired Trevor to paint the walls of the spacious one-bedroom flat a brilliant white, and she had gone out straight away to purchase bright and cheerful readymade drapes in rust and red that she had seen in a shop window in the Stratford East market. And so, right at that moment, as Anna sunbathed in her back garden, mother and son were in the flat above Prima Pasta, having washed away any sign or smell of Bridget.

Later that evening, while watching a Harold Pinter 'Play For Today' on television, Anna smiled at the thought of the look on Frank's face at Prima, knowing that Trevor and his mum were settled above while he and Bridget were working below. She had to admit that there was possibly a little more than just kindness in her motives when she had come up with the idea — a touch of malice had its place in there too.

While she was enjoying the irony of it all the phone rang, interrupting her lovely mood. She couldn't believe that this was going to be Frank in a telephone booth shooting his mouth off again. It was in fact Trevor. He asked her if it would be all right for him and his mother to come around with a bottle of sparkling white wine as a thank-you gesture for letting him move into his new home. Naturally, she wanted the company and a bit of celebration, no matter what the given reason. She replaced the receiver and immediately went next door to Rachel to ask if she would like to pop in and join the small family in their little revelry.

Half an hour later, Anna was opening the door to Trevor and Rose, both in celebratory mood, as well as her lovely neighbour. She welcomed them in, and once in the sitting room Trevor took over. He insisted that the women sit down while he found everything he needed in Anna's kitchen – a corkscrew and four wine glasses, and little dishes for the crisps and peanuts that he had brought with him. And to help it all go with a bit of a swing, Anna put on one of her and Frank's latest long-playing records – Cat Stevens' 'Teaser and the Firecat'.

Chapter Ten

With Trevor and Rose settled in the flat, Anna was beginning to feel on top of things. Today, Rachel was baby-sitting the twins for a couple of hours and she was getting herself ready to hail a cab and pay a return visit to Rose. After that, she was going to a street close by to the restaurant, where she knew that her and Frank's car would be parked. She had broached the subject with Frank of them buying a smaller runaround car for her so that she could move about more freely with the twins and visit her family. She gave him what she considered to be sound reasons for needing it now that they were separated, but he had simply shrugged it off, saying that it was an unnecessary expense.

Anna wasn't sure whether he just wasn't prepared to pay for a second car from their joint account, or whether he simply didn't want her to be too free to come and go. Clearly, he intended to continue using their dark blue Volvo Estate himself. She knew he wasn't using it to travel to work from the Tower Hill flat because her sisters had told her that he was still taking black cabs – as he had always done so as to be able to drink while working. Knowing that it would be difficult for him to park long-term in the tourist area of Tower Hill, where he was working today, she felt sure that he must have left the Volvo in a back street close to Prima. She couldn't fathom what was behind his behaviour, other than his stubbornness in not letting go, and she wasn't prepared to ask him for a third time to return the car to where it was usually parked, in a turning near their house, so that she could use it.

So, with the lovely Rachel coming in, and with Jackie in the wings to help out should the need arise, Anna was all set. Jackie the entrepreneur was now working on a part-time basis as a copy typist in the city, and getting stuck in to her growing business of not only selling Avon products from home, but jewellery and fancy lingerie too.

George had told Anna that she could phone him if ever she needed a lift anywhere, but she was too independent for this. She knew he would understand because he had been brilliant about everything since the day she went to Prima to sort Bridget out. He had called round now and then, as well as phoning, to make sure she was all right. His support was a comfort to her, as was the fact that she had her babies and no one could take them away from her, and she was no longer crying herself to sleep at night.

On her way to Prima in the taxi, Anna was not only relishing the fact that she was about to hijack the car, but was also looking forward to seeing Trevor's mother – after she had enjoyed a cup of frothy coffee in the restaurant below. She couldn't wait to stroll into her restaurant to meet up with her sisters as arranged, and then click her fingers at Bridget for attention. She had phoned her sisters the previous day and told them her plan, and they were only too happy to come along and give her some moral support. She also knew that George would be there at this time of day.

Anna got out of the cab in warm sunshine and strolled towards the entrance of Prima Pasta. She couldn't have been more pleased to see her sisters with George at their usual long table by the window. Greeted by a song from Simon and Garfunkel playing on the jukebox, she looked at George, and from the way he looked back at her, it seemed that he was conveying a message through the lyrics that filled the space between them: 'If you need a friend I'm sailing right behind. Like a bridge over troubled water I will ease your mind.' This brought a lump to Anna's throat and tears to the back of her eyes and she wasn't sure why.

The blood rose to her cheeks when she caught sight of Bridget, who was leaning against the bar and sipping a glass of white wine while looking from George to Anna with one eyebrow raised and a sly smile. Her expression said it all. She would report this little intimate cameo to Frank when she got back to Tower Hill that night.

'Take the weight off of your feet, sweetheart,' said Linda with a welcoming smile. 'And once you've ordered something to eat you can tell us why you're looking a touch on the smug side.'

'I don't want anything to eat.'

'Are you sure? Because this pasta with mushrooms and fresh prawns is delicious.'

'I'm not hungry. And as for looking smug ... once I've been up to see Rose I'm going to search the little side turning for our car. And if it's not there I'm taking a cab to Tower Hill, where it might be. Once I find it, I'm driving it back home.'

There was a silence all round as the other three exchanged looks. This was the kind of thing that any one of them would have done themselves without batting an eyelid. But Anna? The most docile of Ivy's three daughters? It didn't sit right.

'You won't have to search far, babe,' said Hazel. 'It's been parked in the same place for days, halfway along the turning. And you'll know why if you think about it. Frank likes his daytime drink and I guess he's been sipping more wine than usual lately. I hate to think how much he's paying out in taxi fares with his toing and froing, but then that never did bother him in any case, did it?'

'He can do what he wants,' said Anna, 'so long as I've got my transport back. He's kept the car away from me deliberately to get his own back. He's still livid about Trevor moving into the flat.'

Linda chuckled. Whether she agreed with her sister or not didn't matter. She had a lovely determined expression on her face and that was what they had been waiting for. 'You're bang on right, sweetheart. Let the bastard stew in his own juice and good for you for waking up at last. It's about fucking time. Now then, wave Fanny La-La over for today's menu and get some food inside yer. George is entertaining us with more stories about the Krays.'

'As if you don't know already.' Anna was amused. 'And I told you, I'm not hungry.' She looked at George and said, 'Well, go on then, storyteller. I haven't seen you for days so now you can entertain me as well as my sisters.'

George looked away from her gaze and picked uncomfortably at his pasta. 'It's not that interesting, babe, I was just killing time that's all. I was just about to tell the girls about the Krays' first fight in the ring when they wore old worn-out boxing gloves. They gave such a good show by all accounts that their wages for a fight went up to seven and sixpence.'

'It's a pity they didn't stick to professional boxing then, isn't it. Then they wouldn't have had to face a murder charge, would they?'

'Maybe not. But the twins were known as tough gang leaders by the time they was sixteen, babe. They used knives, choppers, swords – you name it. There were a lot of rival fights in those early days.' Sighing as if he was bored with his own conversation, he leaned back in his chair and looked away. Just seeing Anna sitting there was pulling at his heartstrings. 'They were heroes to us younger lads, even though they were five-foot nothing.'

'It was the way they walked about as if they were kings of the patch that made others of their kind fear or respect them,' said Hazel. 'Reggie was the better boxer of the two, but they both fought at the Albert Hall at one time or another apparently.'

Anna received this information with a quizzical expression, then said, 'Changing the subject to something a bit nicer, I would love a frothy coffee.' She smiled, and winked at George who was looking at her again, and then clicked her fingers for attention. The look on Bridget's face was priceless. As much as she wanted to ignore the summons, even she knew that she had little choice other than to be at the beck and call of the customers. Very slowly, she slipped off the bar stool with anger blazing in the dark brown eyes that went so well with her bright ginger hair.

'She's gonna love the clicking of fingers, Anna,' said Hazel. 'Mind she doesn't accidentally spill hot coffee over you when it comes.'

'Don't bank on her coming over,' said Linda. 'She'll send one of the kitchen staff if necessary because there's no way she's gonna wait on *you*, sweetheart.'

Linda wasn't far off the mark, but even though Bridget was desperate to click her own fingers at one of the other waiters, they were all far too busy serving at their own tables. She had little choice but to stroll over in her high heels and take Anna's order. She looked at Anna with apathy bordering on insolence – and might have got away with this and managed to provoke an angry response – but her nose was still bruised and a bit swollen, and Anna could hardly stop herself from grinning as she ordered her frothy coffee with a small brandy on the side. Once Bridget had gone off to the back to place the order, George spoke.

'Come on, girls,' he said. 'Give her a break for Christ's sake.' He then gave Anna a meaningful look. 'She coped with having her nose put out of joint. Now lay off.'

'Well, you would side with her, George, wouldn't you.' Hazel smiled. 'She's done you a favour where our Anna's concerned. When's the next little trip down to Kent for the pair of you, then?'

George took a gulp of lager and said, 'It's the sign of ageing, Hazel – gossiping like old women.'

'As it happens,' said Anna, 'we had a lovely day out. I loved it down in Kent. And you'll never believe it, but there's a vacancy at a children's home close to Tonbridge for a secretary-cum-matron.' She looked at Linda and shrugged. 'Life in the country has to be better for the twins than life in the East End.'

This bit of news out of the blue went down like a damp squib and brought instant silence. 'And what about your little house?' said Linda, coldly. 'Frank will be in straight away with you know who. You're living in a dream world, Anna. Get real.'

'And how do you know all of this about this children's home?' said Hazel. She hated the idea of not only losing her sister to the sticks but her twin nephews too. 'Been down there again by yourself, have you?'

'Trevor picked up some leaflets from the library to do with schools all over England looking for resident sports teachers. And there it was, children's home and boarding school. The very one that we learned about on our day out, George. Remember?'

'No, I can't say that I do.'

'Trevor's gonna look into it for himself, and while he's at it he'll find out about the secretarial post for me.'

'Did you say it was close to Tonbridge, Anna? This school?' said George, still picking at his pasta even though he had lost his appetite.

'I did indeed, George. When Trev showed me the leaflet I could hardly believe it.' Anna suddenly seemed to be glowing. 'Ever since you took me down there I've not been able to get that bit of the countryside out of my mind. Then Trevor goes and picks up a leaflet about a boarding school-cum-children's home that are looking for staff no more than fifteen minutes away from where the converted huts are.'

A silence fell, and again the others looked sheepishly at each other, wondering what was going to come next. As it turned out, it was Bridget, with the coffee and brandy. Placing it in front of Anna, she stared at her and managed a condescending smile before she walked away, wiggling her arse more than usual.

'It's not as exciting as George's news,' said Linda, cutting through the silence while making a brave attempt to get her sister off the subject of the children's home and Trevor. She wasn't the only one at the table who was gutted to think that Anna would even consider the thought of moving out – never mind shacking up with Bridget's husband. Which is how all their minds were working.

Anna turned to George. 'What's your news then? Come on. Out with it. What's the secret you've deemed not to tell me?'

'I've handed in my notice at the Met, babe. That's all. No big deal.'

'And the rest,' said Linda. 'He'll soon be off to the South of Spain to live like a lord.'

'Give it a break, Linda,' said George, clearly uncomfortable with his life being discussed as if on the open market.

'You're going to live in Spain?' Anna could hardly believe it. 'How come you never told me? Is this why you've been keeping yourself out of the way? I've not heard a peep from you nor seen hide or hair of you for days.'

'I thought that Trevor and his mum were keeping you company, Anna. You've been busy helping them get the flat up there all nice and cosy. Anyway, Spain's out of the picture, but I am going to see someone about the Kent project.'

'Oh my God! Is that the time!' exclaimed Linda, giving Hazel a gentle slap on the shoulder. 'Come on you. We've got clients due in thirty-five minutes. You're gonna have to put your foot down and show what that red Jaguar can do when push comes to shove, babe.'

'Christ Almighty. Why couldn't you 'ave made the appointment an hour or so later?'

'Because when a judge who stands at the Old Bailey whistles his tune for a naughty dance, we jig to it.' Linda laughed. With that she brushed a kiss across Anna's face and told her to listen to what George had to say about the Kent project.

Once by themselves, Anna, a touch shy all of a sudden, glanced at George, the man who she used to blow kisses to when a young teenager, and smiled. 'I'm not sure what to ask about first. What a dark horse you are.'

George leaned back in his chair and studied her face. 'Ask me whatever you want, Anna,' he said, his voice a touch deadpan. 'I've got no secrets, darling.'

'Are you really gonna leave the force?' she said.

'I've handed in my notice so I suppose the answer to that is yes.'

'Right. So does this mean that you've managed to get a good price on the crumbling mansion in Kent?'

'It's not a mansion and it's not crumbling. And yes, in the end I did get it for a good price. After a lot of negotiating. I'll 'ave to borrow a few grand but it'll be worth it. The bank's gonna give me a loan and keep the deeds of the property as collateral and that's always a good sign.'

'But won't you miss all the excitement?'

'Of being a DI? Not really. It's time for me to go.'

'You might end up twiddling your thumbs.'

'Not me, sweetheart. I've seen too many men who've left the force to take early retirement turn into heavy drinkers or lazy bastards because they've got too much time on their hands. That's when friends fall away. And I don't want that. I don't want to turn into a man who drinks on the sly. You can spot them a mile off. Dark anger just beneath the surface and shifty glazed eyes with guilt written all over their puffy red faces. It's sad to see good people go down that road. A tragedy in fact.'

He raised his eyes and met hers and felt as if his heart was melting. Collecting himself, he got back on track. 'I will be taking a risk with the Kent property but I'm used to taking risks every week of the year in my job. I reckon I could sell it on after three or four years without touching or laying a penny out. But I don't want to do that. I want to work and make a profit at the same time as living out my dream. And I don't care who has a laugh on me if I come unstuck.

'I'll turn that place into a small hotel or upmarket holiday flats. There's a big change on the way, Anna, where the future new rich are concerned. It might take another ten years but at least by then I'll have my place up and running. And if those of us who've got a few bob saved up now don't get in quick and invest, we'll not only miss a golden opportunity, but we'll be out in the cold in a decade or so when it all starts happening. Land is still cheap in East London. In twenty years or so we'll be surrounded by sky-scraping tower offices for people to work in. Now, if I was to find one or two of the old-style hotels in Spain that are run-down and pick them up dirt cheap, I would convert those into holiday flats as well. And before you tell me that I'm running before I can walk, I know I am. But that's how I've been brought up to do things.'

'You'll never be a lazy bastard, George,' said Anna. 'You'll work things out to the nth degree and then go in as if you're a novice and a bit green. I've known you for a long time, don't forget.'

'Anyway ... enough about me. What about you and lover boy?'

'What lover boy? Trevor?'

'If the name fits ...' George shrugged.

'What makes you think he's my lover?' she teased.

'The gossips are not always wrong. And your mum told me that you've been seeing him.'

'She would – and you know why.'

'Do I? I'm not so sure. Anyway, from the look on your face sweetheart, you're happy. So let's leave it at that. He seems a nice chap.'

'Your wife seems a lovely woman.'

'Touché.'

'So she *is* back then?'

'Been and gone. It's over for us, Anna. I won't say it doesn't make me feel sad, it does. But it's all amicable.

She's going off to live on the Isle of Man with her new bloke. Good luck to 'er.'

'The Isle of Man? Isn't that where the rich go so as not to pay too much tax?'

'Exactly. I can't match the pocket of someone who can afford to live there. She's caught herself a millionaire. He's an ugly bastard but a lovely man according to my ex.' After a few seconds of silence George checked his watch as if he had somewhere to go.

'Don't let me keep you,' said Anna, half joking.

'Wouldn't dream of it, sweetheart, but I do have a little appointment to keep. I'm going round your mum's place.'

Taken aback for a second, Anna looked at him puzzled. 'Are you? What for?'

'I'm meeting Horace there to go over a few figures.'

Anna could hardly believe it. She knew who Horace was because Ivy had told her. And, of course, she had kind of hinted that they were in the early throes of courtship. But why would George be meeting up with him?

'I don't get it, George. Did you know Horace before Mum did, then?'

'No. I popped in to see Ivy the other afternoon and he was there with a mate of Gwen's from next door. There was a foursome – the girls were just going out with the boys, and they were about to show the old chap the real East End – especially the pie and mash shop in Bethnal Green.'

'Oh? I don't remember Mum mentioning that to me.'

'Why should she? What's up with you today, Anna? She's in her fifties, for Christ's sake. I think she knows what she's doing, and from what I could see of it the old boy is really taken with her. You haven't got a problem with it, have you?'

'Of course not.' She looked at him, all but staring him out before saying, 'I loved our day out in Kent and I would love to do it again sometime – when you're free that is.'

'When *I'm* free? You've been busy, sweetheart. Sorting out Trevor and his mum.'

'I have been a touch busy, it's true, but I've also been under stress.'

'Course you have. And as for Horace, I like him and I trust him. When he asked what I was in, I told him that I was just about to get out of the police service and then I bent his ear about my pet subject. His attention was grabbed straight away. In fact he was keyed up over it. Thought it was an excellent project. We got talking and he asked if I was looking for a silent partner.'

'And?' Anna was a touch bemused by all this.

'I told him he could be as noisy as he liked because he looked keen.'

'And?'

'I've never seen a more genuine smile in my life. He was so happy at the thought of it that a little tear trickled from the corner of his eye. I burst out laughing and offered my hand and he shook it passionately. He's all right, Anna. A good bloke. Posh but down to earth. The best of his type.'

'So . . . Mum's found a friend that might turn out to be your business partner? I've lost a husband. Trevor's got rid of his whoring wife. You're getting out of the force – and the world goes round and round.'

'And so does money, babe. And as for the Kent project, a bit of old money influencing the horoscope is no bad thing. Plus the old chap wants to do something interesting at sixty going on seventy. And if that's not a man after my own heart I don't know what is.'

Looking into George's handsome smiling face, it dawned on Anna that she had possibly hurt his feelings by not getting in touch enough. She now wondered if she had been too wrapped up in her own little world and her involvement with Trevor and his mother and the flat. Glancing at George's face, she felt as if she was about to lose a friend and this made her stomach churn. 'It seems that some grass has been growing under my feet with all of this going on. I'm sorry, George, I—'

'Don't worry about it, babe. We know each other too well for that.' He stood up, straightening his shoulders, and took a deep breath. 'I'll see you around. You take care of yourself.'

Anna looked up at the tall and handsome sod and said, 'If you walk out of here and leave me feeling like this, George, I don't ever want to see you again.'

'Feeling like what, Anna?' He was getting impatient with her.

'I don't *know*!' She then lowered her voice to a whisper. 'Sit down, for Christ's sake.'

'What for? You're going up to see Trevor's mum, to have a cup of coffee with her until he gets in, and then I suppose you'll come back down here for a candlelit dinner.'

'George, please . . . sit down.' She was close to tears.

'No. I don't think I want to hear what you feel you've got to tell me. Do what you want, Anna, but don't forget that you're on the rebound from Frank. Stay lucky.' He then walked firmly out of Prima Pasta without paying his bill. He hadn't done this intentionally but once outside, when it dawned on him, he smiled to himself and quietly said, 'Fuck you and thank you, Frank. It was a good pasta. Eat your heart out.'

But Anna wasn't going to leave it at that. She was up from the table and outside in a flash, ready to run after him if necessary. She called out to him in a tone of voice that ordered rather than asked him to stop, and her shrill voice was enough to affect even the most hardened plainclothes police officer. But he shrugged it off. 'George! Don't you dare ignore me! Don't you dare walk away from me!' she screamed. 'Wait!' He didn't look back and nor did he show a peacemaking hand.

Standing there as if she were frozen, there was nothing that Anna could do to stop those tears rolling from her eyes and down her cheeks, to then trickle the length of her neck. 'What is it with me?' she asked herself. 'What am I doing wrong?'

It was then that she realised just how much George meant to her. She didn't want him to walk out of her life the way Frank had. She didn't want to wake up in the mornings without his image ever coming into her thoughts – his smiling face and his affectionate wink. She went back inside the restaurant to collect her handbag and saw Bridget leaning against the bar with her arms folded, smirking. She had seen and probably heard it all, and it took every bit of Anna's strength not to rise to the bait and go over and punch her in the face, as she'd wanted to do in the first place when George had stopped her.

Staring back at the girl who had turned her world upside down, she restrained herself from giving Bridget something further to gloat over. Instead, she put on a patronising smile and slowly shook her head, as if she were looking at someone who seriously needed to see a shrink. She then walked out of Prima with her head held high and went up to see Trevor's mother – before going to take from Frank something that she felt sure he treasured more than the silly cow at the bar. His precious car!

Once in her old flat and in the company of Trevor's mother, Anna began to relax again. Knowing this woman the way that she now did, she knew that she would ignore the fact that Anna had shed a few tears and no doubt smudged her mascara.

'The kettle's just boiled, love. Tea or coffee?' Rose asked.

'Coffee please.' Anna smiled warmly at her and then dropped into one of the comfortable arm chairs in the light, bright sitting room. 'I don't know about you, but I'll never fathom men.'

'More importantly, Anna, they'll never fathom us. Bear that in mind and you won't feel quite so bad when you've upset one of them for one reason or another.'

To Anna, Rose seemed as if she had been born to comfort people. 'You and Arthur seemed so easy and happy when I saw you together,' she said. 'Is it an art or does it come naturally?'

'It takes time, Anna. Years. But then, as we know,

not all marriages are made in heaven and those that are don't always stay there, love.'

'Trevor and Bridget's didn't and neither did mine and Frank's. Thanks to Bridget.'

'It takes two to tango, sweetheart. Sugar and milk?'

'One sugar and a little milk. Thanks.' Anna went quiet, because even though she knew that Rose was right and that Frank was just as much to blame, at least he hadn't slept or flirted with women before Bridget came along – as far as she knew. 'The thing is, though, Rose,' she said, a touch wary. 'This isn't the first time that Bridget's all but destroyed a marriage, is it?'

'Ah. So you've found out about the other two men in her life.'

'Trevor told me. At least you can rest assured that he won't ever take her back. You've got a really good son there, you know. I wish I had met him before I had met Frank.'

'Oh?' said Rose, placing the small tray with their hot drinks on the coffee table. She sat down in the other armchair. 'And what makes you say that? You've not fallen for him, have you?'

'It would be hard not to love someone like Trevor. I don't mean in a wild romantic way. He's such a lovely guy. A best mate type that you know you could rely on.'

'Exactly. So what about Frank? Do you think he'll stay with Bridget for long? Or is this just a fling he's having? A fling that's destroyed a marriage.' The tone in Rose's voice had changed from friendly to accusing.

'I don't know. I don't think he so much as looked at another woman before she came along. But then she was a practised man stealer by then from the sound of it, and a clever flirt too – with a smile that's full of promises. Never mind the way she sits, long flowing cheesecloth skirt or not. She might just as well have put a sign up saying, Welcome to the Inn.'

'Really? From what I've heard Frank was all over her from the beginning. But like I said, it takes two to tango.' She glanced covertly at Anna and then said, 'Will you take him back?'

'No. I don't think so. I might have, for the sake of the twins, but I don't think I like him any more. He's changed. I think I still love him though. But hopefully this will wear off as the memories of good times fade into history.'

Rose shook her head thoughtfully. 'That makes me feel better, but I don't know why.' She smiled and shrugged. 'I suppose I was hoping that you and my Trevor might fall in love.'

Taken aback by this confession, Anna let her guard down. For some silly reason she thought that she had been under attack. 'Oh Rose, that's a lovely thing to say. But even if we did feel that we were right for each other, he would be taking on twin babies. Frank's sons.'

'True. I suppose it was just a silly fancy of mine, love, that's all.' She shrugged and gently laughed it off. 'I was being a bit selfish. I'd love you for a daughter-in-law and, if truth be told, I suppose I was kind of trying to engineer things this way. I think that Trevor is going to apply for the position in that children's home you know.'

'Well, if he does, Rose, I might well apply for the position of secretary and matron. So we'll be living under the same roof for a while if we are both accepted. My sister and her chap would rent my house while I gave it a try.'

'I would love it if you did, Anna. Trevor is wonderful with disabled children as well as those with no problems. I've seen him working with them in the local swimming baths. He's got medals for coaching you know.'

'I know he has and I'm sure he deserves them. So who knows? Maybe we *will* be living under the same roof. We'll just have to see how things pan out won't we?' For some reason it was George who came into Anna's mind as they laughingly clinked their coffee cups in a kind of a toast to the future.

'I'll live in hopes, Anna. I'll live in hopes. You're a lovely girl.'

'Thank you, Rose. And you're the best mother that Trevor could have asked for. One day he'll have a family of his own. There's more than one lovely single girl out there that would melt under his gaze. He's tall, broad and handsome, don't forget. Never mind that he's a swimming coach with medals under his belt.'

'We'll see,' said Rose. 'The wind will blow the way it wants to and sow the seeds near, or far and wide. Love for my son might be in the heart of the Kent countryside or right on his own doorstep. Who knows?'

'Nobody. And that's about it really. None of us know, but right now I'm about to go and get in our car and drive it home, come what may.'

'Come what may? Why do you say that, Anna?'

'I'll be doing it behind Frank's back. I want the car. He took it. Now I'm taking it back.'

'Rather you than me,' said Rose. 'Rather you than me.'

Chapter Eleven

As Trevor pulled away from the house Anna glanced sideways at her and Frank's car parked on the opposite side of the road and smiled inwardly. She brought to mind the evening when Frank had phoned to ask if she had dared to take it from where it had been parked up, close to Prima. She had so loved that moment. Immediately her ex had discovered it gone he had put two and two together because he had been told that she had been into the restaurant that day and in a fairly buoyant mood. The best of it, as far as Anna was concerned, was that he hadn't been able to vent his anger openly because even he knew that nobody in their right mind would question the fact that his young wife, the mother of twins, had to have a vehicle so as to get from one place to another.

A fortnight seemed to fly by in Anna's busy day-to-day life as a mother of twins. With the car at her disposal she felt as if she had been liberated again and it felt good – not only that, but it meant that she could go to and from her sisters' place as well as taking the twins to see their grandma. She still hadn't plucked up whatever it needed to go and see Frank's mum. Deep down she didn't want the gentle woman to be dragged into the dirty mess of it all. In an attempt to get some kind of a routine back into her life without a husband there for her, she found an inner strength that she hadn't realised she possessed.

And now, with her babies in Rachel's good hands, she was sitting next to Trevor in his car on a Friday afternoon while hers was parked near her house. They were on their way to the children's home in the heart of the Kent countryside and just a few miles from the small and lovely town of Tonbridge. Anna had purposely timed the day of the interview to coincide with George and Horace's visit to the farmhouse some fifteen minutes drive away from where they were heading. After some discussion, Anna and Trevor had agreed that they really had nothing to lose by applying for the posts, and each had written off to Wymark Hall, mentioning that they knew each other – even though it might have sounded too chummy for comfort. But this didn't seem to have mattered and, as luck would have it, the interviews for both situations were being conducted over two days and it proved easy to arrange things so as to be there at the same time.

With Trevor driving and Anna map reading, they found the boarding school for waifs and strays quite easily and when they arrived at the entrance into the long, wide and curving driveway they were more than impressed by it all. A touch blown away in fact. They reached the grand and beautiful mansion house, which was tucked away and set within glorious gardens, and had to admit that neither of them had expected to find such a magnificent old building or the beautiful sloping grounds, which were almost enclosed by various types of tall trees.

'You *are* sure that we're in the right place, Anna?'

asked Trevor, a little uneasy at these plush surroundings.

'You saw the sign at the entrance gates, Trevor. Wymark Hall.'

He broke into a lovely smile. 'But it's not what I expected. I think I could live here, Anna.'

'You and me both,' she said. 'You, me and probably hundreds of other people. I wonder how many interviews have been held already. I don't think we should get our hopes up.'

'I can't keep them down.' Trevor drove slowly towards the black and white sign which pointed to the parking area. He turned at a wide bend to the rear of the building and was delighted by the sight of boys and girls, in their red and white lightweight summer uniforms, playing on a grassy slope that was interspersed with lovely flower beds filled with different kinds of roses in bloom.

'This looks more like a private boarding school for privileged children, not a home for orphans. We *can't* be in the right place ... can we?' said Anna in disbelief. 'But wouldn't it just be fantastic if we were. If we are looking at orphans ...'

'We are, Anna. Have a bit more faith. There are some people around who've got money and do good things with it.'

'We'll see,' said Anna. 'We'll see. But don't hold your breath.'

No sooner had they parked and got out of the car than two thin little girls, aged about eight or nine, their arms linked, came up to them and showed lovely smiles. One girl had white-blonde hair cut in a bob and the other long, dark brown plaits. Both had rosy cheeks and wore white socks and black plimsolls with their red and white checked cotton frocks. They spoke almost in unison as they said, 'Hello – we're pleased to meet you.'

Laughing appreciatively, Anna said, 'How long did it take you to practise that?'

The girls looked at her for a moment before saying, 'Would you like us to show you around?'

'I'd love it,' said Anna, 'but we have an appointment and we're only just on time.'

'Oh well, thath's all right,' said the blonde girl with a lisp. 'We're allowed to show people to the thecretary'th offith. Come on. It'th thith way.' The girls then did an about turn and walked in step as if they were keeping time.

Anna glanced at Trevor who, like her, was doing his utmost not to laugh. The girls led them through to the gracious entrance hall with polished wooden floors, and an ornate marble fireplace filled with an arrangement of lovely dried flowers. Next to this was an oak door with a black and white sign that said Secretary. One of the little girls knocked on the door and opened it to announce that two visitors had arrived. She then waved Anna and Trevor inside and closed the door after them.

The woman who was clearly in charge of conducting the interviews wore a black and white dogtooth jacket and skirt and a pretty red blouse. As she rose from her seat behind the polished mahogany desk, her rather serious face broke into a warm smile. She held out her hand to Anna, and said, 'Hello. I'm Mrs Page. How do you do.' She then shook Trevor's hand, invited them to sit down, and immediately reeled off what the work involved with no hint of a question as to why the couple had chosen to come together for the interview. When she had finished giving what she obviously felt was a true and honest picture of the hard work and long hours required by both jobs, the woman waited for their reaction. It was Anna who spoke first, asking if she thought that it was feasible for her to carry on the duties involved as matron and secretary even though she had her twins to take care of. Mrs Page smiled at her and nodded.

'I can assure you that you will have many volunteers who will want to wheel your babies around or keep them amused one way or another. Even though we keep strict rules when in the classroom, once outside it, our boys and girls are encouraged to treat this place as if it were home, and I am very happy to be able to say that, believe it or not, they have little trouble in doing so. Grand houses and grounds or not, this place means the same to those from poor backgrounds as it would to those who are, shall we say, more used to grandeur?

'Our children, when they first arrive here, might be a little intimidated at first, but give them an hour or so and they are outside exploring the grounds with those who know all the secret hideaway places. And the swings of course. No matter the colour, creed or age, most of our children settle in very quickly.'

She looked from Anna to Trevor. 'You seem a little taken aback, Mr Plumb. Are we not quite as you expected here at Wymark Hall?'

'You're everything I could possibly have hoped you would be – but I hadn't held my hopes too high. I thought I was going to find shy and sad unwanted children who looked as though they felt they had been dumped.'

'And this disappoints you?' asked the woman.

'No, of course it doesn't disappoint me,' said Trevor, a touch offended. 'I'm not on a mission to save the destitute. I'm here to see if I would fit in as a swimming coach and sports teacher. I would very much like to work with under privileged children but, equally, if this were somewhere for the more fortunate, providing it had the ambience that this place does, I still wouldn't be disappointed.'

'That's a good answer and one I would have hoped to hear. And what about you, Mrs Watson? What are your thoughts on what you have seen so far?'

Anna looked thoughtfully at her and then said, 'I'm impressed – and I'm a little bit overwhelmed if you want the honest answer. The grounds are beautiful and I didn't expect this. The children that we've seen so far, and especially the little girls who showed us the way, seem very much at ease. Very much at home in fact.'

'And this is exactly what we aim for.' She looked from Anna to Trevor and then leaned back in her chair. 'May I presume that you have come on this trip together because you are a couple?'

'No. We're friends,' answered Anna. 'Good friends. But we're certainly not a couple and we would certainly need separate living quarters. It's just coincidence that we've both arrived at a time when we want to work with children. And for my part I know I would fit in here because, from what I pick up, the children that we've seen so far look relaxed and happy and that's the kind of environment I would like my twins to grow up in. There seems to be a lovely atmosphere here.'

'You're right, there is. Our policy is to adhere to the wishes of the founder of this institution who donated this building and the grounds to the poor children of London. We do put character before anything else when inviting people to work with us because, after all, the children who come here have very sad backgrounds, as a rule. They have been either abandoned or beaten or, in some cases, not fed properly and some, although not many, thankfully, have been used as house slaves of one kind or another. Our Victorian benefactor wanted this building to house suffering young souls who could be offered the same opportunities and education as those who have been brought up with a loving family, rich or poor.'

Mrs Page looked from one to the other and smiled. 'If only there were more such gentlemen prepared to give up second homes to neglected children rather than leave everything to their own families, it would be a far better world that we live in – don't you think?'

'Of course it would be,' said Anna. 'I don't know anybody who would argue with that.'

Mrs Page proceeded to ask questions of each of them as to their previous occupations and, where Trevor was concerned, his present work as a sports coach, and before they knew it an hour had flown by. They were then given a lightning tour of the school, the dormitories, and the sickroom and, of course, the enclosed swimming pool and PE hall. After shaking hands and saying their goodbyes Anna, from the expression on the woman's face, felt sure that each of them had come up to expectations.

Once on their way back to the parking area, she was touched by the way the same two girls who had escorted them to the secretary's office were waiting to escort them back to Trevor's car. It was obvious that these two skinny waifs who, she had learned from Mrs Page, had no family coming to visit them at any time, were eager for both Anna and Trevor to return. The shyer of the two, without the lisp, having said goodbye through the open window of the car, quickly added, 'I hope you come and work here. It's really nice and I think you'll like it.'

'We'll just have to wait and see how it pans out.' Anna smiled. 'We may not have passed the interview.' She then looked about herself and lowered her voice to a whisper. 'Have many people been and gone for the position of swimming and PE coach?'

'Yes. Quite a few.'

'And for the job as secretary and matron?'

'No. Not many for that one. A couple of older ladies, that's all.'

'Well, thank you for letting me in on that,' said Anna. 'I won't say you told me. It's our secret.'

'Do you want to come and live here then?' said the girl with the lisp, all hopeful.

'Oh, I shall have to have a good long think about it. I've got twin babies you see and—'

Before she could say any more the girls squealed with delight. 'We could wheel them about in prams!'

Gently, Anna said again, 'We'll just have to wait and see. My mind's not made up yet.' She then climbed into the front seat of the car and waved through the window as Trevor drove slowly through the tree-lined grounds along the wide drive.

'That was a bit mind blowing wasn't it, Anna?' was all he managed to say.

'You're not kidding,' she said. 'I kept feeling on the brink of tears and I'm not really that sure why. I think there are a lot of people out there who would be willing to visit those kids and be adopted parents from afar. I learned from my days of trying to get pregnant, that there are hundreds of couples who, for one reason or another can't have children, and who would love to foster a child.'

'I'm sure,' said Trevor, 'I'm sure there must be.'

Both of them were silent as they rode out of the wide entrance of the majestic grounds and continued on through the winding lanes of Kent, heading for the little commune of Londoners who lived in the huts by the river. Anna wanted to show Trevor another side of life that seemed a million miles away from the East End. She also wanted to look at the property that George was in the process of purchasing.

Of course, George would be there with Ivy's new friend, Horace. Horace the backer, who would be part-owner of the property and who, according to what Ivy had told her, was keen to move out of London himself. It seemed to Anna that fate was playing a very interesting, even bizarre, hand. If she were to be offered the post and accepted it, she could easily end up living just ten or so miles from where George might begin a new life, once he got his dream low-cost holiday hotel up and running.

'I wonder how this is all going to pan out,' she murmured, deep in her own thoughts.

'I'm not with you,' said Trevor. 'Pan out?'

'Will one of us be offered a job and not the other? And if this is the case – should we make a pact now as to what we'll do if this does happen?'

'Of course not. I don't see it as a problem whether both or one of us are accepted. I would be disappointed if I wasn't, but I wouldn't want to stand in your way if you were to be invited back and not me. I think it would be great for you and the twins to live in this environment. Who could wish for a better setting? And if it did turn out that it's just one of us they take on – and if it were me – you could visit at weekends every so often. The cottage that comes with the position is tiny but there are two bedrooms from what I remember of the details. And if this were to be the case, you could leave your car parked at the boarding school and I could drive us out for a Sunday lunch or afternoon tea in Tonbridge. Us and the twins.'

Anna smiled. 'That's a good second option to pave the way for disappointment. I know that you would really love to work there, Trevor, whereas with me . . . well, it's a lovely idea, but that's all at this stage. It's a bit like a fairy story to be honest and I have to keep my feet firmly on the ground.'

'I *would* love to work there myself. You're right. Let's wait and see whether it is an option or not.'

'Absolutely. But I do want you to know that I won't be put out if you are recalled and I'm not. I've got baggage as far as the authorities are concerned, don't forget – and you haven't. You're more or less single and with no ties. Whereas I've got the twins.'

'And a husband who might want you back.'

'Well, he'll be whistling down the wind. It would take a long time for me to be able to trust him again after what he's done.'

Trevor nodded thoughtfully but gave little away. In truth, he desperately wanted this appointment more than anything else in the world and, if he was honest with himself, now that he had seen and listened to the woman who had given a picture of something that dreams were made of, he was ready to give up everything.

Once they reached the little oasis of Hunston, Anna had to rely on memory to direct Trevor along the narrow winding lanes that led to the commune. 'We'll know when we're close to the place, because we'll see smoke rising into the sky from the chimney of the old cookhouse on the common,' she said.

'You are kidding me.' Trevor smiled. 'You told me that the huts had been converted and that they had been fitted out with kitchens.'

'They have been, but they often use the cookhouse when the weather's fine. I told you – it's like up-market camping and they love living this way. It's their bit of paradise and long may it last. George reckons that they grow marijuana in their herb garden. Purely for medicinal purposes of course.'

Trevor slowly shook his head. 'I think he might have been having you on, Anna.'

'No, he wasn't. And why wouldn't they grow it? As I

286

told George at the time, my gran always used to have a plant on the go in her back yard for medicinal purposes. She was given seedlings as a gift by an old-fashioned herbalist who used to live in Wapping before she passed away, aged ninety-eight.'

Peering into the distance while driving and not really taking notice of what Anna was saying, Trevor murmured to himself. 'I can't see any smoke but I can see the sun glinting on some long black corrugated tin rooftops.'

'That'll be it then. We're here. Drive slowly in case any of the old boys are pedalling their ancient bicycles.'

'It's a bit out in the sticks for pensioners isn't it? How on earth do they manage?'

'Well, it's hardly in the outback and there's all the amenities just a car ride away. Wait 'til you see them and then you'll know. They've adapted to the life like ducks to water. They've knocked two huts into one along each block and turned them into little country cottages. You can pull up and park under that big oak tree.'

Sinking into a mood of regret at not having headed directly for London after the interview, Trevor parked and looked ahead at the commune. 'Are you sure that they don't just use the places as holiday homes, Anna? I can't believe they live here season in, season out.'

'Of course they live here. Come on. You'll understand once we're there in that little oasis.' She got out of the car and waited for Trevor to lock the door while she, just like George had done, peered under her hand at the huts and the surrounding fields where masses of wild flowers were now opening. Beyond, in the distance, she could see the river twinkling under the sunshine.

'Come on.' Anna turned to Trevor and smiled at his mystified expression. She couldn't know, of course, that he was at a complete loss as to why Anna and George had been so taken with this place. To him this was just a bunch of people – the older generation – staying on a camping site.

'Are you sure we won't be intruding, Anna, if we go trampling on their privacy?'

'No, of course not, Trevor,' she said. 'It'll be fine. Come on. They'll have seen us by now and will be wanting to know who's arrived.' She gave him a fond nudge with her elbow. 'Come and have a glimpse into what you could be living like once you're a pensioner.'

'I'm not sure that I really want to, Anna – to be honest. I've got the picture from all you've told me and from what I can see. It reminds me of a camping site in the South of France that Bridget and I once drove to for a week's holiday. It was good, but not exactly incredible. And I don't think that I would have liked to have people coming and going and watching us as if we were prehistoric.' He glanced at his watch as if he had somewhere more interesting to go.

'I never saw it like that, Trevor, but I suppose you're right. They don't want us gaping at them.' Disappointed that she wasn't going to enjoy a chat and a cup of tea with the lovely old folk, she shrugged it off and suggested that they move on to the next port of call and look for the farmhouse that George and Horace would be exploring. She couldn't help wondering what the thatched cottage on-site that George said he might move into was like.

'To be honest with you, Anna,' said Trevor, with a faraway look in his eyes, 'I would rather go to a pub on the way home for a pint and a sandwich and chat quietly about the children's home and my future there. Whether you think it would be a good move for me when it really comes down to it. Would I miss London too much for instance?'

This second change of plan was worse than the first. 'You mean that we're not going to try and find the old mansion?'

'Mansion? From what you've told me it's an old farmhouse, Anna, very large and very dilapidated.'

'Well, whatever it is, I really did want to see it. It means a lot to George and to Mum's friend, Horace. George worked really hard to finalise the deal for something they have great plans for. And I know it's not far from here, Trev. I think it's only about ten minutes away from what I remember George saying. We could ask someone. I've got the address in my handbag. And we needn't stop long, just have a lightning tour.'

'But then we'll be shown around, Anna, and by the sound of it both men will want us to see every inch of the place which to them is exciting, of course it is – but to us?'

'Well ... Horace is Mum's friend, so it is important to me. She could even end up living and working there once they've got it up and running.'

Trevor checked his wrist watch and sighed. 'Well, I don't know about you, but I could really kill a pint and a sandwich. Why don't we head for a pub en route home and maybe come down another day as a treat?'

'Okay,' said Anna reluctantly, her desire for excitement now waning in the face of Trevor's lack of enthusiasm. 'Let's go.' She managed a weak smile and followed him to the car. Once they were slowly pulling away she said, 'George was over the moon when he found the place where he used to go hop-picking as a kid. To find that it was being used again, that is. And used in such a terrific way.'

'Nostalgia.' Trevor smiled. 'A trip down memory lane which is great until all the leaves come off the trees in winter. Then it would all look a touch bleak. I'm sorry to be realistic, but facts are facts, Anna.'

'But winter doesn't last for ever. Think of all the blossom in spring and then the fruits in late August and September. Apples, plums and damsons. You can't beat an apple straight off the tree.'

'I think you can. I tried one once and it put my teeth on edge.' He shuddered at the thought of it as he drove along the gravel lane, homeward bound. 'Now, raspberries and strawberries freshly picked is another thing altogether. If you like I'll take you soft-fruit picking. That's a lot of fun. Last year, on a trip back to the Midlands to see Mum and Dad I must have picked about five pounds of raspberries for the freezer. I spent a whole day out there in the sunshine picking. It was wonderful.'

'Mmm ... Perhaps I'll have a try at that one of these days. It sounds really healthy – being out in the fresh air like that and for all those hours.' She said this simply because she couldn't find anything to talk to Trevor about. Not that it mattered too much because he had been more than content to drive in silence for most of the time on the way down. Other than *The Archers*, which he told her he never missed, the radio was switched off. There were no songs from the hit parade belting out and no half-hour comedies to smile at.

She recalled her day out with George, when they had walked along the dirt and gravel track towards the huts, holding hands – two good friends on an outing. He had been enjoying a bit of nostalgia and she had been taking pleasure in having a day off from motherhood and the role of a housewife.

'I'm surprised that George can afford to buy such a large property. If it is as good as it's been made out to be,' said Trevor, as he softly filled the quiet space. 'I know it will need a lot of work to bring it to what he wants it to be, and where will all the funds come from? He can't earn that much as a policeman and he's too young to collect a pension – I would have thought.'

'He's a detective inspector, Trevor,' said Anna. 'I daresay he's got some savings.' Of course, she well knew that he was a bit of a bent copper, but from what she had heard so were others who worked in and around London. It was perks that made up for the long hours and low pay is how most people saw it. It was also exciting, and a little bit of that did nobody harm in the general run of humdrum life. 'I think that George might dabble in a little bit of business that's not strictly above board when working with his cousins.'

'I might have guessed,' said Trevor, slowly shaking his head.

'He risks his life keeping the drug dealers out of the

East End. He's not only hated by the dealers but feared by notorious villains.'

'A bit of a gangster movie star then?' Trevor laughed.

'And he's loved by the old people he keeps an eye on. I've seen for myself how kind he is to them.' She brought to mind the comical sight of George with the lovely old boy who had shown them around the site when they had been there, the one who had reminded her of *The Beverly Hillbillies* on the telly.

The space in the car went quiet again and Anna didn't mind one bit. She was thinking about the place that she had arrived at and then left without saying hello or goodbye to the affectionate people. The old folk had, without doubt, in their own special way created their own tiny village. 'You've got to take your hat off to the people living in the huts though, Trevor, surely. I mean to say, they even turned two of them into a laundry room using six second-hand washing machines that the resident plumber repaired and fitted. And they've got two old tumble dryers donated by a launderette somewhere in South London.'

'Of course I take my hat off to them. It's just that I don't see it through the same eyes as you do. It's a campsite and no more than that.'

'Well, I think that it's romantic. The last of the Romany gypsies in their painted horse-drawn wagons still turn up for the potato and fruit-picking seasons, and they still dress in their traditional clothes from what we were told.'

'Of course they would do. Those that turn up every now and then in the Midlands paint a lovely picture as well, but they also leave an ugly one behind – old rubbish of all sorts. They're a bloody nuisance. Not all of them clear up after themselves.'

'Well, maybe the ones you're referring to are a different kind of travellers and not the Romanies, who always clear up after themselves.'

'Gypsies are gypsies, Anna.' He smiled.

'I suppose so,' said Anna, ending it there. All that she wanted now was to get back home after being more than disappointed at not having another look at the huts or taking the ten-minute drive to see George and Horace in their exciting new world. She wasn't quite sure what excuse she was going to make to them for not turning up. She could hardly say that Trevor couldn't be bothered and that the high point of this trip for him once they had been to the children's home was to go to a pub for a pint and a sandwich. She couldn't help but compare it to when she had been there with George, before he had dropped her off at the lovely tea rooms in Tonbridge while he went to do a bit of business. She had loved everything about that day. She could have stayed for ever with the hotchpotch of old-time Londoners who loved their new life, not to mention her time in the olde-worlde tea rooms.

'A penny for your thoughts,' said Trevor as he glided along the wider road to pick up a bit of speed and get them back into suburbia and a pub for a bite to eat.

'I was thinking about the cottage that was mentioned. I should have asked if I could see it really . . . but then again, if that woman thought that I was what she was looking for, she would have offered to show it to me, wouldn't she?'

'No, I don't think so. The interview was the first

step, Anna. You've got to think about whether it would suit you.'

'I know. I need time to think about it. About everything really. It all sounds idyllic but would I want to move away from my friends and my family? It's not as if I'm unhappy where I am.'

'You need time, that's all. Time to adjust to the fact that you're no longer living with your husband. You're probably still in shock.'

'Do you think so? And what about you, Trev, are you still in shock?'

'No. Don't forget that Frank's not the first. Deep down I think I knew it was only a matter of time before she would leave for good. I just wish I had been the one to make the move, that I had thrown her out before she chose to go of her own accord.'

Anna slowly shook her head and sighed. 'If someone had told me a year ago that this was all going to be happening to me I would have laughed in their face. I suppose this is what people refer to as the twists and turns of life.'

'I think so. And there's nothing we can do to stop what is coming because we have no idea what the next day will bring. For all we know, right now we could be lying in a mortuary tomorrow having been killed in a car crash – in this very car.'

'Well, that helps,' said Anna in a wry tone. 'A right bundle of laughs you are today, Trevor, I must say.'

'I'm being realistic. And my feet are firmly on the ground. I'm not one for dreams and never have been. All I hope now is that I will get that position at the children's home. I really want it, Anna. It's as if it's already written in my stars, but I can't begin to make plans in my head in case something else happens to stop what might be on the cards right now.'

Anna slowly nodded. He was right. Life did seem to be a lottery – just like her old neighbour had told her more than once. Not in her wildest dreams would she have imagined that she would be sitting next to Bridget's husband having this conversation – never mind that she and Frank would split up. Even so, she couldn't be too down about things; at least she had learned a lot in a short space of time rather than being cheated on and kept in the dark. She had also seen how the children she had met today, who had mostly been born on the poverty line, were now living in a beautiful mansion house, albeit an orphanage, that they could call home. Really and truly, she had seen enough for one day now that she thought about it. More than enough.

'I don't want to be a killjoy, Trevor,' she murmured, 'but do you think we could go straight home without stopping off at a pub? I've got a headache.' This was a white lie but she couldn't help it. She just didn't want to sit in a pub, surrounded by strangers and with little or nothing to say to Trevor, who was totally preoccupied with whether he would be accepted as swimming instructor and PE coach or not.

'You're not being a killjoy,' said Trevor. 'Don't worry about it. We've had a lovely day out.'

'Yes, we have,' said Anna, relieved that they were heading straight for home. London was where she belonged. London was where she had been born and bred. She did admire the old folk who had opted out in Kent, but she would always want to be able to hear the sound of the hooter from the local beer-bottling factory in the late afternoons telling the workers it was time for them to clock off.

She loved the quiet back street that she lived in and she loved her neighbour Rachel, the woman who had come through two world wars and still had no chip on her shoulder. The woman who was playing grandma to her twin babies. The only thing that was niggling at the back of her mind now was that Ivy might be tempted to move out of London if the romance between her and Horace strengthened. Life wouldn't be the same without her mother there for her and the twins. She checked her wristwatch and then asked Trevor to drop her off at Ivy's flat.

Chapter Twelve

'Oh ... look what the wind's blown in,' said Ivy when she saw her daughter standing on the doorstep. She then looked over Anna's shoulder at the car and the man at the steering wheel. 'He can come in for a cup of tea, you know, Anna. He might not be one of us exactly but that don't mean I can't get to know 'im.'

'He doesn't want to come in, Mum.' She turned to Trevor, smiled and raised a hand, and he waved back at her before pulling away.

'What is he then? Just a friend who don't mind chauffeuring you around or is he a man with a guilty conscience? I hope the fresh air didn't get to the pair of you. It's too soon, Anna. It could be out of the frying pan and into the fire, sweetheart.'

Anna followed Ivy into the kitchen and flopped down onto a chair. 'He gave me a lift to a children's home in Kent, that's all. I was considering Linda's offer. Of renting my house while I languished in the Kent countryside for a while. But I've changed my mind. I would miss you lot too much. You, our friends and my sisters.'

'I could have told you that. Frank's been on the phone by the way.' Ivy filled the kettle. 'He wondered if you were here. Then, when I told 'im you weren't, he asked if I was looking after his twins again.'

'Oh Christ! What did you tell him? I hope you didn't mention Rachel, did you? He'll use that against me if you did.'

'I said that Jackie was baby-sitting them – which she is – with Rachel keeping an ear should she be needed. He's still livid over you taking the car back.'

'Oh really? Good.' The room went quiet as daughter and mother looked at each other. Anna could see that Ivy was worried that she might be pushing Frank just a little bit too hard. She kept her thoughts to herself though.

'He asked if you'd gone to the woods with George or with Trevor. I said you'd gone for a ride out to the countryside with Trevor and that George was with my boyfriend, looking at a property investment in Kent.'

'And what did he have to say to that?'

'He burst out laughing and then said he had to go because one of the two of you had to look after the welfare of the twins. He said he was going in to Jackie's house to see that she was coping all right. Then he put the phone down.'

'Really? So what was he laughing at? Or was it a sarcastic chuckle?'

'I've no idea. He's acting selfish, I think. Doesn't want to think of you having a lovely time, never mind what he's been up to. He phoned ten minutes later to ask if my boyfriend was a gangster – just like George. I said George wasn't a gangster but a detective inspector and that he'd got his facts wrong again. I also told him that George was leaving the force and going into property development with a friend of mine.'

'And?'

Ivy sat down at the table and looked Anna in the face. 'He didn't like that one bit. I don't think he knows who to be jealous of – Trevor or George. What do you think, Anna?'

Anna shrugged with a touch of nonchalance. 'Trevor has really got his heart set on working with underprivileged children Mum. And I think he'll jump at the chance to live and work in the home in Kent. As for George, he isn't in the least bit interested in me other than as a pal from the old days. And that counts a million times more than what Frank's accusing him of. He hasn't come on to me at all. Okay? I am Nora-Nobody's-Sweetheart. All right?'

This brought a lump to Ivy's throat and she swallowed hard. Her youngest daughter, her baby, meant everything to her, and here she was feeling as if she was on the rubbish heap and she was only in her mid-twenties. And the worst of it was there was nothing she could say or do to make her lovely daughter feel better about herself. It was the wrong moment to give her the praise that she so deserved. Ivy felt sure that Frank would want her back but she also knew that Anna had pride – and that pride had been badly bashed about. As for Trevor, she had prayed that he would go off on a mission and not draw Anna into a relationship that to her mind would be one of utter boredom that her youngest in the flock would live to regret. Nice enough chap, though, he was.

George, on the other hand, was the one that Ivy chatted about to the good Lord before settling her head snugly into her pillow. She felt that he would love, cherish and look after her Anna right the way through life and into old age. But dare she try and match-make? No way. She held the silence which hung in the room and reached out to the kitchen dresser for a small tin of shortbread biscuits. She was biding time and giving Anna the opportunity to talk if she wanted to. Her patience paid off, because not only was her daughter ready to talk but tears were softly trickling down her face – and this is what Ivy had been waiting for. Anna had been holding in her emotions so that no one would know what she was going through for far too long. Ivy was no fool. She knew that her daughter had been broken-hearted when she found out about Bridget, never mind the fact that Frank had now left her and the twins and shacked up with the little bitch. Still Ivy said nothing as she sat down at the table and gently pushed the tin of Anna's favourite biscuits towards her.

'This time last year everything was so wonderful,' Anna only just managed to say. 'We were looking forward to the twins and we loved each other. How can it all change in such a short time?'

'This time last year you were five months pregnant and Frank was fucking that woman in the flat above the restaurant, Anna.' Ivy was determined not to let this opportunity slip by, even though the stance she was taking was tearing her apart.

'If you hadn't had a visit from your sisters to urge you on, Anna, he and that waitress would still be laughing behind your back. As it is, as it's turned out, this isn't the case. Frank's ashamed and wants you back. Bridget's had a smack on the nose and she's lost Trevor for good. She must know that her days are numbered and that Frank will sling her out with the rubbish. All that he's hanging around for is to see you weaken and forgive him and forget what's happened.'

'Well,' said Anna, between sobs, 'he's got a long wait. I won't ever be able to get it out of my head that he was fucking that woman in *our* bed, time after time. He was touching another woman's body and she was touching his. I hate him, Mum. I hate her. I don't ever want to be in the same room as either of them.'

Ivy got up from her chair again, speaking quietly and saying, 'I think it's time for something a little stronger than coffee. A drop of best brandy will do you the world of good, sweetheart.'

'Yes please, Mum.'

This is what she had been waiting for. This is what she wanted. An hour later Ivy was still in the kitchen and still having to watch her daughter languishing over a lost way of life. And then, to top all of her wishes, she heard George pulling up and parking outside. She could recognise the sound of his beautiful car anywhere.

She glanced at Anna and could tell that she wasn't in any fit condition to hear anything other than her own crying, and her cursing at her swine of a husband. She didn't stop her and she didn't say why she was leaving the room. She just left her to get on with it. As quietly as she could, she opened the door and waited for George and Horace to arrive on the doorstep. She placed a finger on her lips to give them both a clear message not to say anything.

Once they were in the kitchen, Ivy leaned on the dresser, her arms folded and looked sadly at her daughter who was now sobbing into her hands again. This emotional scene was too much for George. He was pinching his lips together tightly, trying to contain his strong feelings of sorrow at seeing the woman he loved in this much misery and pain.

'Oh dear, oh dear, oh dearie me,' said Horace, all fatherly. 'We can't be having this, dear child. Dear me no. At this rate you'll be having us all in fits of tears and crying rivers.' He then winked at Ivy and gave George a look to say, *Leave this to me. Leave the kitchen.*

Ivy nodded, led the way out and into the sitting room. And George was only too pleased for the chance to escape from the kitchen that was so charged with emotion – in particular, uncorked grief.

Once alone with the daughter of a woman he thought was just wonderful, Horace sat on the kitchen chair, held out his hands to Anna, and cupped hers in his own. He spoke gently to her, saying, 'My dear sweet girl . . . you have every reason in the world to cry and I cannot think of a better place than around your mother's kitchen table because, for one thing, you are quite close to the sink should the tears become a flood.'

This brought a feeble smile from Anna, who tried to say something but just couldn't get her words out – it seemed as if her throat was closing up. She shook her head miserably and the pained expression on her face and in her eyes was more than even an old acting veteran could cope with. Horace did his best to stay his own tears and, without thinking, he picked up Anna's glass of brandy and drank it down in one. This unintentional diversion made her giggle softly through her tears. Whether the kindly gentleman had done this deliberately or without thinking really didn't matter. It had done the trick. Horace in his own way was bringing her out of her misery.

Reaching across the table to take her hands again he looked into her eyes and said, 'Now I know you will think this an old and worn-out cliché from an old and worn-out actor, Anna, but please do believe me that this little honest outburst of yours is part of the beginning of healing your broken heart. Not one soul whom I knew in or out of the acting profession, but especially those in the theatre, who had gone through what you suffer now, did not escape without a sudden rush and flood of tears every now and then. Anger is actually the best of all cures, sometimes, and this no doubt will follow quite soon – which is possibly why your mother as well as the man who I believe loves you dearly, have both run for the comfort of the living room.'

This made Anna laugh as well as cry. 'Oh, Horace, I do hope that you don't walk away and hurt Mum the way she's been hurt before. Because this dark feeling of pain inside is awful.' The tears trickled again, but she carried on. 'I know you're only friends, but she does like you a lot, and I don't want her to go through this. I don't have a cut or a bruise to lay a wet flannel or wrap a bandage around but I hurt so badly inside at times.' It was now as if a tap had been turned on full because there was a steady stream of tears.

Anna placed a hand beneath the centre of her ribcage. 'This is where it's worse. It feels as if there is a dark sickening hole and the feeling of dread keeps on coming and going.'

Horace offered both arms and Anna was ready for

them. She stood up and fell into them, holding on tightly as he patted her back the way a caring father might. He spoke very quietly, saying, 'I know you won't be able to absorb any of my well-intentioned words at this moment in time, dear child, but please do try and trust me when I say that this awful unendurable pain *will* ease, and you will feel better for having suffered it now and not later on. Deep down, you will have known what was going on between your husband and that hussy all of the time – but you weren't brave enough or ready to accept that one of your worst nightmares was a reality. So *do* be angry, Anna. Be jealous. Be vengeful. Be anything that will help to shift that dark knot of pain until it gradually fades away altogether.'

Drawing breath and gently pulling away from him so as to look into his face, she managed to say, 'What on earth must I look like?'

'As beautiful and as innocent as the day you were born into this world. And in any case, who gives a monkey's great-aunt what you look like, my dear. It is you, Anna, who this family and fold of friends love and want so much to see happy. And if I may be so bold as to give advice, I would say to you: pay attention to the fact that under this roof and within just a one-brick wall division, is a very good and decent young man who loves you as no other could.'

'George?' said Anna, dabbing her nose with her handkerchief. 'No. He's a family friend. I suppose we've always loved each other, but more like cousins than anything else.'

'I could not disagree with you more, child,' said Horace. He then eased her back down onto the kitchen chair, and sat himself down opposite her. 'This is all I will say on the subject, Anna. But you know ... George was very disappointed that you didn't turn up at our beautiful old tumbling manor house.'

'Tumbling? Oh, Horace ... it's not really that bad is it? You and George haven't made a big mistake, have you?'

'No, indeed we have not. And if you will forgive an old veteran for repeating himself, George was so looking forward to you seeing it. He wanted to share a glass of sparkling champagne with you – and of course the person called Trevor.'

'Trevor wasn't interested, Horace. He wouldn't even walk with me to the old folk from the car, once we'd parked. Those who were living in the huts that I was telling you about the other day. He just wanted to get away from it all.' She started to shed a tear or two again.

'I presume you mean the huts which I have already seen?'

Anna could hardly believe her ears. 'Have you seen them? When? And why would you want to?'

'Why? Because George wanted me to see how simply people could live.'

'Well, it sounds as if you had a better day than I did then. We did go to the children's home for the interviews though and that was very nice. A bit sad and happy all rolled into one. But I'm really glad I went.'

'I can't imagine how you coped. It must have been emotionally charged, Anna. You were in an orphanage after all is said and done. Do you not think that your tears might well have been brought on by all that you saw and heard while there? You have just come from a place where there are children who have no parents to love them, after all. And you, deep down, of all people must know a little of what this feels like. Your mother told me about your father leaving you and I can see for myself how close to Ivy you and your sisters are. This is something that cannot be matched by anything. Wealth and notoriety kneel at the feet of this kind of precious love.'

'We are close, it's true,' Anna murmured as she dried her eyes. 'Look at me. What have I got to cry over? I've got my family and I've got my babies. And soon I'm going to get back in touch with all of my old friends. And I won't be ashamed to tell them that I'm a single parent now. That Frank's left me. That we're getting divorced.'

Horace drew a slow and trembling breath as he leaned over the table. 'I shouldn't start to use that divorce word yet, Anna. I wouldn't trouble trouble until it troubles you. Your husband has separated himself from you. Leave it at that for now. But enjoy this time of changing fortunes and just wait and see how things pan out.'

'"Don't jump in – or out, as the case may be – with two feet," is what you're saying?'

'Well, not exactly. I think it's more a case of just don't jump out of anything yet. Take it easy and bide your time. Legal matters and court procedures and divorce papers … let it lie. Enjoy life and see what drops onto your doormat in the mornings. I never pay a bill, you know, until the very last red warning letter.'

This made Anna smile. 'No wonder you get on so

well with Mum. That's just what she does even though she's got the money in the post office ready to pay.'

'Well there we are. When you're in bed at night and can't sleep, mull this kind of an attitude over and I think you'll see what I'm trying to say, even though I'm not making a very good job of it.'

'You are doing *very* well, Horace. I do know what you're saying. Live and let be?'

'Whenever possible – yes. Now then, why don't I run you home in my car? How does that sound?'

'Perfect. If you're sure you don't mind?'

'I would not have suggested it otherwise. From the East End I shall drive homeward bound to the West End. From East to West.' He chuckled. 'It sounds like the title of a film, doesn't it.'

'It probably is,' said Anna, as she stood up to leave. 'I'll just go and say bye-bye to George and Mum. I can't wait to hold each of my babies. I miss them even after just a half day or so. It's a funny old world, isn't it? Sometimes I feel as if I can't keep up with what's going on inside my own head, let alone out there. I used to be ahead with the fashion and what was going on but not any more.'

'This is because you don't need such trivia, my dear. And you are not as behind as the debutantes who attend Ascot when it comes to fashion. They do not seem to have caught on to the new fashion. The new look – hot pants. The Chelsea Pensioners have little else to gaze at with joy. Long may hot pants survive and swiftly may the memory of flower power and men in girls' clothes die.'

307

The ride through to Stepney Green and to Anna's house had been really pleasant. Horace entertained Anna with amusing stories from his theatre days, and before they knew it they had arrived in her street. She didn't have to ask if her knight in shining armour wanted to come in for a cup of tea because he had already assumed that he would. He was out of the car and opening her door before she could even begin to thank him for the lift.

Gently holding her by the arm as he saw them both across the quiet narrow road, he admired the tree-lined pavements on either side. 'I had no idea that the back streets of the East End were so pleasant,' he said.

'What were you expecting?' said Anna as she pushed the key into the door. 'Thieves and vagabonds?'

'Well, as a matter of fact, in a way I suppose I was. Not quite true Dickensian in this day and age, but where are the shifty people with shifty eyes?'

'Here, there and everywhere, but spread out all over the world, Horace.' She opened the door wide and waved him in. By the look on his face she could see that he was not only impressed with the inside of her house but a touch amazed.

'Why, Anna ... it's such a lovely little house. And I do so love the way you've decorated it. William Morris has always been a favourite designer of mine.' He stood and admired the pale pink and green honeysuckle wallpaper in the passage, reflecting the beautiful coloured light coming from the stained-glass window above the doorway. He then drifted into the kitchen where Anna said, 'I'll put the kettle on for a cup of tea while you sit in the sunshine in our back garden. It's small but lovely.'

'I should like that. I shall think of the new designer Zandra Rhodes in Notting Hill and the clothes she designs for the hippy generation, and thank God for Jean Muir who continues to produce the best of English clothes. Classic, simple and elegantly expensive.' Horace was deliberately side-tracking because he had seen through the window exactly who was in the garden. 'This is how I see you, child.'

Anna switched on her chrome electric kettle, feeling lighter and happier now that she was back in her little house. 'You didn't expect to see an overflowing dustbin and rats running around did you?' she joked.

'No Anna, I did not. But then neither did I expect to see who I can only presume to be your husband ... who seems to have the undivided attention of a beautiful young girl.'

Anna spun around and felt as if an icy electric shock had struck right through her entire being. She stared at Horace and then slowly stepped to the window to see who was in her garden. Surely to God he wouldn't bring Bridget here!

It *was* Frank – but it wasn't the whore with him. It was Jackie, her young friend the Avon rep. They were each in a deckchair and almost close to touching and she was looking into Frank's face and smiling. Smiling, and by the look of things, hanging onto her husband's every word.

'Now let's not jump to any conclusions, Anna ...' said Horace.

'I don't need to.' She turned to face him. 'I'm going

to go out there and very quietly ask him to leave. I don't want to know any ins and outs, and until Jackie's explained herself I'm going to give her the benefit of the doubt. Please don't feel you need to stay, Horace. In fact, if you wouldn't mind too much, I would really prefer it if you left now because I don't want Frank to see you here. He'll use you as a diversion and probably even accuse you of being my sugar daddy just to get himself off the hook.'

'I shall leave, and absolutely agree that this is the right thing to do. But please don't be too irrational. That is a very innocent scene. Don't give him any reason to accuse you of being a nasty suspicious wife.'

Anna sighed deeply. 'You are *so* on the ball, Horace. You're absolutely right. The twins are probably upstairs fast asleep. This is still Frank's house as well as mine and he's entitled to be in the garden with Jackie.'

'My thoughts entirely, Anna,' said Horace. 'Well done, you. Play this impassively and without suspicion.' With that he quietly took his leave.

Anna turned to look at the innocent scene again and suddenly felt as though there was another hand at work here, that maybe one of her guardian angels wanted her to see Frank in action. He was pulling in someone as lovely and innocent as Jackie – she could tell by the way he had just leaned closer and taken her hand in his. She wondered just how long he had been reeling her in, baiting her with his good looks while going through the Avon catalogue with her.

With a sudden urgent need to get out of the house before her presence was felt, Anna left and closed the door silently behind her. She only just managed to catch the attention of Horace who was pulling away. She waved her arms to get his attention and he made an excellent emergency stop. She opened the passenger door and slipped in beside him short of breath. 'Another thirty minutes away from my babies will be worth what I'm about to do. Drive off, Horace. Please take me back to Mum's place.'

He said nothing, and drove away with no intention of asking what she had in mind or what had gone on in the house once he had left it. But he could see the determined look on her face that had replaced her earlier sorrow. Fate had a very strange way of working, he thought.

Ivy was in the sitting room enjoying a cup of tea with George, Gwen, and her chap, Wilfred, when Linda opened the door to Anna. She hadn't expected her sister to be there and smiled as she fell into Linda's arms. 'You don't know how pleased I am that you're here,' she whispered.

'Really?' said Linda. 'Why? I only popped round to give Horace the once-over.' She looked from her baby sister to her mother's boyfriend. 'Well, you look all right, but are your intentions honourable is what me and Hazel need to know.'

Horace was amused and touched by her forthright manner. 'Scratch the surface, my dear sweet child, and you will find that I am dreadfully sensitive. Please *do* be nice to me.' His acting ability was to the fore and he was enjoying himself. 'See me off if you really feel you ought – but don't hit me, I beg you.'

'Silly bastard.' Linda laughed. 'You'll do. Go on, get

into the sitting room, the pair of you, and give us the latest. Frank's been on the phone.'

'What?' said Anna. 'Already?' She looked at Horace and shrugged. 'I didn't think he even realised that we were there. What can he be up to?'

'You tell us,' said Linda. 'He just asked if you were back from the trip out to Kent with Trevor, the budgerigar who you're training to talk in long sentences.'

'Oh right. He was possibly making sure that I wasn't about to disturb him while he was making a move to shag Jackie in our house.'

Horace left the girls to themselves and made his way into the sitting room, thinking to himself that life in the East End was certainly stranger than any play that he had ever been part of. And certainly stranger than any fiction he had read.

'Listen,' said Anna, lowering her voice and taking both Linda's hands in her own. 'I'm gonna have to work like lightning. Frank's up to something. And I'm not talking about the flirting that's going on right now with young Jackie. She'll be all right. She'll see right through him. But he's gonna move back into the house if I'm not careful, and from the way he's been behaving lately it wouldn't surprise me if he changes the locks.'

'Oh come on, Anna. He wouldn't dare do that. Lock out his twins and their mother? No way.'

'That's not what I said. He'll lock me out but keep my babies with him. He's already hinted that he'd report me to the authorities as a bad mother who keeps leaving the twins with strangers to look after.'

'I'll fucking kill him if he even hints at that. The fucking little toe-rag.'

'Never mind all that. Just listen and do as I say.' She looked directly into her sister's eyes. 'I'm deadly serious here, Linda. Keep on track. Right?'

'Well, go on then ... what do you want us to do?'

'This week you move into my house with me. Then, together we'll pack up mine and the twins' things, hire a van and a driver, and then later on we'll move me temporarily into the flat above Prima.'

'Get off it! You're not living with that jerk, Trevor.'

'No I'm not. And he's not a jerk. He's a lovely guy but not one of us, that's all. He's different and we mustn't knock that. He's already looking for another flat for himself. He doesn't want to live up there any more while madam is down below crossing and uncrossing her legs at the bar. And anyway, I think he'll be taken on for the job at the children's home.'

There was a pause while Anna allowed Linda to take it all in. 'Go on then,' Linda finally said. 'So you'll live in that one-bedroom flat ...'

'Yes. You live in my house and pay me the rent we mentioned. I'll be more than happy, living above the shop as it were. And I'll have company in the evenings, won't I?'

'What? You're gonna sit in the restaurant in a corner like a sad old bag lady are you?'

'No. I'll be upstairs and I think that George might come and go more than he feels he can if I was to stay at the house.'

'That makes sense.'

'I know you're gonna say that this is all on the

rebound, but it's not. I don't think that either of us realised it, but we've always kind of loved one another. Even Horace in there picked up on it. The old boy saw it straight away.'

'But you're more like brother and sister. George is our adopted brother.'

'Neither of us knew what the other was thinking, so for all of these years we've left it at that. I do love George, and do you know how I know this?'

'You're obviously gonna tell me, sweetheart, so spit it out.'

'Because the thought of maybe never seeing him again if he were to go and live in Spain, which he's mentioned as part of his plan to do with property and all that – I would be gutted. Heartbroken. Whereas if Frank was to go off and marry Bridget I would feel really hurt, but it wouldn't be as bad as George never being there again for me. I don't want Frank to get my house. I want you to be living there and guarding it for me.'

'And where is Frank supposed to live?'

'The flat at Tower Hill where he's living now with the slut Bridget. Why change it? Once we get divorced, the courts will decide how things are divided up. Let them do the dirty work.'

'And George? What if he wants you to move into his house in Chigwell now that his wife's gone? He's yours if you want him – but don't go there if you don't feel the same way about him. Don't break the poor sod's heart, Anna. We already love him as if he's one of the family.'

'So do I – and more. I thought that I'd lost him the

other day when he walked away from me at Prima. I all but begged him to come back and talk but no way.'

'And do you know why? Because actions speak louder than words. Get in there and let the bloke know that you love him or back off.'

'Shush! Someone's coming.'

'Anna, do you want me to run you back home?' said George, deadpan. 'I'm off back to Chigwell and the old boy's going back to his pad.' He looked from her to Linda. 'Or are you gonna give her a lift, Linda?'

'Whatever fits in,' said Linda and left the kitchen to go into the sitting room.

George studied Anna's face as she looked at him and smiled. Neither of them said a word and the atmosphere could have warmed butter straight from the fridge. Emotions filled the small space between them and it was all that George could do to stop himself shedding a rare tear. Still neither of them said anything. Then, drawing in air, Anna pinched her lips together and slowly nodded her head as a few special words drifted into her mind. But could she say them aloud? No. Instead, she blew him a kiss, the way she used to many years back when she was just fourteen . . . and he caught it in his hand and placed it in his jacket pocket, the way he used to do.

Clearly doing his best to control his emotions, George was lost for anything to say, but it was all right because Anna was taking those all important first steps towards him and only stopped once their hands touched. He cupped her face, looked into her lovely soft green eyes, and then murmured, 'I love you, Anna.'

The seconds ticked by and, with a solitary tear rolling

down her cheek, she only just managed to whisper, 'And I love you, George Blake.'

'Good. Because your birthday is only a few days away, and so we can have a double celebration.'

'And what might the second celebration be for?'

'Well, if you say yes, I would like to slip a diamond ring on the third finger of your left hand.'

'And if I say no?'

'I'll slip it onto the third finger of your right hand . . . and wait patiently for you to say that you will marry me once your divorce comes through. Yours and mine.'

'Put like that – how could any girl in her right mind say no?'

'Good. I'll take that as a yes, then?'

There was no need for Anna to say anything, which was just as well because she was too choked up for words. She closed her eyes and hugged him and that faint smell of aftershave that she had picked up on so many times before was now against her skin. 'I think I've always secretly loved you, George.'

'Well, then you should have said, because I've loved you since you were only sixteen.' He cupped her chin and kissed her lightly on the lips. 'Dreams don't normally come true, babe, but mine has. Don't break my heart, will you.'

'No, George. I won't break your heart. Kiss me again.'

So there, in Ivy's kitchen where many problems over many years had been discussed many times, there really was no need for words and no more to be said.

Sally Worboyes

Sally Worboyes' novels effortlessly evoke an East London which is now just a memory. Anna's vibrant community in *Lipstick & Powder* is not so very different from Sally's own background. She grew up in 1950's Bethnal Green in a typically sprawling East End family. As well as five siblings she had numerous aunts and uncles and she and her cousins and friends were always in and out of each other's homes.

Although her family were working class with no money to spare for toys, Sally and her brothers and sisters didn't want for love and attention, and every summer the whole family had a working holiday in Kent, hop-picking. Her memories of life in

Every summer the whole family had a working holiday in Kent, hop-picking

that colourful corner of London imbue her novels with a rare sense of authenticity and magic.

What made you start writing?

Being one of six children and from a working-class family I didn't have a box of toys, but I did have a make-believe world and a precious toy shopkeeper's till. I played in my bedroom with this for hours on end. My make-believe regulars were drawn from neighbours, aunts and uncles, school friends and a few famous film stars.

My imagination held me in good stead throughout my childhood until I could read library books, and this was when the scribbling kicked in. I had to get the stories out of my head so tried to write a book but it took too long because I had to keep on sharpening my pencil with Mum's blunt bread knife. So I decided to produce shows in our block of flats. The concrete staircase served as seating and the bay window on the second floor, where I lived, became our stage. Most of the kids on the block wanted to be in the plays so the audience was a bit thin at times!

I didn't have a box of toys, but I did have a make-believe world

How much of the stories are fictional and how much is based on fact?

I am pedantic when it comes to fact. I can't bear to miss anything and it pains me on the rare occasion when I might not have got it right. I not only scour history books at the library but also get my son, Rob, to search the internet and collect information on the period I'm writing about. The rest, which probably amounts to eighty per cent, is fiction – part of which is the sheer joy of living out a little of my own secret fantasies.

What were your family and your upbringing like?

My sister, four brothers and myself were part of a close and an extended family of first and second cousins, aunts, uncles. All of the elders worked hard to make ends meet but still they managed to get together for a beer party every so often as well as a drink in the local pub on a Saturday night. We kids played outside of the pub, calling in now and

> *We kids played outside of the pub, calling in now and then for a bag of crisps*

then for a bag of crisps or glass of lemonade. It was fun, mostly because we were very close and cared about each other. Clothes in general were handed down to whichever brother, sister or cousin would fit into them. Nobody cared if something was patched or stitched so long as it was clean. And they were. Our Grandma Lizzie, who boiled her whites until they gleamed, saw to that. Garments could be stitched but they were not allowed to be dirty.

For you how has the East End changed? What do you remember most about the East End that has disappeared?

I grew up on the border of Bethnal Green and Stepney. My best friend Margaret and I used to roller skate from Bethnal Green Gardens, through the backstreets and alleyways to the Tower of London. Sadly, though, the city has now spread like a cobweb into the East End with high-rise office blocks and wide new roads replacing some of the old turnings. It would be a rare thing to see a child skating through it all. The markets are still there, Bethnal Green, Whitechapel, Aldgate, but it's no longer a mix of

I used to roller skate from Bethnal Green Gardens, through the backstreets and alleyways

religion and race the way it used to be.

I recently walked from Aldgate station to Whitechapel market and couldn't quite make out what was different. Then it dawned on me. The Jewish traders were very thin on the ground. The small tailors, the run-down pawn shops, the old-fashioned jewellers had practically all gone. Even worse was that the old London cockneys calling out their prices were nowhere to be seen. The Salvation Army wasn't playing outside of Whitechapel railway station and there were no slippery bookies on street corners ready to take illicit bets. Bobbies on the beat have been replaced with police officers wearing flat caps and looking far more official somehow. The way of life that I and thousands of others knew has gone for ever.

There were no slippery bookies on street corners ready to take illicit bets

What prompted you to move out of London to the countryside?

My memories of hop-picking. Pure and simple. The way of life when my family and relatives lived in huts in the heart of the Kent countryside for at least six weeks of the year came to an end with the arrival of picking machines. I wanted to bring some of that way of life back. Moving to an old farm in Norfolk with barns and outbuildings in the early Seventies was the next best thing, and I loved living there. It was a bit dilapidated and we cooked on an open fire outside at first until reality kicked in and the house was re-wired. We had an electric oven for everyday use but we also had an old-fashioned wood- and coal-fired oven in the kitchen for cooking the Christmas turkey and roast vegetables. My children grew up there and thankfully they had a taste of country life: the village shop-cum-post office, the church, the village hall.

A number of your stories are set in the 1960s. What do you remember most vividly about that time?

The excitement of an era changing. No more Brylcreem for the lads and the outmoded Teddy Boys were married and raising families. We had the Beatles, we had the fashion guru Mary Quant with affordable clothes (or copies) and there were free-for-all parties going on into the wee small hours in every direction. Needless to say, my

London might have been swinging but the East End was thumping its heart out

friends and I did not miss the best of them if we could help it. We had choices every Saturday night, when it was brilliant to stroll from one fashionable pub to another to where the pick of the lads in their Italian suits would eye up the goods. My friends Pat and Carol and I had a whale of a time. Sometimes we would go from one party to the next in search of the boys we were deeply in love with who were too cool to approach us for fear of rejection. London might have been swinging but the East End was thumping its heart out. There was a fantastic sense of fun and freedom for my generation. Better than all of it was that there was no more talk of the war and the suffering and how easy us post-war babies had it. We had moved on and it was great.

Anna dreams of visiting Biba in *Lipstick & Powder*. Were you into fashion in the 1960s?

Absolutely. I started working in the city in 1961 when I was just fifteen. I didn't earn much at first because of my age but I knew which stalls to go to in the Roman Road market

I knew which stalls to go to in the Roman Road market for cheap copies of the latest fashion designers

for cheap copies of the latest fashion designers. I adored my first pair of slingback shoes with handbag to match and my Prince of Wales check, Italian-styled suit, which gave me the up-to-the-minute Mod look. I wore pan stick make-up, very pale Corn Silk lipstick, eye-shadow and lots and lots of black mascara (the spit and rub on to the brush type).

As for Biba, which was the place to shop if you could afford to, just like Anna in *Lipstick & Powder*, I never made it there. But I was more than happy with the copies purchased from that market stall.

How often did husbands cheat on their wives in the East End? Were the women as strong and determined as Anna?

I don't think that East Enders, husbands or wives, did cheat any more than anyone else. Possibly less in fact. The women were tough and gutsy and pulled together in times of crisis. Families were important at the end of the day, as were neighbours. I remember my Nan saying that some men and women, even though they enjoy their own cake, are bound to be tempted to taste another with a different flavour to it.

Women were tough and gutsy and pulled together in times of crisis

I think that most women were probably as strong as Anna deep down and although harmless flirtation would have been seen as okay, too much of it in the same direction and then the knives and forks would come out!

Have you ever had to overcome any of the problems that Anna faces?

I did have one major problem that Anna faced in that I needed to have the fertility drug, after two years of trying to get pregnant. I remember my GP quietly looking at me when I sat in the chair in his surgery weeping. He asked if I could afford to go private. I said that I was thinking of buying a 21-inch colour television set but I would much sooner have a baby. He slowly nodded and then said, 'I'm going to recommend you to the best man for the cause and I will arrange for the fertility drug to come via the NHS. You will have to pay for your visits to his offices in Harley Street. How does this sound?'

I said that I was thinking of buying a 21-inch television set but I would much sooner have a baby

I wept for joy and thanked my doctor from the bottom of my heart. I so wanted to have a baby.

I was pregnant within six months with my first son, Duncan, in 1972. I then had my second baby, Esther, without any fertility drugs in 1974 and stopped at number three when my adorable baby, Robin, was born in 1977. Unlike Anna in *Lipstick & Powder*, I had my babies one at a time. I now have my first grandchild and I love her to bits.

Describe your typical writing day.

When I am in full swing I write when I am awake – during the day or the night. In between, I eat what I fancy, watch *EastEnders*, *Deal or No Deal* and property programmes. I also love watching holiday programmes because I imagine I am there and then at the end am thankful that I'm not and can curl up in my own bed after a soak in my own bath.

I love watching holiday programmes because I imagine I am there

Who is your favourite author?

It continues to be Charles Dickens, whose world I lived in as a child – via his fiction, of course. I do browse through the book stores and buy new novels in paperback but hardly ever get round to reading them. I do love my Sunday morning papers and all the lovely magazines you get with them. I make them last the week out. I hardly ever read fiction when I'm writing a book and I'm writing for most of the time. I do like to watch a good play on the TV though. Or a good film. Or a bit of side-splitting comedy . . . when you can get it.

What do you like to do in your free time?

Play with my baby granddaughter, Phoebe. Visit my daughter and my two sons. See my friends. Swim. Go for lovely long walks with the dogs or by myself. Sit in the garden at home by the river where I don't write but watch the wildlife with a glass of wine in my hand or a cup of coffee if it's too early in the day for alcohol … she quickly adds.